John Sweeney is an award-winning journalist and a former long-serving BBC reporter for Panorama and Newsnight. He is the author of eleven books, including three novels: the 200,000-copy bestseller *Elephant Moon* and two modern-day political thrillers, *Cold* and *Road*. His non-fiction work books include *Murder on the Malta Express – Who Killed Daphne Caruana Galizia?*, an investigation into the murder of the great Maltese investigative journalist Daphne Caruana Galizia, an examination of the Church of Scientology, *The Church of Fear – Inside the Weird World of Scientology*, and an account of his time spent undercover in North Korea, *North Korea Undercover*. He tweets from @johnsweeneyroar.

The Useful Idiot

John Sweeney

SILVERTAIL BOOKS • *London*

'Any report of a famine in Russia is today an exaggeration or malignant propaganda.'
— Walter Duranty, *New York Times*, 1933

'One of the most monstrous crimes in history, so terrible that people in the future will scarcely be able to believe it ever happened.'
— Malcolm Muggeridge, 1933

'There is no bread.'
— Ukrainian peasant to Gareth Jones, 1933

Chapter One

Maerdy, South Wales
January 1927

Drizzle fell in the faces of the returning men, soaked their clothes, and made the once proud banners behind which they walked yet more sodden. Hobnailed boots clattered on cobbles and the men tramped onward with their eyes straight ahead, not looking at the shop windows they had long shunned, not looking at the eyes of the children bunking off school, not looking at their women watching them. They had fought for longer than anyone else but they had lost and they were all but broken.

The great wheels above the pit had not turned for eight months but now the spokes of the winding gear scissored the sky. The overseers were underground checking for gas in the tunnels, preparing for the first shift. At the colliery gates a mass of police stood in capes, gleaming dully with the wet. Protected from the rain by the eaves of the lodge was a blackboard, pinned on it a type-written list of the men the owners thought fit to return to work. Missing from the list were the names of the troublemakers, the hard-core union men, the Communists, the men who would never work at the pit again.

The line of men came to a stop at the colliery lodge, broke ranks and mingled about. In silence, those at the very front read the list. They moved away, then more and more men came to take in the mineowners' decree: this man can work, that man can starve. A fresh shudder of rain came in from the black hills, its noise rattling on the tin roof and drowning out the start of the disquiet below.

Soon the disquiet grew. One of the non-men, not on the list, tried to walk through the lodge gate into the colliery and was pushed back by an overseer so forcefully that he fell over, bashing the back of his head on a brick. There he lolled in the mud, groggy and groaning, the whites of his eyes flickering in their sockets. A few of his friends picked him up and took him back to see a doctor but the rest stayed by the lodge, their anger growing. A second overseer started barking orders, giving voice to the silent division written on the blackboard. A pole bearing the Mardy colliery banner smacked down on his head.

As he crashed to the ground, the police moved in a great wet shoal towards the men – and the riot began.

It lasted for hours, a great mess of shoves and pushes, bricks thrown and windows smashed, bones broken and skulls fractured, the men getting the better of the fight for most of the day. There were more than a thousand of them, and only two hundred police.

Towards the end of the day, police reinforcements came from Somerset and Gloucestshire, dozens and dozens of them. That was when things started to look hopeless for the men.

A police van sped downhill to be met by a hail of bricks and stones. It stopped and a lad, but fourteen years old, went to ram a steel pole in the spokes of the van's back wheel. As he did so, he slipped on the wet, the pole tumbling downhill – and the boy fell awkwardly on the asphalt.

Moments later, a fresh hail of bricks pelted down – and the police driver wrenched the van into reverse, crushing the boy's skull beneath the rear wheel, sluicing blood and brains over the road. At the sight of it, a young police officer started to retch in the gutter.

A flashgun sparked and a police sergeant came running up to the man with the camera who had captured the accident. The sergeant raised his truncheon to bring it down on the man's head.

"Give me the camera, butt," the sergeant said, "or there'll be hell to pay."

"Stop!" came the reply. "I'm a reporter from the *Western Mail!*"

"Don't be stupid, butt," said the policeman, and the world turned to black.

In the morning, the drizzle was finer but no less depressing. The boy's house was in one of the poorest streets in the pit village, black drapes in the windows, a black ribbon tied on the door knocker.

Resting his bicycle against the wall, he tapped gently on the knocker and, after a time, the door opened to reveal a tiny girl in a black cotton dress like a doll from Victorian times. For a time, she stared at his face solemnly; then she turned on her heels, and he followed her down a dank unlit corridor to the kitchen at the back of the house. Here, two boys and two girls – all dressed in black, all thin, the oldest no more than ten – sat around a table, their mother tending a kettle on an iron stove.

Without turning around she said, "So?"

"I'm a reporter from the *Western Mail*."

"You ever worked down the pit?"

"No. I suffer from claustrophobia."

"What's that?"

"Fear of confined spaces."

Still with her back to him, she said, "We don't talk to those who haven't been down the pit. Too many lies have been written about us."

"Please, I want to tell the story of what happened. I want to report the truth."

"Listen, mister, I don't know who you are or which bloody newspaper you work for but this poor house has seen trouble enough." She turned around and instantly her voice faltered as she studied his face. "Who did that to you?"

A livid blue-black bruise ran from just below his right eyebrow to his jawline, the right lens of his owlish spectacles cracked from side to side. He was short, tough, a little swarthy – "a touch of the gypsy" was how his district editor put it – but he had a sweet, innocent smile that was all the more winning because of the bruising.

He didn't reply.

"They told me," she said, "there was a reporter there who took a photograph of my boy when he'd been run over. They say the police beat him senseless and took his camera."

3

"That was me. My name is Gareth Jones."

"Are you going to write a story about what happened, the truth mind?"

"Yes. The truth."

"His da died in the pit last year, just before the strike. Roof collapse, they said. His da was buried alive scratching a living for his little ones – and the boy they killed yesterday, he was our only hope. Strong lad, like his da, full of mischief. Our only hope and they killed him."

"It was an... an... an..." Jones' stammer always came at the worst moments, "an horrible accident," he finally said. "I saw it with my own eyes."

She invited him to sit down at their table, made him tea and opened up her heart to him. There were times, moved by the passion of her words and the stillness of the children as they sat, listening to every word, that he had to reach for his handkerchief and blow his nose, to hide his emotion. When they had finished talking, the little girl led him down the dank corridor again. As Jones stood by the door, he palmed a five-pound note – almost a month's wages for him, far more than he could afford – into the girl's hand. She stared at him curiously as he walked out into the rain.

Jones returned to the district office, cycling the way back to Aberdare, and tapped out his story in dogged silence, the other cub reporters watching him with a kind of awe. When he was finished he stood up, walked over to the district editor and handed him his story.

The district editor had been passed over for promotion to head office in Cardiff so a sourness often gnawed into his soul. After reading the story twice, he shook his head and placed his copy on the spike. "No-one's going to be bothered about a road accident in Little Moscow," he said. "Write up that report of the ways and means committee, sharpish."

A stillness in the office as everybody watched for Jones' reaction.

4

For a time he stared at his boots in silence, then picked up a pencil and played with it.

"Mr Jones, are you going to do that story on the ways and means committee," the district editor asked, "or are you going to walk out of this office and never come back?"

The pencil snapped.

Jones said nothing and moved his chair closer to his desk and started typing: "The meeting of the Ways and Means committee..."

That evening, he went to the local library just before closing time and put in a request on a card for a book he had been thinking about reading for a long time. The librarian had a sympathetic face.

"You may have to wait a week or two, Mr Jones," she said. "*Das Kapital* by Karl Marx, it's very popular these days."

Chapter Two

Moscow
October, 1932

The short walk from the hotel had already taken an hour, more, and if Jones didn't find Kurskaya station in the next seven minutes he would miss the special train and so the opening of the Lenin Dam. With the dying of the light, the fog that cloaked the city was turning red and through it something was coming at him fast, metal squealing on metal, a monster from a child's nightmare. Glancing down, Gareth Jones realised he was standing on a rail, a yard in front its sister. He stepped backwards and the tram brushed by him, inches from his face.

Loudspeakers on street corners Jones couldn't see cackled the same phrase, over and over again. Shaking from the brush with the tram, he bumped into a man in a flat cap and dark black overcoat, fraying at the sleeves. Jones mumbled sorry, checked his watch and asked the man the way to Kurskaya station in his poor, clumsy Russian. The man was in his sixties, short, thick-set, his eyes red-raw. He made a sound and Jones, at first, thought he was laughing at a private joke. Then Jones realised that the man was crying. The contrast between the man's solid appearance and him weeping was, like the fog, bewildering. Jones asked his question again.

"It's *gdye nakhoditsya Kurskaya stantsiya*, you daft sod," the man, replied, then took out a handkerchief and blew his nose.

"You're British?" asked Jones.

"I am. Harold Attercliffe from Barnsley. And who might you be?"

"Gareth Jones, *Western Mail*."

The man nodded slowly. "Saw you at the hotel this morning. Bloody reporters. Can't trust a reporter. Needs must though. You a socialist?"

"I am a man of the left. I'm sorry, I'm in a frantic hurry, I'm going to miss a train."

"If you want to find the station in this muck you follow the tram tracks."

Jones headed off to the right.

"No, not that way! Look, I'll come with you."

They walked between the tracks through the fog.

Oumansky, the official at the foreign ministry, had warned Jones in his pedantic, irritating way that the special train for the opening of the Lenin Dam in Dnepropetrovsk would leave on the dot of five o'clock. The loudspeakers clacked again.

"What is that phrase they keep on repeating?" asked Jones.

"The liquidation of cowlessness," said Attercliffe.

"That's gibberish."

"Watch what you say out loud son. Or the GPU" – he pronounced it the Gay-Pay-Oo – "will be after you."

"What's the GPU?"

"Never you mind."

They walked in silence. The freezing air, poisoned by a hundred factory chimneys, tasted of burnt milk.

"Station's here," said Attercliffe.

"Thanks," breathed Jones.

"Can I trust you, as one socialist to another?"

Jones hesitated.

The question came again. "Can I trust you?"

"Yes."

"Good. Then give this envelope to someone at the British Embassy. No-one else, mind. It's important."

Attercliffe handed him a slim brown envelope, which Jones placed in the inside pocket of his jacket.

"Only one thing more..." Attercliffe continued – but at that moment he was cut off by the arrival of another tram punching through the fog, its bell clanging.

A surge of disembarking passengers parted the two men. By the time they had cleared, Attercliffe had been swallowed up – and, although Jones called out his name, climbing to the top of the station steps to call out again, it was all in vain. In reply, there was only the sound of the tram's bell clanging and the soft footfall of unseen people threading their way through the murk.

The ticket hall had the feel of a marbled ballroom past its prime, gloomy apart from the place where a spotlit Stalin smiled down, the benevolent stationmaster. Across the quiet of the concourse, Jones ran helter-skelter, tumbling over his own feet as he made haste down a flight of steps into the train shed.

Down here, railings at head-height guarded the platforms. A crowd clutching cardboard suitcases and bags made out of blankets tied with string choked the single narrow gate to the platforms. At the gates, tickets and passes were being checked by a railway inspector, then checked again by soldiers – not regular Red Army, but special troops in khaki great coats with blue trimmings and red stars. The fur hats they wore, folded up into spikes, reminded Jones of the drawings he'd seen in Pears Encyclopaedia of the warriors of Genghis Khan.

By platform one stood a train, its seven carriages a forbidding black, with red hammers and sickles brightly painted on each carriage. Up and down its full length, soldiers at every ten paces.

Two minutes to five.

The engine puffed out a fat plume of steam. Jones clutched his Gladstone bag and charged into the mass of people, crying out "Sorry, sorry!" – but the crowd was having none of it. Blocked, he backed out and approached one of the soldiers on the outer rim of the crowd, pleading with him in English for permission to pass through.

"Nyet!" spat the soldier.

Jones trotted away from him, running parallel with the railings guarding the platform. Then, he stopped dead. Pivoting, he lifted his bag and hung it by its strap onto one of the spikes – and, grabbing hold of two vertical railings, found a toe-hold at thigh height. To cries of "Nyet! Nyet!" from behind, he launched himself up onto the sturdy horizontal cross-bar. He almost fell, balanced himself, stayed up, just.

Whistles blew. Soldiers barked. Rifles pointed their snouts at him, the guard at his back continuing to roar "Nyet!"

It was no use. The carriage was still too far. Finally, Jones lifted his hands high above his head and froze, a statue of surrender.

An officer, rolls of fat backing up over the collar of his uniform, walked down the platform towards Jones. Pork sausage fingers pried open his leather holster and he pointed his revolver directly at Jones.

As Jones hung there, the officer came closer, closer still. Thirty feet from Jones, his face broke into a smile that did not reach his eyes.

Twenty feet...

Fifteen...

"Press, press!" Jones shouted.

The officer's shiny boots went click-clack on the platform, then stopped. He was ten feet away, if that.

"I'm Gareth Jones, Moscow reporter for the *Western Mail*." His Welsh lilt was so thick it was almost as if he sang rather than spoke. Smile faltering, then dying; hands lifted higher, higher still. Jones closed his eyes and waited for the shot.

Chapter Three

Someone started to clap, slowly, the applause echoing around the engine shed. Jones opened his eyes to see a man slip out from the shadow of the last carriage, a cigarette dangling from his lips, his hands still coming together. Something was said in Russian, something commanding and to the point.

Slight, balding, physically not impressive, the new arrival nevertheless had a quality that drew focus to him. The officer lowered his revolver and waddled back up the platform.

"Bravo, bravo!" cried Jones' saviour, still clapping. "What an extraordinary entrance! Well done, comrade, well done."

Jones leapt down from his plinth, retrieved his bag from the railings and hurried over to thank the man.

"Jones, eh? Welcome to Moscow, old boy. Welcome to the not-so-shining city on the Moskva." His voice was amused, his eyes a glittering grey. "The name's Duranty, Walter, from the *New York Times*." His accent was a curious but pleasant blend of top table Algonquin and Scouse.

"The Great Duranty?"

"You make me sound like a wizard. I'm supposed to be the hotshot reporter around here – but I've never made an entrance like that. Clearly, you're a young man to watch."

"Thank you ever so much."

"Gratitude is a dog's disease."

"Who said that?"

"Stalin."

"That seems a little mean."

"Sssh, you'll get us all taken away."

"Well, this young man is in your debt, Master."

"For God's sake man, don't call me Master. Not here, not these days. You'll get us all into no end of trouble," said Duranty, a twinkle in his eye. "You can buy me a drink, one day. But not on this train. Food and drinks are on the house. The thing about Soviet Man is that he's brutal and sometimes just plain wrong... but he does know how to throw a party."

An anxiety in a grey suit, with a cowlick of hair plastered over his skull, trotted towards them at speed.

"Mr Duranty," said Oumansky, the man from the Foreign Ministry Jones had met the day before. "The train is leaving. We must stick to schedule religiously."

Duranty's eyes shone with malice. "Religiously, you say, Mr Oumansky? Isn't religion what Marx said was the opium of the masses? Does Comrade Stalin hold with this priestly talk?"

Oumansky breathed out a sigh freighted with worry. Dozens of faces peered out from the train's windows, drawn by the commotion.

"Oh, come on, Constantine, lighten up!" said Duranty. "Let's give our man here some champagne. Welcome aboard the Soviet Express. Choo-choo! Choo-choo!"

As they were speaking, the engine sounded a piercing whistle and, behind them, the train started to inch away. Oumansky and Jones jumped aboard as the train began to pick up speed. Duranty, slow with his bad leg, hobbled towards the train, now accelerating away from him – and, jumping off again, Jones whisked him up in his boxer's arms and lifted Duranty on to a mini-platform at the very end of the train. Running now, running fast, he leapt and landed helplessly on a prone Duranty – and the two men collapsed in a heap, Jones' trilby falling off his head, tumbling towards the tracks. It was a gift from his mother, the initials G.J. stitched into the band lest he lose it. That wasn't going to happen, not on his first day. He caught the trilby just in the nick of time.

When their laughter faded, Duranty said, "You shouldn't have troubled yourself, old cock. You see, the Soviets want diplomatic recognition from the US of A and they want it bad. There's a professor from Yale, Cornelius Aubyn, on board to tell Roosevelt everything is hunky-dory. If the *New York Times* misses the train, they'll shoot the stationmaster."

A shadow floated over Jones' face and Duranty tweaked his arm playfully. "Forgive me, son. I saw too much death in the war to take anything seriously, especially missing a bloody train. Come on soldier, no harm done, let's get that champagne."

Jones helped Duranty to his feet and the two men headed towards the restaurant car, Duranty steadying himself when the carriages wobbled over signalling points. Inside, it was warm, unpleasantly so. Each carriage had an oil-heating stove going at full throttle. The fittings and fixtures were extraordinarily plush, the carpet underfoot a rich pile, the bunks dressed with fresh white linen.

"Built for the Tsar," said Duranty. "Lovely locomotive. Made in Glasgow in 1913. It's Stalin's special train. When he's no got use for it, they let us workers have a play. That's socialism for you."

The older man stopped at a compartment and opened the sliding door. "Talking of fraternity, you're sharing a pit with me, old chap. Dump your bag and let's get that drink."

Duranty waved Jones in. "You take the top bunk. I can't get up there with my gammy leg. Besides, you can reach it in one jump. Keeping up the acrobat stuff, eh?"

Grinning, Jones heaved his bag onto the top bunk. Then they set out again, passing through a carriage cluttered higgledy-piggledy with boxes of equipment.

"German motion picture crew, here to capture the opening of the dam for posterity. I hope you've brought your make-up."

"Make-up? No," replied Jones before he realised he was being teased.

A young man – tall, almost gangly, with a Mr Punch nose and a blue bow-tie – emerged from a cabin, his face knotted, carrying a German newspaper in one hand and a box camera in the other.

"Max Borodin, Gareth Jones." Duranty introduced the two men, then said, "What's with the cheerful expression, Max?"

"News from Berlin," Borodin replied, lifting his paper an inch or two. His voice had a natural melancholy.

"What news?"

"Adolf, again."

"What's he been saying this time?"

Borodin read from the newspaper. "Raising his voice to its highest pitch, Hitler thundered, 'I have one advantage over my adversary. He is 85 and I am 43.'" Shaking his head, Borodin said quietly, "The difficulty is that, for once, every word Herr Hitler says is true."

"Oh, I wouldn't worry too much about old man Hindenburg versus Hitler," Duranty replied, before quickly adding, "Oh, Borodin, I forgot who your people are."

Borodin turned to go but thought better of it. "Duranty, remember – I might be half-German Jew, half-Russian atheist, but I've got two good legs and I can kick you with both." He turned his head, gestured to the box camera in his hand and said to Jones, "Have you been an acrobat for long?"

"My first day. May I ask, what model is that?"

"ICA Kinamo," said Borodin, "the smallest movie camera on the market. It was created to catch such moments of pure athleticism. Next time you plan to jump like that, you let me know beforehand."

"I have no plans to jump like that ever again," said Jones.

"Pity. Mr Jones, one word of advice. In Russia you must be especially careful of the company you keep."

Borodin smiled malevolently at Duranty, then was gone.

"Cheeky sod," said Duranty. "In Germany, his ilk is in trouble."

"Ilk?" asked Jones.

"The Jew. Borodin is a film director. Russian father, German mother, Jewish and a big Social Democrat family to boot. Hitler's not yet in power but the pressure on his people is growing by the day. He's had to say 'auf wiedersehen' to all the lovely girls who want to be in the movies and has been making money doing boring advertising films for German engineering companies. The way things are going in Berlin for his kind he's going to be the clapper-boy next."

"Why would the Germans want to film the opening of the Lenin Dam?" asked Jones. "The Soviets and the Germans don't like each other."

"Depends which Germans. The Weimar crowd, the Social Democrats, don't like Stalin so much – but their days are numbered. The Junkers, the army, Hitler's people, the moneymen, they admire how things are being done here. No liberal nonsense about the rule of law. Got to feel sorry for Borodin, now that man with the little moustache is getting stronger."

"The German conservatives," said Jones, "people say they're planning to get rid of Herr Hitler."

"Maybe, maybe not." Duranty paused. "I need that champagne. Talk of Adolf always makes me thirsty."

The train clattered along at a stately pace. Soon the fog was lifting, making way for a wine dark sky broken by a brilliant shaft of red light, which fell across muddy streets and brick factories. The city thinned out, then stopped – and, after that, the train cut through endless fields, every now and then passing strings of little wooden shacks so flimsy and fairy-tale they seemed to be made out of gingerbread.

The restaurant car was sumptuous, tables set with white table-cloths and gleaming silver cutlery. Lenin and Stalin looked down from respective oil paintings, Lenin disapproving, Stalin's mocking smile never leaving his lips.

"Ladies and gentlemen," Duranty boomed, the circus ringmaster, "I give you the only one of us, on his very first day on the Moscow beat, who has the courage, the acrobatic skill, the sheer bloody balls to solve the problem of the great Russian train station queue. You simply jump six feet in the air and hey presto! You've beaten every-one to it. Ladies and gentlemen, be upstanding please for our very own amazing acrobat, Mr Gareth Jones of the Welsh Morning Doodah."

"*Western Mail*," Jones corrected, blinking. The company got to its feet, cheering.

"Champagne!" yelled Duranty, and a flurry of waiters appeared with champagne bottles and flutes. "Ladies and gentlemen, a toast, to the Flying Welshman!"

A trio of drinkers at the far end of the restaurant car started to sing "For he's a jolly good Soviet and so say all of us!", a song the carriage took up.

Throughout it all, Jones studied his feet, his cheeks burning bright pink – until, at last, the singing ended and Duranty led the way to the end of the carriage, where two wide divans faced each other. Here he made space for himself and Jones between two Russian women, one dark and severe, the other blond and smiling. Opposite them were the three singers. Duranty introduced the men first. "Here are the three wise monkeys of the Moscow press corps. On the left, Lou Fischer of the *Baltimore Sun*. Lou has a few skeletons in his cupboard but nothing the Kremlin doesn't know about."

Fischer, a thick-set, fleshy man, opened his mouth but no sound came out.

"In the middle, Eugene Lyons, United Press. Gene's got so many skeletons you can't fit them into any cupboard."

Lyons grinned feebly. Short, well-dressed, with a mop of unruly light brown hair, he sported a broken nose and a thoughtful face.

"And the third monkey, Linton Wells, International News Service. He's just a skeleton."

Wells had the look of a greyhound no longer raced for money. He eyed Jones soulfully.

"Boys and girls," Duranty continued, "don't be fooled by the spectacles and the shyness. He's a young little owl, our Mr Jones, but he's up for the right kind of trouble, aren't you, eh Jonesy? Twit-twoo? He's the owl and maybe one of you two girls are going to be his pussycat? The owl and the pussycat, eh? Natasha? Evgenia?"

He pointed in turn to the smiling blond and the gloomy brunette. "Natasha is pure Russian but Evgenia's from Kiev."

"Stalino," replied Evgenia, curtly.

"Where's Stalino?" asked Jones.

"South of here," replied Duranty, "in Soviet Ukraine. Coal town. A dump."

Evgenia showed her teeth, white and sharp. It could have been a smile.

"Vot is owl and puzzycad?" asked Natasha, leaning forward to get a light for her cigarette from Lyons. As she did so, she held herself steady by resting the fingernails of her left hand on Jones' thigh. Her hair was done in bangs, with a black choker around her neck, red stiletto shoes and a black spangly dress, short for Moscow, short for anywhere. Cigarette lit, she leaned back and blew out a halo of blue smoke.

"The Owl and the Pussycat is a nonsense poem of interest only to people like Mr Duranty, who think nonsense clever," said Evgenia. The voice was soft and hesitant, yet somehow it carried a spirit of resistance to Duranty's power over the company.

While Natasha was sporting the very latest Parisian fashion, Evgenia could not have been more plainly attired. She wore a dark brown dress that went to her ankles and plain black boots. She had long dark brown hair to the waist, a sallow face and perhaps the darkest brown eyes Jones had ever come across. Jones noticed that she seemed to be surveying the world with her head slightly turned away but with her eyes looking back, as if she struggling against a physical compulsion to be somewhere else entirely. He found himself staring at her and she returned his gaze steadily, until, embarrassed, he looked away. She was uncommonly beautiful.

"Bravo old girl, bravo!" said Duranty. "Now I need more nonsense juice. Champagne! A man could die of thirst here. What's the point of having a revolution if a worker can't have a drink when he needs one?"

He stood up, not so steady on his feet, and bawled at a waiter fussing over a dining table at the other end of the carriage, "More champagne, if you please!" Then he sank back on the divan and moaned, softly, to himself, "Service in Russia is not what it used to be, said the Tsar to the Tsarina."

The waiter, an elderly silver-haired man with kind eyes, vanished and returned within seconds, bearing three bottles of Veuve Clichy and seven fresh champagne flutes. He popped a cork, spilling not a sip, and then poured the drinks. "What's your name, comrade?" Duranty asked him.

"Comrade Gazdanov, comrade."

"We're all equals here, comrade. Comrade Gazdanov, can you get us poor workers some caviar and blini with sour cream, please. A man's got to eat." Duranty patted his stomach. The waiter nodded and departed.

Soon, Oumansky joined them, sitting on the edge of the divan with the three newspapermen, his neck craning this way and that, never at rest.

"So, Jonesy, what's your prize here?" asked Duranty, his eyes full of laughter. "What are you going to do in Mother Russia to make your name?"

The train clattered over a signal and the carriage swung drunkenly this way and that. Natasha reached out for Jones' thigh to steady herself, again, but when the carriage righted itself it stayed there.

"What do you suggest?" Jones replied.

"My readers," said Duranty, "are ordinary people, the salt of the American earth and they're interested in only three things. If you knock out a story that combines all three, you'll do fine."

"What are they?" asked Jones.

"Sex, blood and gold," Duranty repeated the phrase, relishing it. "You want to make your name as a newspaperman, you write about those three and not much else."

Jones smiled, coughed and said, "May I ask, what's the GPU?"

Natasha removed her hand. The bright lights of the carriage died, leaving their faces bathed in the reddening light. A silence prickled.

"Why do you ask that?" said Lyons, eventually.

"I came across a British engineer in my hotel, a Mr Attercliffe from Sheffield. He translated a phrase for me that was being repeated by the loudspeakers, 'the liquidation of cowlessness'. I told him that it was gibberish and he said that I should watch what I say, lest the GPU hear about it. He pronounced it Gay-Pay-Ooo. Attercliffe wouldn't tell me. So what's the GPU?"

"Haha," snorted Duranty, recovering first, "good question, my young owl. No better question here in the Soviet Union. Lyons, are you going to tell him? You're the expert on them. Or is it the other way round?"

Lyons shrugged.

"Wells, answer the man's question, damn you? What's the Gay-Pay-Doodah?"

Wells stared at Duranty coldly but he, too, said nothing.

"Mr Fischer?"

Fischer opened and shut his mouth, a goldfish out of his bowl. The two women stared at the floor. Oumansky gazed fixedly out of the window. Framed against the last rays of the sun, a stallion galloped alongside the train, its mane on fire.

The illusion was broken when the train crossed a bridge over a swollen river. Below the train tracks, two men, monolith-still, were lost in their fishing. In the dying light the pasture gave way to a forest of silver birch, bone pale, continuing without end.

Duranty studied Oumansky's absorption in the coming darkness and then, winking at Jones, said, "it seems you've asked the very best kind of a question, one that no-one wants to answer."

"And, you, Duranty," said Jones, "if I were to ask you point blank what the GPU is, what would say?"

The carriage lights, small but beautifully cut chandeliers, came back on.

"Out loud I'd tell you it's like the Mothers' Union," he said, his voice a languid drawl.

Jones smiled straight back at Duranty and said, "Like the Mother's Union, eh? I see."

That was the first moment when Duranty had a glimmer that this young man might be trouble. "Little Owl, are you making mischief with me?"

"Not at all," said Jones. Outside, the silver birches marched into the night – but, caught in the reflection from the window, he saw Evgenia's eyes flash in delight.

"I'd still like to know about this GPU," said Jones.

Duranty's voice dropped a register. "I'll answer your question. First, during the Revolution, Lenin's armed fist was called the Cheka, short form for the Extraordinary Commission. Cheka, in English, would be Exco, a nice cold hard ring to it. They mean business and some. In the early '20s, after perhaps too many people got shot, they rebranded the Cheka the Gay-Pay-Oo, the State Political Directorate. Now, officially, it's the OGPU. It stands for the Joint State blah-blah, but everybody still calls it the Gay-Pay-Oo or the Three Letters – or, best of all, because it's never really changed, the Cheka, the officers the Chekists. They're the political police and their job is to keep the Soviet show on the road while every capitalist on the planet is out to wreck it. They're based in the Lubyanka. In the old days, under the Tsar, it was an insurance company. Now they insure against the defeat of Communism. They can be rough, too rough, but the way they see it, they're fighting a war and one they have no certainty of winning." His eyes narrowed a fraction. Then he donned his sardonic mask again and his voice returned to normal. "But have you come all this way to pick holes in the great Soviet experiment, Little Owl? Two thousand miles from London is a long way to travel just to play the bourgeois wrecker, no?"

Jones turned back from the silver birch and shook his head. "No. I was a reporter in the valleys when the mineworkers struck for months in 1926. The Conservatives were cruel, Winston Churchill a total bastard."

The engine whistle blew sorrowfully, mourning the dusk.

"In Maerdy pit they lasted until 1927. The pit village was so left wing, the hatred for the mineowners so strong, the locals called it Little Moscow. The day they tried to go back to work," Jones continued, "it soon became apparent that the mine bosses had played a dirty trick. Most men could return. But some had lost their jobs for good. Naturally, there was trouble, not just from the men who'd gone back to work only to discover they'd been sacked. A young lad, no more than fourteen, he found a steel pole and tried to jam it in the wheel of a police van. Somehow, he slipped. The police van stopped because others were throwing stones at it. It started to reverse. The young lad didn't stand a chance. He couldn't get out of the way in time and it ran him over... There and then, I decided to read *Das Kapital*. After that, I knew I had to come to Big Moscow, to the Soviet Union, to see this noble experiment for myself."

"You mentioned Churchill, Jones," said Duranty, softly. "He sent British soldiers to join the Whites in 1918 to crush the revolution, to help the counter-revolutionaries. That's why the Soviet Union has got to have the Cheka or something like it. You can't make an omelette without breaking eggs. And I'm afraid to say, you can't break eggs without the use of force."

Jones nodded. The train slowed down to something approaching walking pace, allowing a man and a woman on a horse-driven cart to overtake them. Duranty gestured to the cart riding alongside.

"Progress, Jones, means the railway over the horse and cart. But progress can be painful." He smacked his left leg below the knee and it gave off a soft wooden thunk. "Lost my leg below the knee in a train wreck. Hurts like hell sometimes, especially in the cold and wet. But that's how life is. No pain, no progress."

Swigging back the last of his champagne with a flourish, he poured himself a fresh glass and topped up Jones'. Outside, the cart pulled off on a diagonal tack and slid into the night.

"That said," Duranty continued, "these people here are fighting like tigers to make the world a better, fairer place and there are so many powerful forces out to stop them. It goes against the grain to watch them bullied out of their dream. Perhaps going to Harrow makes me want to help Stalin & Co. Something about cricket, fair play, makes me stand up for the Soviet experiment. I'm not a passionate believer. But I'm on their side."

The train went over some roughly-laid track. Swaying, they sipped their champagne in a comradely silence, broken only by a tinkling from the chandeliers.

"Jones, you were asking about the Cheka," said Duranty. "You've had the theory, now here's the practice."

With a very slight tilt of his head, he gestured towards two men coming down the carriage towards the party. The first was roughly the same age as Jones, shorter than average, shaggy-haired, wearing a blue suit, white shirt and red tie. In poor light, Jones and the newcomer could easily be mistaken for each other.

The second was the fat officer who had, scant hours before, pointed his revolver at Jones.

Jones' double introduced himself as "Colonel Leonid Ivanovich Zakovsky." His voice was high-pitched, the squeal of a piglet on the run from the butcher's knife. Turning to his deputy, he introduced him as Kapitan Genrikh Samoilovich Lyushkov. Zakovsky then squeaked a long speech in Russian which Evgenia translated, her head askance. "Colonel Zakovsky would like to tender his apologies to you, Mr Jones, for the unfortunate misunderstanding at Kursk station today. But he says you gave the impression that you were a saboteur and he says his deputy Kapitan Lyushkov was right to place the security of Professor Aubyn and the other members of the Moscow press corps first and foremost. We are most grateful to Mr Duranty for his assistance, and Kapitan Lyushkov would like to say that he's pleased that no harm came to you."

Lyushkov's voice was a low rumble. He kneaded the pale dough of his face into a smile.

"He doesn't sound very pleased that no harm came to me," said Jones, unhelpfully. "What did he say exactly?"

"It was by way of an apology," replied Evgenia, guardedly. Duranty chuckled to himself. Now Zakovsky was squeaking again and Evgenia translated. "Colonel Zakovsky says that you, Mr Jones, are most welcome to the Soviet Union and he hopes that your time in our great country will be fruitful for both parties."

As Zakovsky moved forward, Jones stood up and the two men shook hands. Then Zakovsky spoke some more, his tone less friendly. Jones waited for the translation.

"Colonel Zakovsky says," said Evgenia, "that the Soviet Union is under constant attack from bourgeois fascists, social fascists and Hitlerites. The GPU are the armed fist of the revolution and no-one, not even our friends in the western press, should be under any illusion that, if they endanger the revolution in any way, they will be smashed to a pulp."

"Smashing," said Jones.

Zakovsky bowed, Lyushkov beamed piggishly, then the two Chekists took their seats at a table in the middle of the carriage, out of earshot but in sight.

"See, just like the Mother's Union," said Duranty dryly. "Right then, boys, let's play a game. Who is the biggest name you've interviewed? The winner gets" – he fished out a silver cigarette lighter from his pocket and flourished it in front of them – "this."

Fischer picked it up, examined the inscription and then smirked to himself.

"Calvin Coolidge," offered Wells.

"Boring and out of power," snapped Duranty.

"Al Capone," said Fischer.

"Tax cheats don't count."

To Jones, Duranty seemed very intent on keeping his lighter.

"Stalin," said Lyons.

"Ah, now we're talking," said the ringmaster.

Jones said, "Tell me about Stalin, Lyons. What's he like as a human being?"

"Once I'd got in the Kremlin it was easy," said Lyons, "Stalin met me at the door of his state apartments and shook hands, smiling. There was a certain shyness about him. He was remarkably unlike the scowling, self-important dictator of popular imagination. 'Comrade Stalin,' I began, 'may I quote you to the effect that you have not been assassinated?' The old boy laughed and said, 'Yes, you may – except that I hate to take the bread out of the mouth of the Riga correspondents.'"

Jones frowned, puzzled.

Duranty explained, "Riga, the Latvian capital, is the town where all the Red-baiting flotsam and jetsam end up. Hitler-loving reporters, White Russians and western espionage agents send messages to London, Washington and Paris, suggesting that the Soviet experiment is soon going to die – and, rather too often, that Stalin himself is dead. They've killed him off a dozen times. So the Vozhd has a sense of humour about the drivel his enemies write about him."

Lyons lifted a hand in air, calling for calm, then said, "So between us, the present company has met Stalin, a US President and a gangster. Whoever tops that wins Duranty's lighter."

After a pause, Duranty raised his arm. "I was in Paris just before the war and messed about with Aleister Crowley. I'd say the Great Beast trumps all other cards in the deck."

The rest of the company fell silent. Duranty's sway over the other newspapermen seemed absolute.

"So the Great Beast wins?" asked Duranty.

Jones coughed, his eyes mildly amused.

"Mr Jones, who have you met?" asked Evgenia in black-eyed innocence.

"Adolf Hitler," Jones said and – except for Duranty – the company roared their approval.

"So, how did you get the scoop of the century?" asked Lyons.

"I wouldn't call it a scoop. I didn't interview him properly," said Jones. "Or have much time with him, just a few words. But I observed him as best I could. Close up? Unimpressive. His car arrived at the airfield in Berlin and he stepped out, a slight figure in a shapeless black hat, wearing a light mackintosh. He raised his arm flabbily to greet those who'd assembled to see him. So here was the leader of the most volcanic nationalist awakening which the world has seen and yet he was a mild nobody. I was mystified. The bodyguards were more striking. The uniform is black with silver brocade. On their hats there is a silver skull and crossbones, the cavities of the eyes in the skull being bright red. The SS ooze violence, barely suppressed." Jones gestured to the two Chekists. "Like our friends here."

"Likening Hitler's SS with the Cheka isn't the done thing in the Soviet Union," said Duranty through a thin smile.

"Perseus wore a magic cap that the monsters he hunted down might not see him," said Jones, enigmatically. "We draw the magic cap down over eyes and ears as a make-believe that there are no monsters."

"What?" said Duranty, incredulous.

"It's from *Das Kapital.* Monsters do exist, in the Cheka and the SS."

For a second time Duranty understood that Jones could be dangerous.

"So," Lyons interrupted the argument, "who is the bigger beast, that self-styled nitwit and writer of mediocre necromancy... or Adolf Hitler?"

No-one said anything but Duranty pushed the lighter towards Jones.

"No thank you, Duranty, I don't smoke. It's only a game."

"No, you must. It would be an insult if you didn't collect your winnings. I insist."

There was something hard about Duranty's tone that left Jones feeling it would be wrong to resist him, but also that Duranty would not forget this moment. His hand reached out to inspect it. On one side was the inscription, "To W.D. All my darkness, A.C."

"This was given to you by Aleister Crowley himself?"

"It was so."

"What was he like?"

"A mesmerising fraud."

"Just like Hitler then," and the company laughed.

The waiter returned bearing a tray with plates, cutlery, pots of caviar resting in a bed of ice, blini, and a silver pot holding sour cream. Natasha took control and showed Jones how to spread the cream on the blini and then cover it with caviar, a mix of red and black eggs. Jones had forgotten how hungry he was. Breakfast at his hotel had been a miserable affair of black tea, one sad hard-boiled egg and a lump of black bread as hard as teak. He wolfed the blini, caviar and all.

"Yum-yum," he said and Natasha toyed with the phrase, "yoom-yoom", giving it a sensuality entirely lacking in Jones' version.

"What's your office's telegram address?" asked Duranty.

"WesternMailNews. Why do you ask?"

"Just in case there's some dreadful accident."

Jones looked a little downcast.

"Only jesting, old boy, only jesting."

The company concentrated on the caviar and blini, all except one. Out of the side of his eyes, Jones observed that Evgenia wasn't eating. Her hand went to the bottle of red and she poured herself a glass of wine, holding it up to her nose to savour its taste. As she did so, the light from the chandelier shone through the wine, bathing her face a deep red.

"Savouring the bouquet is bourgeois, Evgenia," said Duranty, his eyes on fire.

Evgenia blushed to her roots, put the glass down and stood up. To leave, she had to squeeze past Jones. Shrinking from physical contact with her, he edged sideways and upwards in his seat, making an exhibition of himself.

After she'd left the table, Duranty smiled pleasantly, running his finger around the top of the champagne flute. "You're acting as if Evgenia has some physically deformity, Jones. Is that the case?"

"Yes, no," he stammered.

Before he was obliged to say more, a waiter tapped a glass with a fork, announcing dinner. The company, about twenty in all with the German film crew, sat down at tables decorated with candles in the shape of red stars. They were served fresh Astrakhan caviar washed down with pre-war vodka, white bread and butter, borscht soup spiked with sherry, grilled salmon, roast partridge and chicken served with vintage burgundy and cakes of every kind, fine Russian cheese, hot-house grapes, old port and older cognac.

When Evgenia returned she took a small bowl of borscht. The others fell on the feast as if they had never seen its like. Jones began to wonder whether this fare wasn't easily available in the ordinary way. That would square with the pitifully poor food he had put up with at his Moscow hotel.

A thin-lipped blond man in a black polo neck sweater slipped into the carriage and sat at a table on his own, furthest away from the reporters. His cheekbones were so sharply defined they looked as though they had been cut by an ice-axe. Scowling at the carriage, he pecked at his soup.

"Who's that?" asked Jones.

"That's Dr Limner," said Duranty, "Professor Aubyn's personal factotum."

"Where's the great man?"

"He likes to keep himself to himself," said Duranty. "Tomorrow they're taking us to a collective farm so we'll see quite a lot of him then."

"May I ask another question?" said Jones, tentatively.

Duranty's eyes flickered with their habitual amusement. "Go ahead old boy, go ahead."

"Back in Britain, in the right-wing press, there's talk of famine here in Russia. Is there any truth in that?"

Fischer seemed as if he was girding himself to say something – but Duranty leaned forward, colliding with Natasha and spilling red wine over her frock. The clean-up operation was diverting and involved a fair amount of mockery from Lyons, Fischer and Wells.

Once order had been restored, Jones tried again.

"So, this talk of famine?"

Gesturing to Natasha and Evgenia, Duranty smiled. "George Bernard Shaw came to Russia just a few months ago on a fact-finding trip. These two ladies were his translators. What did you make of him, girls?"

Natasha looked at Oumansky, who was staring at his feet, then spoke. "For a westerner, George Bernard Shaw has a fine analytical command of the problems that the Soviet Union faces. But..." She gave a sly glance at Oumansky, checking that he was still lost in his boots. "He didn't do yoom-yoom." Her delivery of the phrase made it sound indecent, provoking yet more laughs from the newspapermen. "I prefer the Flying Welsh," she added, and with that she rested her hand on Jones' thigh, again.

"Evgenia?" prompted Duranty.

She was staring out into the darkness.

"Evgenia?" Duranty repeated, this time a command.

She put her fingers of her right hand to her neck and ran them along her jawline but said nothing.

"What did you make of George Bernard Shaw's line on famine, Evgenia?" pressed Duranty.

"Most memorably," she replied, "George Bernard Shaw said, 'I did not see a single under-nourished person in Russia, young or old. Were they padded? Were their hollow cheeks distended by pieces of India rubber inside?'"

"That's what he said, girl," Duranty snapped back, "not what you made of him."

"It is for others to judge. My function is simply to be the people's translator, Mr Duranty. I do not wish to trespass beyond my position. That would be a disservice to the revolution and to the Party."

"Bravo, old girl, bravo," Duranty replied.

"And you, Duranty? What do you make of these famine rumours?" Jones asked.

"Look at this feast. We're supposed to be going through the dead centre of the very worst of the famine zone, according to the propagandist press which hates the Russians. I'll wager you won't see anyone starving."

The train pulled to a halt at a primitive station, lit feebly by a few lamps. The restaurant car had become unpleasantly stuffy. Zakovsky, chicken leg in hand, stood up to open a window to allow some fresh air in. He nibbled on the leg but something about it displeased him and he lobbed the remains out of the open window. The engine sprang back into life and the carriages concertinaed as the train got under way once more.

Looking up from his plate, Jones made out six or seven small boys emerge from the outer darkness, racing for the officer's chicken leg. A small, very thin boy got there first – but he was pole-axed by a punch from the biggest lad of all. The thin boy lay on the ground, a pool of blood by his head. Jones craned forward to see the end of the scene, hoping that he would get up – but the train picked up speed and what happened next was swallowed up by the night.

*

Perhaps it was the lack of motion that woke him. Jones was disorientated at first, his neck cricked, but slowly he took in his surroundings, the dining car empty apart from Oumansky and Lyons talking quietly over glasses of vodka on a separate table. Through the window, Jones made out a sickle moon, ringed by cloud. It cast a feeble, silvery glow onto the dark forest outside.

The train had stopped. It was two o'clock.

Standing up, he stretched and headed towards the train compartment he was sharing with Duranty. Once outside, he tapped once on the door and, hearing no reply, slid it open a fraction. There was no light inside the compartment. Before his eyes adjusted, he heard a low animal grunt of a man in ecstasy, then made out the form of Duranty, sitting in the lounge chair by the window. Kneeling in front of him, but unidentifiable in the scant moonlight, was a woman, half-naked, her hands tied behind her back with some black cloth, her head dipping low into his groin.

"Well, you found the sex old boy," Duranty's voice was amused. "Blood and gold next. Won't be too long. Come back in half an hour."

Jones slid the door tight shut and hurried down to the end of the carriage, where the maid with the potato face smiled at him thinly. He stepped outside onto the footplate. The cold scoured his throat. Hoarfrost had turned the silver birch trees into a ghost army frozen in motion. Except for the soft chug of the locomotive's idling engine, the night was still.

Who was she?

The more he turned it over in his mind, the more he wondered whether it might – it couldn't be – Evgenia. Jealousy, self-loathing and doubt tumbled inside him. He felt tempted to jump off the train and march off into the frozen emptiness, never to be heard of again. His parents would care, but no-one else.

"Evgenia. Evgenia. Evgenia."

Repeating her name didn't soothe him, didn't answer his stupid, revolting question. Had it been her with Duranty?

Soldiers in Genghis helmets came out of the dark, walking fast towards the front of the train, moving past him in silence. Shrinking back into the shadows on the footplate, he stopped counting when he got to a hundred. At the end came a small knot of civilians, well-dressed for the cold. Jones noted one family, a massive red-bearded father, an accordion around his neck, a handsome mother and a plump boy with rosy apple cheeks coming along behind. Then came more soldiers shouldering two wooden carts covered with cloth.

Freezing, bewildered, he watched the last of the soldiers file past him, then returned to the restaurant car, knowing he'd rather spend the night there than in Duranty's compartment. He called for vodka from Gazdanov, the waiter.

When a glass arrived, he knocked it back in one and ordered a second, then a third. For the fourth, Jones watched as Gazdanov returned with a litre bottle and two glasses. The waiter poured two shots, one for Jones and one for himself. They clinked glasses and drank, after which the waiter left Jones the bottle and bid him goodnight. Jones worked the bottle mechanically after that. It was three quarters empty by the time the train gave a shrug and pulled itself nonchalantly forwards.

Shortly, they passed through a city – but, by this time, Jones was drunk. The vodka bottle and little glass bobbed up and down before his eyes. Looking up through the windows, he made out a great railway station, brilliantly lit, empty of people apart from a knot of well-fed and warm-looking civilians gathered around two carts laden with food. His eyes closed and opened and he took in what was laid out on one cart: oranges, chicken, blinis, sausage, bread – and, beside it, a plump boy dancing a jig while stuffing an enormous sandwich into his mouth. It was the same boy Jones had seen earlier that night, walking besides the halted train. He couldn't get the name of the city on the station platform because it was in Cyrillic but clumsily he took out his notebook and tried to write what it looked like in Roman script. It took him three goes, but eventually he got it roughly right: "Xapkob". Jones had a Russian-English dictionary but it was in his bag and that was in the compartment with Duranty. He wasn't going back there tonight.

Nothing made much sense. He fell asleep, dreaming that his old district editor in Aberdare wanted a story from Moscow's ways and means committee and the only thing he had to file was a story about an old man in blood red fog weeping, weeping without control while a boy danced a jig.

The train jolted to a halt and Jones woke up. For some reason – anxiety, perhaps – he checked his pocket and found the envelope

Attercliffe had given him at the station, something he had quite forgotten. Opening it with clumsy fingers, he found a black and white
photograph of a tank by a road sign. The road sign was in Cyrillic.
The photograph had been taken in Russia.

Lined up with their backs against the tank's tracks were a number
of officers in uniform. Some wore scuttle-shaped helmets.
Germans, thought Jones. Their leader was a thin, tall man, with
silver hair cut very short and hooded eyes staring directly into the
camera. Around him, others wore brown uniforms, baggy trousers
and flat hats. Red Army, Jones realised.

He turned the photograph over, to find the date that was written
there. 1ˢᵗ August, 1932. Jones breathed deeply. Here was incontro-
vertible evidence of a straight breach of the Treaty of Versailles,
banning Germany from developing tank warfare.

Gravely troubled, Jones looked up and found that Lyushkov had
entered the restaurant car while he had been asleep. The fat officer
was staring at him, hard.

This was unsettling because he was second from right in the photograph.

Chapter Four

Stalin floated above a mist that hugged the hollows of the earth, the eeriest thing that Jones had ever seen. The train came to a halt, a whistle blew and the mist thinned to reveal the heads of a throng of peasants, stocky and well-fed. The fat boy who Jones had seen dancing a jig at the station in the middle of the night was there, along with red beard, his accordion strapped to his chest, his wife by his side.

The mist swirled, thickened, then faded. The train doors opened and film crew, reporters, translators and minders stepped down, walking one hundred yards towards the airbound god and his devotees. As they grew nearer, a plinth for the *Vozhd* emerged, and behind that a smart, newly-built red brick building. This was the collective farm they were to visit.

Seven young women, their hair plaited, stood holding freshly cut flowers, sheaves of wheat, freshly baked loaves and little bowls of salt. Young and slender, they stood with their toes at ten-to-two on the clock. Jones wondered for a second that they might all be ballerinas from the Bolshoi shipped in for the occasion, but then dismissed his suspicion as absurd.

The mist was turning from pink to gold as the sun climbed in the east and Borodin directed the film crew. Hurrying into position, they framed the seven young women with their loaves and salt. Then a clapperboard snapped, and Borodin shouted, "Action!"

A crow squawked, hopping from one chimney to the next.

"Action!"

Once again, nothing happened.

"Action!"

Furious, Brodin ran over to Oumansky, shouted at him, and

waited as the official trotted all the way back to the train and entered the first carriage. After a delay, Oumansky came out and held out his thumb.

"Action," yelled Borodin once more – and this time a small knot of dignitaries emerged at the front carriage, stepped down and began the walk to the collective farm. Oumansky led the way, with Zakovsky, Lyushkov and Dr Limner bringing up the rear. After a pause, Professor Aubyn emerged into the light, sporting a black Lenin cap set at a jaunty angle on his head, black coat, black trousers and ballroom shoes. A sparse man with a sparse beard, his once blonde hair now faded to grey, Aubyn had the air of an angel who had lost his way back to heaven and was rather cross about it.

As the cameras rolled, two of the young women stepped forward, bouncing on their toes, and presented the professor with bread and salt. Aubyn froze, stupefied. Oumansky sidled up and whispered something and Aubyn very gingerly broke off a little tab of bread, dipped it into the salt and then held it in the air, inspecting it in the manner of a laboratory technician peering at a Petri dish with an unwelcome batch of mould.

Borodin yelled, "Cut!" and hissed something to Oumansky, who mimed "Eat it!" to Aubyn. Aubyn was about to do so when Borodin yelled "Wait!", then cried "Action!" – at which point, the professor ate the tab and then broke into an aimless smile. Around him, the horde of well-wishers broke into a spasm of joy, red beard squeezing out the Kalinka on the accordion, young men dancing, the young women clapping and cheering. The group entered through a gateway and, beyond that, ploughed earth could be seen tapering away to the edge of the mist.

Close by was an asphalted parade ground. Shortly, a ballet of six tractors trundled in, criss-crossing the parade ground and each other, each one loaded with smiling workers holding sheaves of wheat. Jones didn't know much about farming but it was October and the harvest should have been brought in a month before. And another thing that troubled him: in Wales, every farmer he'd ever met was a miserable sod, forever complaining. All of these farmers were smiling, all of the time.

After the tractors came twenty horses, led by their grooms, then a herd of fat cows, then three very fat pigs, led by the nose by three young women holding fat carrots tantalisingly just in front of their snouts. They trotted across the asphalt, the cleverest and seemingly the most compliant of all the animals.

Duranty sidled up to Jones and said, through the side of his mouth, "Old Macdonald had a farm, E-I-E-I-O." Jones, still troubled from what had happened last night, could not help but smile. Duranty had the charm of the devil himself.

The third pig, a brindled old sow, truculent and strong-minded, was proving to be a Trotskyist. While the young woman over-concentrated on smiling at the dignitaries, the sow trotted forward with an unexpected burst of speed and gobbled up the carrot, almost taking off her fingers in the process. Then, as the other two pigs left the arena, the sow reversed and started to grub up the horse and cow dung left by the previous actors.

"Cut!" Borodin hissed at Oumansky. "Do you think a pig eating shit best conveys New Soviet Man?"

Oumansky shook his head.

Meanwhile, the young woman seemed to be losing her conviction that she was any kind of swineherd. Everytime she got within a few feet, the sow eyed her with menace and she backed off. Finally, one of the male farmers, a strapping fellow, came to her assistance. He waved a rake in the sow's general direction but the sow was having none of it. Zakovsky shot a look at Lyushkov, who disappeared around the far corner. Shortly afterwards, an old man emerged. Sour-faced, strikingly thin and poorly shod in cloth boots, he was carrying a stout stick, which he promptly used to wallop the sow on her rump, showing all the lack of charity you would expect from a true swineherd. Meekly, the sow followed the thin man off the display area.

Once more, Borodin cried, "Action!" and then a wrath of cackling geese appeared. Then came a duck, waddling through the display ground, followed by twenty ducklings, bringing forth a series of oohs and aahs at the sweetness of the scene. "Cut!" yelled Borodin and the hosts seemed to sigh with relief that nothing else had gone wrong.

Soon, the sun broke through the mist and the party were led around a corner to find an apple orchard – and, beneath the trees, three rows of tables, laden with bread, hams, cheeses and fruit, bottles of vodka at every other place. By the top table was a small wooden podium, to which Professor Aubyn was led by Oumansky. A short speech and then they could all enjoy breakfast. That would have been the plan.

The collective farmers cheered as he mounted the steps of the podium. Evgenia appeared by his side, standing demurely one step below him. Aubyn coughed twice – someone passed him a glass of water – and then started to speak. His voice was high-pitched, scholarly, upper class.

"Comrades," he began, "it behoves me to bear witness today to these remarkable fruits of New Soviet Man. This is a miracle..." He hesitated and Evgenia took the opportunity to translate his words into Russian. While she did so, he looked somewhat peeved – as if the act of translation was breaking his train of thought. "...As I was saying... a miracle of wheat, a miracle of beef, a miracle of pork. And do not forget the noble duck, still less the workers' goat..."

He hesitated once more. Evgenia leapt into the gap, her translation of the last phrase "the workers' goat" bringing forward a titter of laughter from the rougher, thinner-looking collective farmers assembled at the back of the throng. Lyushkov detached himself from the dignitaries and walked slowly towards the back of the crowd. The tittering stopped as if it had been switched off at the mains.

"...together our brother animals labour, too, for the common weal. But there are enemies afoot. Joseph Stalin himself has put it like this..."

He droned on and on, Evgenia translating, for another thirty minutes. Then, though he may not have come to an end, Zakovsky started clapping, Lyushkov followed suit and soon the whole collective was roaring their approval. From around a corner came a throng of children wearing red scarves. They started to mob the professor, as a pack of wolflings might savage an elderly bear. Aubyn half-smiled. The speechifying was over.

"Ah, the Little Octobrists," said Duranty to Jones, the two of them alone in a small alcove. "They can always be relied upon to liven up the party. They're the Soviet version of the Boy Scouts. At nine they become Young Pioneers, at fourteen Komsomols, Young Communists."

"When do they stop being Young Communists?"

"That happens at 28."

"And then?"

"Well, if they're lucky and well connected and have no known bourgeois blemish on their character, then they may get to join the Cheka. These are the larvae, the Cheka the fully-fledged butterflies. Pretty little killers, eh?"

Jones studied him, hesitating to speak.

"Out with it?"

"Yesterday, when I asked about the GPU, the Cheka, you – all of you – were very cautious. Now you're cracking jokes about them, without a care. Why?"

"Ah, very good, young Jonesy. A good reporter should always sniff out an anomaly. Today, right now, there's just you and me. Yesterday, we were in company, lots of Russians, lots of colleagues. You never know. The Cheka, they've got ears. There'a joke: a Russian looks at himself in the mirror and says, one of us must be an informer."

"You don't trust your colleagues?"

"Not all of them."

"Any of them?"

"No."

"Who do you trust the least?"

"Well, me, frankly."

Jones burst out laughing. There was something extraordinary about this man, how he was so shameless about his lack of shame. It was undefeatable and there was something admirable about this quality. Jones, conflicted, uneasy with himself, felt in awe.

"But you trust me?" asked Jones.

"You've got an honest face. And, besides, you're new."

The throng attacked breakfast with a passion that startled Jones. No grace and no graces were heard or seen as the collective farmers wolfed the food in front of them. Jones looked around for the sour-faced swineherd but he could see no trace of him, nor of Lyushkov.

"Evgenia?" She had found an empty place next to him.

"Yes, Mr Jones?"

"There's one thing that happened last night that I was wondering whether you could explain."

Duranty, sitting opposite, took in the conversation and held his head to one side, eyes glittering with curiosity.

"How can I be of assistance, Mr Jones?" Her voice, soft and low, dropped an octave.

"Evgenia, in the middle of the night..."

"Yes?"

Her eyes truly were the blackest shade of brown he'd ever seen.

"We passed through a big station. I've got a note here of the spelling of the station in Roman script." Fishing out his notebook, Jones showed her the page on which he'd written the name down three times.

She giggled and said, "Your handwriting is a little difficult to make out, Mr Jones."

"I'm so sorry."

She handed the notebook back to him. "What does it say?"

He squinted at the letters drifting across the page. "I think I wrote Xapkob, Evgenia."

"Not Xapkob. The Cyrillic letters means you pronounce it Kharkov, Mr Jones. It's the capital of Soviet Ukraine."

"Thank you so much, Evgenia. As we passed through the station, the people were dancing and eating on the platform." He paused. "I'd love to go back to Kharkov one day to see more of it."

"Perhaps, one day, I may able to escort you there, Mr Jones, the work of the party permitting."

"The work of the party must come first, of course, Evgenia."

She smiled at him so bleakly that Jones wondered to himself whether he'd ever met a woman who disliked him so much.

Chapter Five

Dark, fat clouds shifted up in the sky, occasionally letting a cone of sunlight poke through.

Beneath those dark, trembling clouds, the Lenin Dam was a fat concrete thumb jamming the mighty Dnieper. To the north, upstream, it had created an inland sea stretching to the horizon and beyond. Along the course of the dam, red flags snapped in the breeze. To the south the river, far punier than before, trickled along its ancient course. Marching in step with it were spindly electricity pylons running power lines to the new factories.

Professor Aubyn, Dr Limner and the great and the good from Moscow were decanted from their limousines onto a specially built wooden platform overlooking the dam. Horse-drawn artillery, stewarded by GPU troops, trotted towards them, their cannon pointed at the reservoir. A thick black cloud shifted and, as if on cue, the sun came out, illuminating a man in a suit – a minister of this and that, Jones never caught his title, still less his name – who stood on a podium and began to orate.

Jones' Russian couldn't begin to follow the speech but Evgenia provided a running translation for those journalists who wanted to get down every word: "Under the Wise Direction of Our Great Genius Leader and Teacher Stalin... a man of iron, a warrior of steel, a Leninist of bronze and a Bolshevik of granite..."

The speaker droned on. "Thanks to his inspiration, the seven rapids, which made our great river a hazard for the ancients, have now been inundated. Such is the gloriousness of the true path of Marxism-Leninism as defined by General Secretary Josif Stalin that the very force of nature falls on its knees in homage..."

Jones' attention wandered from Evgenia's translation to the

hectic craftsmanship of Borodin's film crew. They worked the two main cameras and the little Kinamo, filming the whole speech, changing reels at frantic speed to capture as much as possible. They had performed as they had done at the collective farm but this was a far bigger occasion. Borodin was the master, the cameramen the first, second and third mates, and the clapper-board man the ship's boy. All three had assistants and the assistants had assistants too. The whole thing looked like a nest of ants having a nervous breakdown. And yet it worked. They filmed from afar. That would be the long-shot. They stopped, change reels, then scampered within thirty feet or so of the podium, lined up on the great orator, whoever he was, and started over again. The mid-shot. For the finale of the great speech, they raced to the podium and captured the climax.

When the great man ended his speech, he waved his fist, the cannon boomed, a flock of cranes lifted from their nests, a band played The Internationale – and everyone stood up and applauded rapturously. The crowd waited for the dam to start to thunder. Nothing happened. Not a drip of water fell. The applause carried on as if, thought Jones, they had been ordered on pain of death not to stop. Hurrahs came and went. Still clapping, the audience craned their necks, wondering what they might have done wrong.

Oumansky hurried up onto the platform to talk to Borodin. The two men jabbed each other in the chest with their fingers. The applause rolled on and on, while Borodin and his crew trotted with their equipment to the cannons. Readying the two big cameras to get side-shots of the cannons, Borodin engaged the artillery officer in a long conversation. Then the clapper-board man went clappety-clap, Borodin raised his hand – and the officer roared a command. Once again, the cannon fired, the band played the Internationale, and the crowd went wild with excitement, just as before.

Still the dam stayed dry, and still the crowd clapped. The camera crew jogged to the bandstand, lined up on the tubas, trombones and drummer, waited for the clapper-board man's authority, and then filmed the Internationale being played, long-shot, mid-shot, close-up. By now the applause was getting feebler and feebler. The clouds had gone, the sun was glaring and the heat of the day cast a sleepy spell on everyone.

The camera crew walked at no great pace to the top of the dam while the applause pattered on. By now, the audience understood that there was little point in slamming their hands against each other until the clapper-board man had done his thing. The crew lined up for a side-shot of the great dam's sluice gates, the clapper-board man clackety-clacked and a great tap was opened in the innards of the dam's workings. Moments later, spouts of water thundered down three hundred feet onto the river bed below.

Two Young Pioneers gave flowers to the man in the suit. One was a blond girl with plaited hair, the other a plump boy with apple cheeks – the same boy, Jones dully realised, he had seen walking silently beside the train in the middle of the night, eating a sandwich at Kharkov station and dancing a jig and playing a peasant's boy at the collective farm.

As the camera crew sluggishly walked back to the podium to capture the flower-giving and jig-dancing, Jones asked, "Where's Stalin?"

It was Duranty, standing beyond Lyons and Fischer, who replied, "Jones, old boy, I think that – what, with building socialism all the time – Uncle Joe decided that it was about time he had a nice day off and went for a drink."

The others sniggered while Jones reddened. He was the new boy and he'd better know his place. That was the message.

As the camera crew got their last shots, the applause dribbled to a stop. Someone closed the dam sluice gates and the water did likewise. Soon, the Soviet and other dignitaries started to head for their limousines, Professor Aubyn and Dr Limner bringing up the rear, as if they'd all been alerted that the show was over by some hidden signal. After a short confusion, the foreign consuls, observers and journalists stood up and headed for their vehicles too. As Jones dallied slowly behind the others, a dapper man emerged and walked with him in step.

"Mr Jones? I suppose I should introduce myself. My name's Wallace Ilver. I'm the commercial attache at the British Embassy."

He wore a natty blue suit, white shirt, dark grey tie and shoes so shiny that the sunlight gleamed off them. Balding with a light brown goatee, his face had somehow not enough flesh on it – as if his first layer of skin had been scraped off. His voice was beguiling. "Enjoying the... er... festivities?"

"It all rather went on a bit, what with the filming and all."

"Such is the way of the New Man. Who would have known such joy was to be had from concrete?" There was something rather likeable about the diplomat's mannered lament. Jones found himself grinning.

"Oh, crikey," Ilver continued, "there's my opposite number from Germany. I'm afraid I ought to go and a have a natter with him, talk shop, that sort of thing." Ilver made to hurry on. Then he half-turned and said, *sotto voce*, "Jones, old boy, keep an eye on things here. Watch your back but, if you chance on anything that might strike us as interesting, there's a cup of Earl Grey in it for you at the embassy. Oh, and a biscuit, of course. If I can ever be any help, just pop by. If I'm not in, leave your card. It's probably best not to telephone."

"Does that mean that someone is listening in?" asked Jones.

"It's probably best not to telephone," repeated Ilver. "Don't forget, tea and biscuits whenever you fancy." His smiled lacked sincerity. "I must dash. Toodle pip."

"What do you actually do at the embassy, Mr Ilver?" asked Jones.

Ilver pivoted on himself. "I'm the commercial attache, Mr Jones."

"This is the world's first truly Communist state. Commerce is dead in the Soviet Union. What do you actually do at the embassy, Mr Ilver?"

"How can I help you, Mr Jones?"

"I've been asked to give a photograph to someone at the British Embassy."

"What does the photograph show?"

"A tank in Russia. Leaning against it a bunch of officers, some German, some Soviet. I'm no expert but the tank looks German to me."

"The date of the photograph?"

"August this year. It could be faked but one of the Soviet officers leaning against the tank is Kapitan Lyushkov. He looks no different in real life."

"So, leaving the date aside, recent?"

"I'd say this year, yes."

"A photograph that is evidence of a present and very direct breach of German promises at the Treaty of Versailles not to develop tank warfare?" snapped Ilver. "A photograph that could start a second world war?"

"Indeed," said Jones.

The others had gone far ahead. "Where is this photograph?"

"In my pocket."

"May I have it?"

"Of course."

Ilver turned, inflecting his body, covering Jones from scrutiny. He produced a silver cigarette case and opened it.

"Cigarette?"

"I don't smoke."

"Don't be dim, Mr Jones. Cigarette?"

"Yes, please." Ilver leaned into Jones, handed over a cigarette and fished out a lighter. As he did so, Jones proffered the envelope which Ilver pocketed. Ilver lit the cigarette in Jones' mouth and immediately Jones started to cough, helplessly.

"Can't you pretend to smoke?"

"No."

"Never mind. Nobody's watching, thank God. Put it out, if you will."

Jones threw away the cigarette.

"Thank you very much, Mr Jones. Her Majesty's Government is in your debt. Can you tell me who gave this photograph to you?"

"A British engineer, a Mr Attercliffe."

"First name?"

"Harold."

Ilver's eyes narrowed. "So, once again, thanks ever so. Now I really must dash. But Jones. Have a care. Don't mention this to anyone. The less said, the better for all concerned. Understood?"

"Understood."

"And, Mr Jones, Her Majesty's Government is in your debt."

Ilver made to hurry ahead, but before he had gone very far, a limousine caught up with them. It was a box with chrome shark's teeth for a radiator grille. Lyushkov was at the wheel, Zakovsky in the front passenger seat.

"Care for a lift?" asked Zakovsky.

"Certainly," said Ilver.

"You too, Mr Jones?"

Jones stiffened. The GPU were the very last people he wanted a lift from but to say no seemed frankly discourteous. He collected his thoughts, smiled handsomely and said: "thank you ever so much." Ilver gave him a bleak smile as if to say, don't overdo it, old boy.

In the back of the seven-seater limo was a man in late middle age with short silver hair and hooded eyes. He wasn't in uniform but wearing a black frock coat, unmistakeably the senior German figure in Attercliffe's photograph.

"Mr Ilver, Mr Jones, may I introduce Herr Verbling, the German military attache?" said Zakovsky.

Verbling nodded stiffly.

"Hello, Ernst, we've met before," said Ilver. "May I introduce Mr Gareth Jones of the *Western Mail*?"

"Pleased to meet you, Herr Verbling," said Jones.

Verbling nodded stiffly once more and sank back into the upholstery, saying nothing.

"What kind of car is this?" asked Jones.

"It's a ZIS L-1, made exclusively in the Stalin Industries Factory," said Zakovsky. He turned to Lyushkov and they talked loudly and animatedly in Russian. Verbling had been staring out of the window but he turned to Ilver and Jones and said softly in crisp English, "It's a Buick 90, shipped out in parts to Leningrad. They managed to tighten the wheelnuts."

Verbling turned back to his study of the countryside. The rest of the journey passed in silence.

*

Darkness gripped Jones, as if he lay bound and gagged at the bottom of a deep well. Sweeping aside the bedclothes, he ripped open the curtains to see that night had fallen. From somewhere below, he could hear faint sounds of revelry. Dressing hurriedly, he nodded to the floor concierge, shunned the lift and tripped down three flights of stairs.

From behind two grand doors, he could hear a hubbub and music, a band crucifying elderly hits from America. Jones made to open the door but, at that moment, was stopped by Lyushkov dressed up to the nines in full dress uniform, his chest jingling with medals.

"Can I join the party?"

"Nyet."

That rumble again, the slow movement of a great stone.

"Please may I join the party?"

"Nyet."

"Why can't I join the party?"

"Net chernogo galstuka, net vkhoda."

"I don't understand you, Kapitan."

"Net chernogo galstuka, net vkhoda." The voice belonged to Duranty. "No black tie, no entry."

Jones turned to the great man. "Isn't that a trifle bourgeois?"

Duranty was dressed in a black tuxedo, a glass of champagne in one hand, Natasha and Evgenia on either arm.

"It is, old boy, it is, but he's a hard man, our Kapitan."

"Can you persuade him?"

Duranty machine-gunned words at Lyushkov in Russian. The Kapitan made a stony reply, only to suffer a further attack from Duranty. Still Lyushkov wouldn't budge. Duranty opened the door into the ballroom and slipped inside. In twenty seconds he returned with Zakovsky, who took in the situation in a flash, smiled at Jones and squealed at Lyushkov. The door to the ballroom opened.

"I didn't know we had to dress up," said Jones.

Duranty grinned. "No need to at all, old boy. As I've said before, Soviet Man loves a party – but he is quite backwards sometimes, almost Neanderthal. There's a problem with Kapitan Lyushkov too. He's a little too rigid."

"Beautiful voice," said Jones.

"Yes, true."

"But the Kapitan is a thug," said Jones.

Duranty stared at Jones, his smile warm, his eyes reptilian. His head tilted to one side and he said softly, "Remember who he works for, Mr Jones." The smile crept into his eyes. "The dam is a great excuse for a bunfight. Come and sit with us."

In the main ballroom two dozen tables were laid out, overlooked by twin portraits of Stalin and Lenin. The room was packed. Everyone from the train was there, together with local dignitaries and their women. The locals were marked out by their well-worn suits and out-of-fashion dresses. The exotic was supplied by a handful of consular officials in uniform: German, British, Polish. The most operatic of all was wearing a white tropical uniform and a butchered swan on his head. That would be, could only be, the Italian consul.

On a platform at the far end of the room a gypsy band sawed away at a tune. Jones took a long moment before he worked out the melody they were murdering: "Yes! We Have No Bananas." A few couples were dancing robotically but most of the company was gorging on the free food. Lyons and Fischer were both deep in conversation with two women who suggested, by their body language, that they were listening to the tongues of angels. Wells was sipping vodka on his own.

To one side, Ilver from the British embassy was leaning against a pillar, his tie undone, chatting to a strikingly handsome youth. In front of him Borodin was arguing passionately with Oumansky – something of a fixture, Jones was beginning to realise. Professor Aubyn and Dr Limner were sitting with Zakovsky who was smiling – and Lyushkov, who wasn't.

Duranty led the way, nodding to and swapping jokes with some of the other guests as they passed by. Once the party had sat down, waiters swarmed over them, offering wine and a starter of the finest beluga caviar. Jones, who was sick of the stuff by now, waved them away. He found himself sat between Duranty and Evgenia. She was wearing a black full-length dress that both hid and didn't hide her figure.

Zakovsky came over and stood by Jones, his normal stern demeanour softened – whether by the occasion or drink, it was hard to tell. He squeaked something fast and incomprehensible and Jones smiled idiotically.

"The Colonel wants to know whether you're married, Mr Jones? Do you have any children?"

Jones admitted that he was neither married nor a father. This was the cue for Zakovsky to open his wallet and show a black and white photograph of Zakovsky Junior, trussed up in the uniform of a Young Pioneer and staring at the camera.

"A bonny lad," said Jones. "What's his name?"

"Marlen."

"An unusual name."

"It's a combination of the first three letters of Marx and Lenin," Zakovsky beamed and wandered off to show his progeny to others.

Duranty leaned over to Jones and said, "The way things are going, perhaps it might have been smarter to call the boy Stalen. But maybe that would be seen as being too close to home."

Conversation in the ballroom faltered as the gypsy band finished their set and the entertainment began. Red Beard had donned Cossack dress and had exchanged the accordion for a balalaika. Taking to the stage, followed by his woman and the plump boy, he started strumming the Kalinka on the balalaika, at which the plump boy did his jolly jig. Next was the Volga Boat Song, the man squeezing out the tune on the accordion, the boy tapping to it with his feet. For an encore, all three of them did a fast run through of Tchaikovsky's 1812 symphony on squeezebox and balalaika, to bravos from the assembled guests.

"Enjoying this?" Jones asked Evgenia as the applause started to fade.

"It's very Russian."

"Nothing Ukrainian?"

"Not yet."

She smiled weakly at him and he smiled weakly back.

Moments later, Oumansky came over, a syrupy smile on his face. "Congratulations, Mr Jones, on a most excellent article on the great Soviet achievement of the construction of the dam. Very finely written."

"What?" said Jones. Duranty nudged him sharply with his elbow.

"In fact, we're so pleased with your insight into our struggle," Oumansky continued, "that we have arranged for you to have a seat at the upcoming trial of the coal saboteurs."

Oumansky, puzzled at Jones' confusion, explained, "Seats are extremely rare at this trial so this is a sign that you've got off to an excellent start in building fruitful relations with us."

Again Duranty jabbed him with his elbow. Jones said, "Thank you very much, Mr Oumansky. That's very civil of you."

Oumansky toddled off and Jones turned to Duranty. "What have I written?" he demanded.

Duranty chuckled. "Listen, kid, it takes a while to get used to Soviet ways, especially the censors at the Foreign Ministry. They have their own rhythms of working. They like us to write exactly what they say and woe betide anyone who strays too far from the party line. Over the years, I've got used to how it works over here. You're the new kid on the block and I didn't want you to get off on the wrong footing."

"So you wrote a piece using my name and sent it? Without, that is, my say-so?"

There was ice in Jones' question.

"It was Evgenia's idea. She's worked with young reporters before and seen them fall foul with the censors so quickly that they have to leave Russia under a cloud."

"Is that true, Evgenia?" asked Jones.

"Yes, it was all my idea," she said. "It's best to stay the right side of them, especially when you first come here. After a time, once they've got to know you, you can do your own thing. But to begin with, it's best to please them. I think you owe Walter a thank you."

Jones started to stammer, "I...I...I..." and then, finally, found his fluency. "I'm so sorry I'm forgetting everything. Duranty, you saved my bacon at the station – and now you've got me into the Kremlin's good books."

"Not the Kremlin, that's much, much harder. The Foreign Ministry's good books."

"I'm very grateful. Have you got a copy of this piece I've written so I can paste it into my scrapbook?"

Duranty handed him a carbon copy of the piece he'd knocked out. Jones read it in silence and then said, "This is rather good. I think I might have a future in journalism."

Duranty and Evgenia laughed long and loud and Natasha tickled Jones' knee underneath the table.

Shortly, the man he'd guessed was the Italian consul approached. Duranty made the introductions. "Gareth Jones of the *Western Mail*, may I introduce His Excellency Andreas Corazza, The Most High Plenipotentiary for the Fascist Kingdom of Italy."

The tickling continued, moving slowly up his thigh.

"Cut the crap Duranty," replied Corazza in a New Jersey accent that could angle-grind Manhattan granite if the money was right. Corazza was stolid, not tall, absurd in his fancy dress regalia – but wearing a smile that told the world he knew it and didn't care. He turned to Jones. "So you're the cub reporter who's training for the high jump? All your rivals are as mad as hell at you and that, in this revolution, isn't a good place to be. Welcome to Russia, Mr Jones."

Jones, not knowing what to say, gulped and offered his slow sweet smile.

On stage, Lyushkov called in English for some songs from "our international friends". Underneath the table Jones caught hold of Natasha's hand and gently moved it away from his thigh. Lyushkov gestured to Verbling who stood up, bowed, then said something quietly in Russian.

Corazza leaned into Jones' ear and said, "The Crucco's running scared. Says his voice has packed in."

"Crucco?" asked Jones.

"Italian for Hun," snapped Corazza.

The MC next pointed to Corazza, who bowed and whispered low into Jones' ear. "Once you've played Hoboken, then Dnipropetrovsk holds no fear."

The Italian walked up to the stage with the self-confident swagger of Il Duce marching on Rome and launched into "O sole mio". He had a fine baritone and left the stage to hurrahs.

After he was finished, Lyushkov regained the spotlight. "Is there any other international friend who would like to perform?"

To his left, Jones made out Natasha jab Duranty with her elbows. The American stood up and said in his deep, rich voice, "Just one song from the United States?"

Duranty limped through the tables, the crowd sympathetic, hushed, expectant. There was an extraordinary animal magnetism about this man, Jones reflected, that he could make people hold their breath while he just walked through a room. Clambering up the side-steps to the stage awkwardly, he got to the microphone stand and smiled beatifically before singing "Say It Isn't So", a mawkish melody of a lover's fear that she is being cheated. The applause was rapturous, louder and wilder than that for the Italian.

Evgenia turned to Jones and challenged him. "So, Mr Jones, can you sing?"

"I'm Welsh, Evgenia. Everyone from Wales can sing."

As Lyushkov asked the audience for any more international contributions, Jones cried out, "One more!"

Jones hurried through the tables and, shunning the steps, vaulted onto the stage to ribald cheers from his fellow reporters. Standing in front of the microphone, he caught his breath and made that slow sweet smile of his. Then he sang Myfanwy in Welsh, his eyes closed, his voice throbbing with passion.

At the end of the song, the crowd roared and clapped and stamped their approval. It took a while for Jones to return to his seat, such was the acclaim from the audience. When he got back, he found both Evgenia and Duranty had left. They didn't come back so he drank and drank and drank some more. Natasha tried to kiss him but, when he turned away, she walked off into the arms of Max Borodin, who danced with her a while. After the next song finished, Borodin returned and sat with Jones while Natasha wandered off again.

"So, the grand opening of the Lenin Dam, Mr Jones? What did you make of it?"

Borodin's question lifted him out of his gloom, a little.

"Very impressive," said Jones.

Borodin laughed out loud. "Here, under that guy," he nodded towards a picture of Stalin on the wall, smiling benignly at all and sundry, "it's not quite the case that the cat has got Russia's tongue. People still talk. But meaning has been hollowed out. I think we can trust each other, Mr Jones. I'm not going to betray your confidences as I am sure you will not mine."

"Where was Stalin today?" asked Jones, bluntly.

Borodin smiled, weakly. Jones pursed his lips, mockingly.

"The convention in polite society is that, if you praise him," Borodin's eyes flicked to the portrait on the wall, "you mention his name with all the honorifics. If praise doesn't flow naturally, it's best to make a veiled allusion. Gorky says, in Russia, even the stones sing."

"Aha," replied Jones and the two men clinked their vodka glasses and drank.

At the far edge of the room Natasha had found Lyushkov's lap. She wriggled on it while staring intensely in Jones' direction. Zakovsky was smiling over a bottle of vodka.

"This dam wasn't..." Borodin's eyes flicked to the portrait "...his idea."

"Then whose was it?"

"Another name. Not one to be mentioned in polite or, in fact, any kind of society."

"Trotsky?"

"Sssh! Not even as a joke, Mr Acrobat. So no-one's too surprised that..." His eyes flicked once more towards the portrait "...found something else to do today."

"I see."

"Internationally, the Lenin Dam is still a very big deal for the Soviet Union. Hence all of this." Borodin waved at the room with his vodka glass, taking in the band, the banquet, the foreign dignitaries and journalists and, in the corner, the two Chekist officers. "But within the walls of the Kremlin, our new dam is a bad victory."

"I heard that you are half-Russian, half-German, Mr Borodin. How is that these days?"

Borodin was ordinarily a mournful man but Jones' question seemed to sink him even deeper into despair. "Not good. Not good here. Worse there. My younger brother Ralf was a Social Democrat in Germany in charge of the party's youth wing. Times were tough, the Nazis were fighting them in the streets, sending thugs into their meetings, threatening them with violence. But Ralf, he was a brilliant organiser and always sunny. 'The Nazis will never hold power in Germany,' he always used to say. He was a much more optimistic man than I."

"And then?"

"Then the Comintern annouced that the Social Democrats were in fact 'Social Fascists' and urged the Communists, the KPD, to devote their energies to the destruction of the moderate left. So last year, in '31, in the Prussian regional election, the Nazis joined forces with the KPD to beat the Social Democrats. In other words, Mr Jones, that guy" – his eyes flicked once more to the portrait of Stalin on the wall – "is doing his best to help Adolf Hitler take power. The switch by the KPD is destroying the resistance to the Nazis. They're growing stronger by the day."

Borodin fell silent. The melancholy of the night closed in on them. On the tables, the ruins of the banquet stood: empty bottles, dishes licked spotlessly clean. On the dance floor, couples danced to a slow, moody number, somehow adding to the sense of failure of the two men at the table.

"Ralf wasn't just a young politician," Borodin went on. "He was also a journalist. He got a scoop. Published it on the front page of the Social Democrat youth newspaper. It was a great story, the text of the Comintern letter to the KPD, ordering them to side with the Nazis against the Social Democrats. Two days later, he fell from his window. Suicide was the official verdict. One police officer, a decent man, came to my mother and told her in confidence that they had a snout who said it was murder, that it wasn't the Nazis but those loyal to..." He stopped talking and nodded, once more, at the oil painting of Josef Stalin on the wall. "The future, Mr Jones, belongs to the Reds and the Browns."

The band played a fatuous song about love and hope. Jones waited for it to end.

"One more question. Where's Evgenia?"

"I suspect she's with Mr Duranty, Mr Jones. Good night."

As Borodin got up and left, Jones lowered his eyes and sank deeper to the embrace of Madame Vodka.

*

53

The curtains had been left wide open from the night before and his room was now bathed in a ghostly white light. Jones got up to see a world transformed. Snow smothered abandoned churches, houses, railings, trees with a thick carpet of white turning pink where the rising sun hit it head on. Bent figures trudged below him, bleakness in motion, leaving their tracks in the snow.

One hundred feet away stood Lenin, one arm outstretched, his coattails flapping in an iron wind, all of his upper surfaces coated in snow. A woman in black, pitifully thin, carrying an infant, walked up to the statue and knelt before him. She lay the baby down at Lenin's iron feet and crossed herself over and over again. It was the strangest of gestures in that place and time – and, upon seeing it, Jones' mouth ran dry. He desperately needed to drink some water but he couldn't leave the window.

A GPU officer on the far side of the square started shouting at the woman, roaring with all the power of his voice – but the woman in black ignored him, then unwrapped the baby from its clothes. Only now did Jones realise that the baby was dead. She laid the naked infant down before Lenin and stood up and crossed herself again and again. The officer started running towards Lenin, followed by four or five more soldiers, and still she crossed herself. The soldiers were one hundred yards from her...

Fifty...

Thirty...

The scream – an animal's cry – ripped through the quiet of the morning,. The GPU officer reached the woman and, facing her, put his arms around her with a tenderness that astonished Jones. It was then that the screaming stopped. A truck hurried up to the statue and braked sharply, spilling out more GPU troops. The officer led the woman to the truck and helped her climb into the back of it. Then he returned, picked up the dead baby and carried it to the back of the truck, where it was taken by someone else. All of this completed, he walked round to the cab and got in and the truck drove off.

A town square mantled in snow, people hurrying to and fro to get out of the cold. Lenin looked on, unmoved. Apart from the woman's tracks in the snow and the shallow dip where the baby had been placed before the statue, everything was as before.

*

Breakfast was a banquet. Inside a Plaster of Paris swan lay a nest of hard-boiled eggs, slivers of roast beef, plates of bacon and ham, caviar, sturgeon, salmon, trout and something hideously ugly with sprouting barbels Jones didn't recognise. Around this there was so much more: fruits and berries, bread and curls of butter, vodka, champagne, burgundy, tea, coffee.

Jones sat down at the table where the other journalists were at trough. Natasha and Evgenia were here too, Professor Aubyn and Dr Limner seated on their own at a side-table. A waiter hovered like a hummingbird close by, until Jones – with a harshness out of character – shooed him away. Pouring himself a black tea, he said, "So, did you see it?"

Duranty was toying with a spoon, dipping into a soft-boiled egg with one hand, a glass of vodka nestled securely in the other, "See what, Little Owl?"

Something about the coy mockery of Duranty's remark stung Jones. "Did you see the mother dump her dead baby in front of the Lenin statue? Did you see it?"

Dr Limner looked up and studied Jones. Professor Aubyn seemed oblivious. Knives and forks clattered on porcelain for a second or two, then fell quiet. Someone coughed. Then there was silence. Pale-faced, Jones repeated his question word for word, taking undue care lest he stumble. "Did you see the mother dump her dead baby in front of the Lenin statue?"

Nothing.

"Did you see it?" snapped Jones.

Duranty's spoon dug deeper into his soft-boiled egg, scooped out the yolk, then tucked it into his mouth before replying. "No, we didn't see it," he said. "Sounds like you had a nightmare, old boy. My advice, Little Owl, better go easy on the sauce."

Natasha sniggered. At another table, Borodin and Oumansky started to bicker noisily, turning heads keen for distraction.

Jones got up to return to his room. Unsteadily, he walked the wrong way, towards the kitchen – until a humbug of waiters put him right. Turning, he walked back past the table where Duranty smiled into his soft-boiled egg. On the stairwell, waiting for him, was Evgenia. As she brushed past him, she stopped.

"Daliwch eich tafod, ffwl." She was talking in Welsh, the words spoken so quietly they were on the edge of hearing. "Daliwch eich tafod neu byddwch yn difetha popeth. Cofiwch fod popeth a ddangosant i chi yn gelwydd. Popeth."

"Hold your tongue, fool," she'd said. "Hold your tongue or you will spoil everything. Remember that everything they show you is a lie. Everything. "

She hurried past him, back into the breakfast room.

Chapter Six

Christmas Eve, 1932 and outside his window at the Hotel Lux the whole of Moscow was shrouded in white. Inside, Jones crouched over his Olivetti typewriter, holding a glass vodka full to the brim and staring at a blank sheet of paper. The woman in black walked across the blank sheet, laying her dead baby in front of the Lenin statue. The scene haunted him, a nightmare that would suddenly run in his mind's eye in broad daylight.

Through the window he could see a little park, draped in white. From nowhere, a tabby cat trotted through the snow, making Jones' mood a touch less annihilatingly bleak. He hadn't heard of or seen Evgenia for two and a half months. He went to the gramophone and put on Eric Satie's Gnossienne No 1, a Christmas present to himself that he could barely afford. The melancholy of the piano notes soothed him. He couldn't explain why.

"Revolutions are the locomotives of history." He had recalled the quote when taking part in a heavily chaperoned visit to a locomotive factory in Moscow. Oumansky had looked at him as if he had gone mad. There were times when Jones wondered whether he was the only person in the whole of the Soviet Union who had read any Marx. It was hard to define why, but the visit was depressing, the immediate source of his bleak mood. Everywhere he'd gone in the factory, more than a mile long, he'd been accompanied by a cloud of officials, flies hovering over a dead dog. Oumansky was perpetually at his side.

Jones had dutifully written down in his notebook Oumansky's brisks translations of the various officials in charge, detailing the astonishing rises in production, the enthusiasm of the workers for subscribing to Soviet bonds to better secure the revolution, their reported joy in leaps and bounds in production. The two things he didn't see were any newly-made locomotives – and any joy. When Oumansky left to visit the bathroom, a Russian engineer, his face as white as candle wax, had whispered to him in bad French that the workers were hungry, so hungry they couldn't work.

"May I quote you on that?" replied Jones in French.

"Mon Dieu, non, absoluement non."

After that, the engineer hurried off and retreated to the far edge of the official party. Every now and then, Jones glanced at him to see him downcast, gnawing on his fingers. Jones felt he couldn't report the exchange for fear of what might happen to the engineer. Besides, a chance remark from one nervy engineer was not enough for him to do down the whole noble Soviet experiment and bring down Oumansky's wrath on his head to boot. And yet his unease stayed with him.

Jones took a sip of vodka and started to pound away at the typewriter, explaining to his readers back home in Wales the magnificent work of the locomotive factory, how its production was so improved, how willing the workers were to pay a ten per cent tithe on their wages to buy Soviet bonds. Not a word of his doubts about what was happening in Russia was reflected in his report. None of his reports had done that. There had been no complaint from the office back in Cardiff. Far from it – only the encouragement and excitement of readers willing to give the benefit of the doubt to a different kind of system when capitalism was failing them so badly.

After he had finished typing, Jones removed the original, the carbon paper and the under-copy and placed the original in an envelope. In the morning he would walk to the Foreign Ministry and deliver it to Oumansky or one of his minions for his approval. Only after they had stamped it, then initialled the stamp, could he go to the main post office in Moscow and get the message telegraphed to his office in Cardiff. He drained his vodka, put on a jumper, scarf, coat and his trilby and prepared to celebrate his first Soviet Christmas.

Someone was waiting for him in the hotel lobby. The face wasn't familiar but he had met him, once. It took Jones some moments to realise that it was Attercliffe. With him was a Russian woman, worry written all over her face, and with them three young girls, the oldest, Jones reckoned, twelve years of age. The daughters were all got up in pink dresses, their blond hair plaited. Jones might have been wrong but he suspected that Attercliffe had been idling his time, waiting for him, perhaps for hours.

"Merry Christmas, Mr Jones."

"Merry Christmas, Mr Attercliffe. Is this your wife and family?"

Attercliffe nodded, his ordinarily bleak face breaking into a smile of paternal pride when his daughters smiled hello.

"You've got a beautiful family, Mr Attercliffe," said Jones.

"All down to Mrs Attercliffe, Mr Jones."

Mrs Attercliffe beamed at the compliment and said in a heavy Russian accent, "Father Christmas, Mr Jones."

"No, Yulia," interrupted Attercliffe. "You mean Happy Christmas. Father Christmas is Dyed Moros."

"I am so sorry, my English is..."

"...much better than my Russian," Jones completed the sentence. There was a moment of silence, a silence which grew and filled the lobby.

The hotel receptionist, a man in his forties with a bulbous nose mapped by broken veins, was not watching the group. Such lack of interest was out of character. Ordinarily, from Jones' observation, he stared at anyone new.

But today was different.

Sitting on a sofa on the other side of the lobby were two men also not watching the Attercliffes and Jones. The first was clown-faced and short, with a put-upon air. The second was far bigger, brutal or brutish, his hair dyed black – or so naturally black that it had the sheen of a chemical dye.

Mrs Attercliffe nudged her husband in the ribs.

"Going to the Metropol, Jones?" Attercliffe asked.

"I am."

"Shall we walk together?"

"What about your family?"

"Oh, the girls wouldn't like the Metropol. And they're Orthodox, not like us, so it isn't really Christmas for them."

"And Mrs Attercliffe?"

"She's looking after the girls."

"Very well, then, let's go."

Attercliffe kissed his wife tenderly and said goodbye to his three daughters, who waved in unison like three little clockwork dolls.

Out on the hotel steps, the cold smacked Jones in the throat like a bully. The noises of the city were muffled by the snow, muffled by some unspoken dread.

Attercliffe and Jones walked in silence, their breaths pluming out before them. Down a gloomy side-street they came across three beggars, one standing rock-still, his back to a wall, one kneeling in the snow, a third squatting. Outright begging was illegal so, most often people would sell something to earn a kopek or two. The standing man had a tattered picture album in his black mittens, its red cover pattered with snow. The kneeler was selling an icon in a frame, the glass cracked from side to side; the man squatting had set out in front of him a wooden tray of forks and spoons and a smear of dirty lace. All three were dead.

"It's the famine," said Attercliffe. "It's far, far worse in the countryside but now people are dying here, in the heart of Moscow. The authorities can't keep up. They're getting swamped by the number of the dead."

"These poor bloody people," said Jones.

"Amen to that," replied Attercliffe. "I can't bear these credulous buggers who come over and think it's all hunky-dory. George Bernard Shaw and the like. The rights of workers here? They barely exist. You're late for work by twenty minutes? You face prison. Free movement of labour has been abolished. You can't leave your village, town or city unless you've got an internal passport. That's why they got rid of the Tsar. Well, he's back, only he's got a red star in his crown these days. But if you say that out loud, you can end up in the GPU hot room."

"What's a hot room?"

"In the basement of the Lubyanka. The radiator is on full blast, the room's full of people, twenty in a cell meant for two. They give you salted fish to eat and not enough water. It's a fancy torture but it's torture, no question."

"But they say they're building the future. To do that, you break some things on the way, but it's still worth it."

"You think that?"

"It's what they say."

"Listen, lad. Listen to me. They go on about the electrification of the Soviet Union until the cows come home. For Metro-Vickers, I helped build an entire electric cable factory upstream of a dam on the Volga, not far from Stalingrad. They built a huge shed out of brick in two months. It was an extraordinary achievement. Then the cable-making lathes arrived from Sheffield. Some of the equipment had been damaged in transit. Not on the ship, mind, coming up from the port. But we managed to fix it and we produced one beautiful cable. And then I went off to Moscow for a week, to try and beg for supplies so we could get cracking. That week they opened the dam and a massive reservoir was created virtually overnight. By the time I'd come back, the whole ground floor was underwater. Electrification of the Soviet Union, my arse."

They had gone a little way further on when Jones stepped on a metal drain cover, which clanked under his footfall. They carried on and shortly the same clanking sounded.

"Don't look round," hissed Attercliffe.

"Those men from the lobby, are they following us?"

"That they are lad," said Attercliffe quietly. "They stood in the shadows when we saw the beggars. Everywhere that Mary went, the lamb was sure to go. They're like Mary's Little Lamb. Little fellow with the put-upon face, he's Klachov – and the big chap with dyed black hair, he's Lintz. They follow me everywhere in Kazan, where we live and work. In Moscow, when I come to talk to officials. On the train, everywhere. Their technique is striking. They always follow me at a distance. If I go to a hotel or restaurant, they sit down at a far table and order tea. Never drink, never food. They read *Pravda* from front to back and then from back to front. They never look at me directly. That is the tell-tale test. Normal people are nosy. Normal people want to know who else is around, what they're like an' all. Normal people stare. But my watchers? Never. Not directly. Sometimes, I catch them looking at me via a mirror."

"Have you any idea why you're being followed?"

Attercliffe felt silent. Jones thought he heard the soft footfall of the followers some way behind them. Or perhaps he was imagining it.

"Point is, Mr Jones, that I haven't been followed in all my time in Russia. It started five days after I gave you that photograph. Since then, I'm never alone."

"Jesus Christ," said Jones.

"Don't take the Lord's name in vain, Mr Jones."

"I'm sorry, I'm so sorry."

"You gave the photograph to someone from the embassy?"

"Yes. He was, on behalf of Her Majesty's Government, very grateful."

"When we met in the fog, there was one last thing I wanted to tell you. It was my mistake because I should have said it first. I should have said don't tell anyone my name."

The Metropol stood before them, all lit up. Beyond it, the towers of the Kremlin were lost in gloom.

"Mr Attercliffe, I can't imagine the British diplomatic service—"

"No, I don't think that either. Perhaps they'll get bored and stop. Still, my wife, she's worried sick about it. I just wanted to let you know what was happening. So I'm going to have one drink here and then I'm going to go back to the hotel. It's probably best if I'm not seen socialising with you. Merry Christmas, Mr Jones."

"Merry Christmas, Mr Attercliffe."

The two of them joined a long queue to check in their coats, headed to the bar, then went their separate ways. A jazz band struck up, playing with gusto. They were doing hits from the early '20s, out of date – but no-one seemed to care. The bar was heaving with people, far busier than Jones had ever seen it. Someone had put a holly wreath around the picture of Lenin but Stalin remained unmodified. A pot plant with a miniature pine tree stood in a corner which, depending on your ideological persuasion, could or could not be mistaken for a Christmas tree.

At a far table sat the watchers, Klachov and Lintz, minus their coats and hats, drinking tea, pouring over two copies of *Pravda*. The Chekists must have had their own bespoke cloakroom in the hotel with a faster service.

Duranty was propped at the bar, a vermouth in one hand, Natasha on one arm, an ash-blond on the other. Natasha was wearing a pale blue number and the ash-blond a dress made up of black sequins, shimmering dully like the wing of a dead starling.

"Happy Christmas, Jonesy," said Duranty amiably.

"Happy Christmas," replied Jones.

Duranty, sensitive as always to what was going on around him, sensed Jones' bleak mood. "You seem blue. Don't be an old curmudgeon, Jonesy. It's Christmas, after all. We're talking about the inevitability of Communism."

"Communism is the riddle of history solved, and it knows itself to be this solution," said Jones distantly.

"Who said that?" asked Duranty.

"Starts with M, ends with X," came the reply.

"Never mind him. Slinky here" – he gestured to the ash-blond – "is a believer. If love is blind, faith is both deaf and blind. This, Slinky, is the Metropol bar which is a shrine not to Communism but to Hedonism. Jones, Slinky. Slinky, Jones."

"Hello Slinky," said Jones.

"My name is Morgan Barnard and I'm from Florida," said the ash-blond. She smiled winningly.

"You told me that your name was Slinky," said Duranty, mildly affronted.

"No, I'm Morgan." She nodded to another blond chatting to an American forestry adviser further down the bar. "That's Slinky."

"Slinky, Morgan, let's call the whole thing off," said Duranty and the ash-blond giggled.

Something shallow in Jones wanted to join in the fun. Holding his tongue, he watched as Attercliffe left the bar. Half a minute later, Klashov departed after him, as regular as a clockwork mouse. Lintz stayed put, looking up at the ceiling. Jones sensed that Lintz was, of the two watchers, the bigger fish, so it made him uneasy that he had been selected for that honour. Perhaps it was just cold outside and the boss fancied staying in the warm. Secret policemen were only human. The thought gave him scant consolation.

"You alright old boy?" asked Duranty, oozing fake concern. The ceiling was a mirror. Lintz could watch everyone at the bar without seeming to do so.

"I'm OK. But the world..."

"What's wrong with it?"

"Hitler's on the brink of power in Berlin, the democracies are mired in the Depression and the Soviet experiment isn't quite what it's cracked up to be."

"Looks like you need some champagne."

"I've gone off champagne."

"Come on, have some bubbly."

"Sorry, Duranty, I'm not in a party mood. Forgive me."

Jones smiled an insincere apology, walked down the bar and ordered a beer. There he found himself standing next to a vast shambling man, nursing a bottle of beer and a shot of vodka. When Jones was served, they clinked glasses in companionable silence and said nothing. The big man downed his vodka, and Jones saw for the first time that he had an empty socket where his right eye should have been. For a second he wondered whether the injury was recent, but he quickly realised it had taken place a long time ago. There was something ugly and raw and vulnerable about the lack of a glass eye which made Jones like the big man. He was in his late fifties, hefty, his suit shining with too much use, the cuffs of his shirt frayed.

"I know it's Christmas," Jones ventured, "but can you tell why is it so packed tonight?"

"Ssssh, Winnie's about to sing the song." The big man's voice was deep, gravelly, extraordinarily so.

"What song?"

"Hold your tongue and listen up," growled the big man.

A beautiful black woman threaded her way towards the band, wearing a black boiler suit with a red handkerchief festooned in a top pocket, a bowler hat and sparkling red shoes. She whispered into the mic, "Merry Christmas boys." Her voice was smoky, sensual, melodic. "This song was sung by my people. And just maybe it's kind of appropriate to some of you, too."

She closed her eyes and sang:

> "When Israel was in Egypt's land,
> Let My people go!"

The bar listened to the negro spiritual in near-silence and then, when the singer had finished, they roared their approval, stamping their feets and banging their bottles of beer on the tables. It wasn't by any means the normal Metropol gang of reporters, diplomats and shady travellers. These people looked much poorer, more desperate. But they had passion. Besides Jones, the big man grinned from ear to ear.

After the cheering had ebbed away, Winnie worked her way through a selection of Christmas carols. As the crowd at the bar listened to *Silent Night* with rapture, Jones wondered what it might be like to be a believer in Communism who had come to Russia and now realised that something was wrong. Winnie finished with *The Internationale*, sung lustily.

"That one was for the Cheka," said the big man. When she had finished, he took one more drink, put down his glass and began to sing in his glorious gravelly bass.

"You will eat, bye and bye..."

Jones had heard the song before but he couldn't quite place it.

"...In that glorious land above the sky..."

That's it: they called it 'The Preacher and The Slave'.
"Anarchist swine!"
The big man's singing stopped as one of the Metropol's oak bar stools connected with his head. Hefty as he was, he was no longer in his prime and he staggered under the blow, cannoning into Jones, spilling his beer. Instinctively, Jones ducked out from under the big man and raised his fists, eyeing the assailant – a tall, thin, red-faced man, a good head taller than Jones. He'd seen the man around, he was certain of it – a young American Communist activist and journalist called Fred Beal. Beal leered at Jones and swung at him, his fist connecting with Jones' right cheek, just below the eye.

Stunned, Jones reeled back, swayed on his feet. For a moment, he feared that he was going to topple over. He staggered like a toddler taking his first uncertain steps, then remembered that he was a boxer and upped his pace. Suddenly he was dancing around the fallen bar stool.

He came at Beal: a left jab to the ribs, a second and a third, a right feint and then a flurry of punches, left, right, left, left, left, finishing off with a haymaker to Beal's jaw that was so powerful the sound of the crack could be heard above the roaring crowd. Somehow still standing, Beal fell back. He turned his torso and, with a crash of breaking glass, he twisted to face Jones once more, a broken bottle of champagne in his hand.

Jones squared up to him, breathing hard. If Beal got lucky with the bottle, he could lose an eye.

Beal's eyes darted to the far corner. Jones followed the direction and saw Lyushkov, taking in everything. Lyushkov glanced at Duranty, who only shook his head. Lyushkov relayed the message with his eyes – and Beal dropped the broken bottle. Seconds later, Dmitry, the biggest of the Metropol doormen, grabbed hold of Beal's wrists and lifted him bodily away. Cheers, whoops and applause greeted the victor. The big man patted Jones gently on the shoulder.

"Some punch you got there, son," said the big man.

Morgan Barnard appeared from nowhere. "Nice shiner."

Jones looked up at the ceiling mirror and saw that his right cheek was turning midnight blue.

Duranty and Natasha joined them. "Come on, Jonesy, introduce me to your friend," said Duranty.

Jones had no idea who the big man was.

"Introduce me to the Secretary-General of the greatest union the United States ever had," said Duranty.

Still Jones had no clue.

"Big Bill was cleared of murdering Frank Steunenberg, ex-governor of Idaho, once Clarence Darrow established that the killer was a paid informant of the Cripple Creek Mine Owners' Association."

"Bill Haywood, the Wobbly defended by Clarence Darrow?" Jones asked.

"Man and boy." The big man got two big beers, handed one to Jones and sunk half of his in one swig. Then, wiping the back of his hand against his mouth, he surveyed the room with his one good eye.

"Merry Christmas, Mr Haywood. I'm Gareth Jones. *Western Mail*, Cardiff."

"Gareth Jones, Fighter," corrected Haywood.

Smiling, Duranty explained to the women that Bill Haywood was the greatest Wobbly that had ever lived.

"Vot Wobbly?" asked Natasha.

"No-one is quite sure where name comes from," Duranty explained. "But the Wobblies were the greatest trade union that ever existed in the United States."

"The Wobblies *are* the greatest trade union," corrected Haywood.

"True," said Duranty, his smile growing broader. "They rose up in the western United States before the First World War. Mine-owners and factory bosses did their utmost to kill the union. Big Bill was framed for the murder of Steunenberg, the former governor of Idaho, even though he hadn't been in the state at the time. Clarence Darrow is America's great defence lawyer and he cleared him."

"Fancy a trial where the defendant is found not guilty," said Haywood, favouring Duranty with his dead eye. "Fancy that, Mr Duranty."

"Quite so," said Duranty and he spied Oumansky near the possible Christmas tree. "Morgan, darling, there's somebody really quite important I'd like you to meet." And, making his excuses, he, Natasha and Morgan moved away.

Jones turned to Haywood. "Do you miss America?" The moment he'd asked it he realised the question was too blunt.

Haywood winced, touched his head where the bar stool had hit him, and said, "Yup."

"What do you miss?"

"The breakfasts. Eggs, ham, maple syrup, hash browns, lashings of it." He leaned in to Jones and whispered, "When we were standing trial, we were in custody in Boise city jailhouse. Fancy banquets aside, food there was mighty better than pretty much every ordinary meal I've have had here."

"Can you go back?"

"No. I ran from the Pinkertons framing me for a second time. I ran from the United States." Again he leaned in to Jones, the conspirator once more. "Turned out I jumped from the frying pan into the fire."

"Why do you say that?"

"Here in the Soviet Union, they have a saying, 'You never know what happened yesterday.' When I first came to Moscow in 1921, I was treated like a God. They fawned on me, hand on foot. Women, whisky, nothing was ever too much for an old Wobbly. But something's changed. Something I did back then is now seen as a piece of badness. I ain't changed. Russia has. Every time I leave my apartment, I'm followed. If I sneeze, three men in mackintoshes write it all down. If I sing Wobbly songs, I get hit. But I'm a Wobbly and I love to sing our old songs. I reckoned that, if I came to the swankiest bar in town on Christmas Eve and started to sing, it would be OK... but I was wrong."

Out of the corner of his eye he noted Ilver, the commercial attaché from the British embassy, leaving the bar. Jones tried to catch up with him but, by the time he'd struggled through the throng, Ilver had disappeared. He returned to his place at the bar next to Haywood.

"May I ask you a question, Mr Jones?" said Haywood.

"Call me Gareth."

"Garry," Haywood went on, and Jones winced, "you report on Russia for your paper, right?"

"I do, Bill."

"You tell the truth, what you see with your eyes and ears?"

Jones said nothing. Haywood reached for his wallet and pulled out a faded cutting from a newspaper.

"Someone gave me this. It's from the London *Times*."

Jones read. "Splendid illustrated magazines... crowds of brightly dressed well-fed happy looking workers are shown with their palatial dwellings... nobody who ever sees these publications will ever believe tales of a half-starved population dwelling in camps under the lash of a ruthless tyrant."

The letter was signed George Bernard Shaw.

"You agree with Shaw?"

"Not necessarily. What is illustrated in magazines may not be true."

"Stop sitting on the fence, Garry. What about what you write? Do you tell your readers about the stuff that doesn't add up? The people crying for no reason? The terror of authority? The beggars? The people starving? The beautiful women who'd fuck anyone so long as they eat and stay out of trouble? You write about the Cheka?"

Jones stared into his beer.

"You a believer?"

"I've read a lot of Marx."

"That ain't any kind of answer to my question."

"Maybe before," said Jones quietly. "Not now."

"You know, high up in the Kremlin circles, they have this phrase that Lenin kicked about and Stalin picked up. They say that people in the West who give the Soviet Union the benefit of the doubt are 'Useful Idiots'. You strike me as an honest man, Garry. You swing an honest punch, that's for sure. But if you don't write the truth about the show trials, the hunger, the Cheka, you're a useful idiot."

Jones drank his beer in silence, turning over what he had seen with his own eyes and heard with his own ears. He thought, too, of what he had glimpsed just five minutes before, of Beal holding the broken bottle of champagne in his hand, looking at Lyushkov who had checked with Duranty. For the thousandth time, he thought about the woman in black, her dead child, and he clawed at the meaning of what Evgenia had said on the hotel staircase in Dnipro. *Everything they show you is a lie. Everything.*

She hadn't taken the special train back to Moscow. She hadn't been at any of the regular haunts used by the foreign journalists, the Foreign Ministry's press room, nor the dead centre of their trade, here at the Metropole. Her absence was a mystery, but so too was what she had said and the way she had said it. Who had taught her to speak Welsh so fluently? His mind wrestled, once more, with what on earth she was getting at when she had warned him that he would ruin everything. Jones knew that, if he could trust just one man in Russia, he could trust this old Wobbly.

"I met a woman, Haywood, a Ukrainian. She spoke my language too. She spoke Welsh beautifully. We both saw something terrible, a starving mother leaving her dead baby by a Lenin statue in Dnipro. She said that everything they showed us was a lie." He trailed off. "It's been months now and, and, and" – he struggled to find the words – "she's vanished."

Haywood finished his beer, wiped the back of his hand against his mouth and said, "Listen, son, in the Soviet Union, in Stalin's Russia, people disappear. Some day I will too."

And, whistling *Let My People Go*, Haywood walked off through the bar and out into the night.

Jones watched him go and nursed his own vodka, lost exploring the depths of his own melancholy. After some time, he was aware of someone drawing close, of great brown eyes watching him.

"May I say that you have the most beautiful voice?" he told Winnie, without looking around.

"You may, darling, you may." She affected a stiff British accent but it didn't quite come off, a failure that made her giggle, deliciously. "You're the new British reporter. You sure can box. Folks say you can jump higher than the moon."

"That's an exaggeration, Winnie. My name is Gareth Jones. Where are you from back in the States?"

"New Orleans."

"Getting used to the snow?"

"No, heavens to Betsy! Had I known how cold it could get here, I would never have left Louisiana."

"*Let My People Go*. Everyone loved it. May I ask, what's the story behind that?"

She nuzzled close to Jones so that what she said couldn't be overheard. "To answer your question, darling. It is Christmas but there's a fair number of folks here, members of the Communist Party of the United States, left-wingers, radicals who came to Russia to see the future. Some folks ain't happy. But they can't go back."

"Why not?"

"The fact that they came to Russia is a great propaganda victory for the big man in the fancy castle."

Jones pulled a face.

"The Kremlin, silly. It's bad news for the Soviet Union if folks go back. So they can't. It's not permitted. When you first arrive, the authorities take your passport. That's fine, who cares? But once you've seen how things really work here, you want to go back to the States, and... you can't. Officially, passports get mislaid. Then there's some who are afraid to go back, on account of being on the run from the law back home. Anyways, folks get homesick. So celebrating Christmas, that's a way of messing with the big man without getting in too much trouble. And listening to little ole me sing *Let My People Go,* that makes Christmas for us all. You see, folks think that the big man in the fancy castle, he's just like the old Pharoah in the song."

"How many American Communists have had their passports mislaid?" asked Jones.

"Hundreds."

"And you Winnie?"

She hesitated, running a finger down the lapel of Jones' jacket.

"Might you be an informer, honey?"

"Certainly not."

"You not going to tell on Winnie, honey?"

"No."

Her fingers twiddled with a button of his shirt.

"I'm trapped. A negress is a jewel for the Comintern, proof of the sickness in American capitalism. The truth is that Winnie would love to go back to the States but she can't."

"I'm so sorry."

"That's all right, Mr British. You want a little relaxation? I can show you some fancy tricks?"

"Oh, Winnie," he sighed. "I'm in love with someone else."

"She in love with you?"

"No."

"Ain't that always the way?" she said and, smiling sweetly at him, she moved away.

Jones had one more solitary drink, then returned to the cloakroom. As he stood in the long queue, a side-door opened, revealing Lintz putting on his coat and, behind him, sitting at a table, was Beal sharing a joke with a bulky figure. Lyushkov turned and, recognising Jones, smiled back.

Chapter Seven

The workers from the Number One Tractor Factory chatted animatedly to one another as they came in, as if they were at the first night of a new play. Apart from the cigarette smoke, everything else was red. Red banners, red carpets, red table cloths covering the tables for the lawyers and the judges, red spotlights playing on portraits of Red Marx, Red Engels, Red Lenin and Red Stalin. Red pillars of light rose up to find the painted ceiling where cherubim and seraphim played, icons from the time before. No-one had yet got round to painting them out.

The journalists were the next to file in, a hundred or more, Russian and foreign. Oumansky had not been over-stating the truth when he had told Jones that seats at the Coal Saboteurs trial were at a premium. The trial had been long delayed but finally it was taking place. Almost the entire Moscow foreign press corps was there: Fischer, Lyons, the whole gang and their interpreters, the latter almost exclusively female. Only Duranty was missing, but everyone one knew he would turn up sooner rather than later. The biggest show in town wouldn't start without him.

Finally, in came the diplomats to relay the spectacle of the people's justice back to London, Rome, Berlin, and Tokyo. Jones looked around for Ilver from the British Embassy but he wasn't present. He was still searching the room when Duranty sidled up and sat down beside him.

"Hello," said Duranty, "enjoying the show?"

"It hasn't started yet," said Jones, gloomily.

"They used to call this place the House of the Nobles," explained Duranty. "This was the ballroom, the Hall of Columns. Word is they had the most fantastic parties here – before the revolution, of course. The nobs would pass the summer in the south of France or on their estates but winter was party time. All the dukes and duchesses would come and dance until their feet bled. Music by Tchaikovsky, Rimsky-Korsakov, Lizst. Tolstoy pictured this room in *War and Peace*. Pushkin wrote about a ball here in his long poem, *Eugene Onegin*. That was then. These days it's where the workers line up to pay their respects to the red dead. Lenin's body lay in state here. And now it's the venue for the people's justice."

"So I see," replied Jones.

Above them a dais was reserved for the lawyers. They filed in, the prosecutors hefting bundles of paperwork, led by the Prosecutor-General, Nikolai Krylenko. The defence followed, elderly pre-Revolution types, "former people", hunch-shouldered, hesitant, playing out their role with threadbare confidence. Above the lawyers on a second, higher dais was the throne of the judges, three men in all – two nobodies on the wings but, in the centre, Professor A. Y. Vishinsky, spectacled, commanding. He banged his gavel, got a subdued hush, then called for the accused to be brought in. A squad of GPU soldiers entered carrying rifles tipped with long, strangely thin bayonets. Fifty-three of them, heads shaved, shabby, their faces grey, bereft of hope. They kept their heads down as they filed into the court, settling meekly behind the forest of bayonets in the dock.

Finally, Prosecutor-General Nikolai Krylenko got to his feet. More dwarf than man, barely five feet tall, his great head was out of proportion with his torso, giving him the appearance of a monstrous toddler. He stroked his chin and then started to talk: "The proletariat thanks the glorious GPU, the unsheathed sword of the revolution, for its splendid work in liquidating this dastardly plot."

Krylenko nodded to the court clerk, who read out the names of the accused in a nervous high pitch. Each defendant stood up, bowed at the judges, said, "Da" and sat down. Then the clerk called out the next one. So it went on and on.

Jones, bored, switched off. He wondered about the men who had stopped following him. He hadn't been tailed since Christmas Eve. The lack of consistency troubled him. Either he was a danger to the Soviet state or he wasn't. The idea that the Cheka would take a casual interest in him, then get bored, was irritating. It meant that he was a bit of nobody. True enough, he thought.

In the courtroom, the clerk got to the letter N.

"Nekrasoff," squeaked the clerk.

No answer.

"Nekrasoff," he repeated.

There was a rising hubbub from the throng. How dare this scum Nekrasoff avoid the people's justice?

"Nekrasoff?"

Krylenko got to his feet. "Comrade Nekrasoff's counsel, will you please explain this insult to the court's dignity?"

Nekrasoff's counsel was tall and old and spindly, a grandfather's clock from another time. Though he formed words, he was so far away from one of the court's three microphones that nobody could hear a thing.

"Speak up man!" snapped Krylenko. "Go to the microphone and explain why your client deems it fit to insult the people's court in this fashion."

He shuffled stiffly to the nearest microphone. "My client is indisposed."

"What? How dare this wrecking scum treat the people in this way!" yelled Krylenko. The crowd cat-called and yelled abuse, so much so that Judge Vishinsky had to work hard with his gavel to create order. Crowd hushed, he gestured to the defence counsel to explain.

"Comrade Nekrasoff is suffering hallucinations and, for his own good, has been placed in a padded cell where he has been screaming about rifles being pointed at his heart. He is prey to paroxysms so, with great respect to the court, it has been decided that it would not further the interests of the people's justice for him to attend."

Jones' translator, Madame Koloshny, gabbled the words out at speed.

"Padded cell? What's that about?" asked Jones.

"Sounds rather fun," said Duranty out of the side of his mouth.

"The counsel advised the court that Comrade Nekrasoff has been placed in a padded cell for his own good," said Madame Koloshny. "Nothing to add. You ask too many questions, Mr Jones."

From the next seat, he heard Duranty suppress a snort of laughter.

Jones and Madame Koloshny didn't hate each other. It was more miserable than that. After a month of working with her, Jones knew her well enough not to press her on the strange fate of the man in the padded cell. Madame Koloshny had been suggested by Oumansky as the perfect person for the role. She had been a beauty, once. Her dark hair was pulled back in a cruel bun, her lips rouged but thin, her cheeks and forehead as pale as porcelain. She was like a china tea set so delicate and refined that you would never want to use it lest you smash the teapot. Yet, somehow, she was hardier, testier than that.

Her English was excellent and, more to the point, she wasn't too expensive. Jones was finding living in the Soviet Union much more costly than he had imagined. Food was far more expensive than it was back in Britain and he'd lost so much weight he had tightened his belt three notches. Far from saving money, he was living well beyond his means and had written to his father, a headmaster back in Barry, Wales, to wire him extra funds. So Madame Koloshny was perfect in every way. That is, except for the fact that she didn't like journalism or Jones one bit. Her mantra was "you ask too many questions, Mr Jones", but the whole point of being a good reporter, he knew, was exactly that. To be precise, journalism meant sniffing out things that didn't feel right, worrying away at the truth like a dog with a bone. In Stalin's Russia, there were so many things that made no sense that to be told "you ask too many questions" was all but unbearable.

The seats were hard and uncomfortable. Jones straightened his back and studied the wretches in the dock.

The defendant that haunted Jones most was Skorutto. He had the long nose, waddling gait and puzzled, silly manner of a duck who had somehow strayed out of its farmyard into the courtroom. Middle-aged, with cropped white hair, he had strong, heavily-calloused hands, and the mildest of manners. Skorutto was not only always pleasant to the GPU guards but also to his fellow prisoners, including the ones who had given evidence against him. He denied his guilt absolutely and with a calmness that made him stand out. Every now and then, while his co-workers were condemning him at length, he would turn to a pudding-faced woman in the audience and smile the sweetest of smiles at her.

Skorutto was supposedly a saboteur who, having spent a lifetime down the mines, first for the Tsar, then the Communist Party, had finally been caught by the authorities. They had revealed the truth about this monster who had worked underground his whole life. The evidence against him was damning. Seventeen of the twenty-four defendants had sworn that he had deliberately wrecked the work of the state. Yet he would not accept the truth. The difference between the weight of the charges and Skorutto's own demeanour was – that word again – bewildering.

After some procedural to-and-fro which Madame Koloshny didn't bother to translate, Prosecutor Krylenko called Comrade Skorutto to take the stand. But Skorutto was different today. The gentle duck had gone. Tottering slowly towards the witness stand, his body trembled and he mumbled something inaudible into the microphone.

"The accused must speak up," demanded Krylenko.

Skorutto eyed Krylenko nervously, coughed and then addressed the microphone. "I have today written out and signed a statement confessing my own guilt. I was part of a conspiracy to wreck the Five Year Plan. With others, I conspired..."

He got no further. His words had barely registered when a scream slashed through the court.

"Kolya, Kolya darling, don't lie! Don't! You know you're innocent!"

It was the pudding-faced woman in the audience. Skorutto slumped against the microphone stand, knocking it over. Judge Vishinsky adjourned the session for ten minutes. The ten minutes turned into an hour, then two.

While they waited, Duranty invited Jones to go outside with him to get some fresh air. Jones thanked him and said that, instead, he would hold the fort. The truth was that Duranty's easy cynicism – which at first acquaintance had seemed so refreshing – now grated on him. So Jones sat tight on his hard wooden seat and thought yet again about Evgenia. She was the mystery of his life, not that Russia was ever easy to read. He was finding it harder and harder to reconcile the fantastic boasts of the Soviet propaganda machine with what he saw with his own eyes. Officially, the Five Year Plan was breaking all records. Officially, more tractors were being built than ever before. Officially, the electrification of the Soviet Union was cracking on apace. Officially, paradise was being built in the Soviet Union.

And unofficially? None of these achievements squared with the dull-eyed beggars from the countryside pleading for bread, most of them pathetically polite and all of them pitifully thin. The ordinary Muscovites queueing outside the food shops from the night before in weather so cold it made your head ache. The corpses in the snow.

In his four months in Russia, a succession of brilliant minds had arrived from the West to bend the knee to Soviet planning. Jones didn't know what to think. There were times the solution was simple: to stop trying to wrestle with the two realities – the official text against the unofficial fact – and just go with the flow. That was easier than forgetting Evgenia. Too often, his mind went back to the train journey to the opening of the Lenin Dam. The moment when she seemed to smile after, a naive innocent, he had asked about the GPU. The deepness of her blush when Duranty picked up on her sniffing the bouquet of the wine. His agony at the thought that it was her pleasuring Duranty under a sickly moon. And, most bewildering of all, what she'd said to him in his native Welsh. How on earth had she mastered the language?

He knew enough by now to know that it was not a good idea to ask about the whereabouts of a citizen of the Soviet Union, whether Russian or Ukrainian, who was no longer around. As far as her existence was concerned, he'd forced himself to suppress his natural instincts.

The stamp of boots interrupted him. The GPU escort clattered in, followed by the defendants trooping back onto the stage, Skorutto visibly limping as he had not been before. As he tottered towards the microphone, Jones screwed his head around to look for his woman's reaction. She was no longer there. In her place was Lyushkov, smiling directly at him. Duranty returned to his seat just in time to hear Skorutto in a flat monotone trot out his confession. He had been a serial wrecker working for foreign powers. Krylenko didn't bark once, occasionally giving him a soft lick with his tongue, a bitch nursing her puppy. When Skorutto had finished, Krylenko, ignoring the accused, stared directly at the workers, his hands on his lapels, the great head framed in the red spotlights and asked softly, "Can Prisoner Skorutto confirm that he makes this confession of his own free will, that there is no question that he was tortured?"

Skorutto smiled to himself and said nothing. Krylenko repeated his question. Skorutto shook his head. Someone in the audience coughed twice, three times. To Jones' ear, there might just possibly have been a tang of irony to the coughing fit.

For a third time, Krylenko repeated his question, adding, "The prisoner needs to articulate his answer to properly honour the majesty of the people's justice."

Skorutto turned directly to the workers, smiled his duck-like smile at them and said, "If the question is raised whether I was tortured during interrogation..."

"That is the question before the court," snapped Krylenko.

"Then I have to say it wasn't me who was tortured. By causing them unnecessary work, I tortured them."

"This is intellectual squeamishness and stupid liberalism!" snapped Krylenko. "These are deviationist meanderings."

"I apologise for my meanderings," said Skorutto with a smile – but the judge banged down his gavel and the court's attention focussed back on Krylenko.

"Prisoner Skorutto, who was it who first recruited you?" asked Krylenko.

"I was first recruited to be a wrecker by Mr Harold Attercliffe, a British mining engineer."

The reporters gave out a collective gasp.

"Bloody hell," said Duranty. "That's big news."

Krylenko held up his palm, signalling for quiet, then said, "The People's Justice will be pleased to learn that, thanks to the unceasing indefatigability of the armed fist of New Soviet Man, we have a fresh suspect to bring before this people's court. Call Harold Attercliffe."

The Yorkshireman was led into court by three GPU guards who towered over him, the thin needles of their bayonets glinting dully as they stepped out of the shadows. Attercliffe was whey-faced, hesitant, limping as he walked to the dock.

"Name?" Krylenko stabbed out the word.

"Harold Attercliffe." His voice was soft, timid.

"Nationality?"

"British."

Jones could barely hear him.

"You are charged with wrecking. How do you plead?"

"Not bloody guilty," snapped Attercliffe, loud and strong. "Call this a trial? None of this is real."

Vishinsky banged his gavel and shouted, "We have our own reality!"

The judge shot a puzzled look at Lyushkov, who was now standing in the aisle to the right of the court. Lyushkov, smiling, shook his head, then moved out of sight into a shadowy recess behind a column.

Then the lights went out.

"This session is now closed," said the judge.

In the darkness, someone shouted, "Smert Stalinu!" – "Death to Stalin!" The cry was taken up by a second, a third, then a dozen voices. The GPU guards barked "Silence!" at the prisoners and the chant was drowned out by fresh chaos as the reporters who worked for the wires rushed from the courtroom, racing to be the first to break the story of a British engineer in the dock of a show trial.

Chairs were knocked over. People went flying. In the middle of it all, Duranty lit a match, his face illuminated as if he was a figure in Rembrandt's Nightwatch. Seconds later, the match died and the old ballroom was once again thrown into darkness.

Standing up, Jones felt in his pocket for the lighter he'd won on the train from Duranty. He'd left it at the hotel. Cursing himself at his own stupidity, he felt his way gingerly along the line of seats. When he came to the end of the line, he groped his away into the void, his fingers alighting on a smooth marble column. He was edging his way round that when a lighter flared directly in front of him. The man holding the light was Ernst Verbling.

"So, Mr Jones, what do you make of the People's Justice?"

"I believe everything but the facts, Herr Verbling."

"To us, the new Germans, it is, for the moment, very satisfactory." Jones said nothing, so Verbling continued, "My light may not last. Would you care to follow me, Mr Jones?"

"I'd rather not, Herr Verbling."

"Very well." Verbling half-smiled, then added, "Mr Jones, we noted what you wrote about Herr Hitler."

"Did you now?"

"You wrote that he was flabby and insignificant."

"I did."

"If you would be so kind to retract those words, the German people would be grateful."

"Perhaps I should have written flabby but significant."

"So you will retract?"

"I'm a reporter, Herr Verbling. I report what I see and hear with my own eyes. At that moment, that day, whatever. That's not to be tampered with."

"Will you retract?"

"That, in my view, is a strange question."

"Will you retract?"

"No."

"Very well. Goodbye, Mr Jones."

Jones waited until the German, lighter held aloft, had left, then stumbled his way slowly towards the lit area outside the Hall of Columns. In the press room in a side-annexe of the main hall, he found a free telephone and dialled the number for the British Embassy. Once the call was connected, he asked to be put through to Ilver. There was a long pause and a certain amount of clicking, then Ilver came on the line. Jones announced himself but, before he could get any further, Ilver cut in. "You do remember our conversation at the dam? The specific point I made."

Jones ignored him. "Attercliffe's just turned up in the dock at the coalmine wreckers' trial."

"When?"

"Five minutes ago. You've got to help him. You've got to-"

"Mr Jones, come to the embassy on Monday morning, January 30th, at ten o'clock sharp. We shall discuss this matter then."

"For God's sake, that's five days away."

"Mr Jones, Monday morning, January 30th, at ten o'clock sharp. Don't be late. Good day to you, sir." And the line went dead.

Jones hung there, desperately searching his memories – but it was no use; he didn't know Attercliffe's address in Kazan, still less had Mrs Attercliffe's telephone number. There was no way of getting her word.

"Hey, Jonesy, you know this guy, Attercliffe, don't you?" asked Lyons. "Didn't I see you with him at the Metropol one time?"

Jones shook his head and hurried for one of the vacant desks. There he sat down in front of his typewriter, inserted two sheets of copy paper and a carbon in the middle, and hammered out a thousand words, setting out all he had seen that day. It was the first honest dispatch he'd written from the Soviet Union and it would be his last. He had had enough.

His last paragraph read:

> This is the truth about this show trial. Soviet justice must be seen not to be believed. As far as this reporter is concerned, it stinks to high heaven. In the higher echelons of the Bolshevik party and inside the Kremlin, the term 'Useful Idiot' is banded about. It means a Western fellow-traveller who, when confronted with the evidence of his own eyes and ears, looks away. For far too long I have been such a 'Useful Idiot', reporting what the Soviet censors want me to write, not what I witness. The truth is that the Soviet Union is a monstrous tyranny where the innocent are framed, where the state tells lies and where hunger is rampant. This useful idiot is one no more. Gareth Jones, Moscow, *Western Mail*.

Ripping the two sheaves of paper out of his typewriter, he pocketed the under-copy, threw the carbon in the wastepaper bin, folded the original and placed it in an envelope which he sealed. Then he got up from his desk in the press room – only to find Duranty standing there, cigarette in hand.

"You filing copy tonight, Duranty?"

"As always. The *New York Times* is a hungry beast."

"Who is the Foreign Ministry censor on watch tonight?"

"Comrade Oumansky."

Jones asked Duranty whether he wouldn't mind handing over his copy too at the same time.

"My pleasure," said Duranty, his eyes on a new translator for a Japanese news service. Jones gave him the original in the sealed envelope.

Oumansky would read it later that evening. He guessed he would get his marching orders to leave the Soviet Union tomorrow morning. Well, so be it. Bowing minimally to Madame Koloshny, Jones headed for the exit. Once outside, he stood on the steps of the House of the Unions, buttoned up his coat, tipped his hat low and breathed in the freezing air.

Since his very first story, the opening of the Lenin Dam, he had been telling lies about the Soviet state. The truth was clear. Skorutto had been tortured to make a false confession. Attercliffe was, could only be, a wronged man. God knows what his poor wife and daughters were going through. To tell his readers the truth, even if he got thrown out of the Soviet Union, was a blessed relief.

Fresh snow had fallen, turning the great drabness into a place of black and white, of cold beauty. A shaft of sunlight tunnelled through the dark grey clouds, igniting the crystals in the snow, making the city all the more beautiful. Trust him, Jones mused to himself, to fall in love with Moscow at the very moment he had written his own letter of resignation.

Something moved to his right and he found himself staring at a woman in a long brown coat on the far side of Theatre Drive. Though she was two hundred yards away from him, he lifted his hat – and, the moment he did that, she held out the flat of her palm, a signal to hold back. Turning on her heels, she started to walk, slowly, away from him, across Revolution Square.

Evgenia.

Chapter Eight

The woman in brown was halfway across the square before Jones followed, picking up his pace. Soon he was pelting across Theatre Drive, provoking roars of anger from the drivers of the droshkies, horse-drawn taxis, as he darted between them.

By the time he reached the square, Evgenia was already at the gates to the Teatralnaya Metro station. She turned to him, the palm of her right hand upright. The message was clear, she wanted him to follow her but not so close that anyone could work out that he was doing so. He did not move an inch as he watched her disappear into Teatralnaya Metro station. Then he walked as slowly as he could bear, looking around him, taking in the sights, the Metropol to the left, the red walls of the Kremlin ahead of him.

The sun disappeared behind thick cloud and the sky began to darken. He passed through the wooden swing-doors of the Metro, but inside there was no sign of her. Perhaps she was down the escalator at platform level. All he needed to get through was ten kopecks for a Metro token – but he didn't have the correct change and the queue for tickets was, as usual, hideously long. He went up to a particularly well-dressed man, offered him a ten-rouble note for a token, fed the token into the machine and tried to walk down the escalator in the normal way, aching to run but not daring to do so.

No sign of her at the bottom.

Arcing to the left, he scoured the platform. Nothing. Then he hurried across to the other track to see a train coming in. Even here there was no sign. As he searched, in vain, for some sight of her, the train doors opened and a crowd of Muscovites piled out.

He jumped high – and there she was, walking away from the train at the very end of the platform, heading towards the signs for the inter-connected Metro at Revolution Square. She certainly wasn't making this game easy for him. Making his way along the platform against the flow of the disgorged crowd was not easy, but at least he had a sense of the rules of the game she was playing.

Broad steps led down to the platform, brass statues on either side. He saw her walk slowly past a brass Alsatian dog, rubbing its snout for good luck. Then she stepped to the left as the roar of an incoming train sounded. Bounding down the steps, he too rubbed the dog's snout for luck, swerved left, and launched himself at the doors just as they were closing.

It was almost too late. Jamming a foot in the door, he tried to force it back open – and, after a lot of cursing and shouting in Russian, the doors relented, sliding back to allow him access within. As they closed again and the train took off, the other passengers in the carriage stared at the idiot foreigner. They could tell from his clothes and the stylish design of his "owl" spectacles that he was not Russian.

She wasn't in his carriage.

At every stop he jumped out of one carriage and walked casually into the next, not daring to do more lest the train doors close on him. Finally, there she was: brown fur hat, brown coat, black boots, sitting down at the far end of the carriage, reading a book, "The Idiot" by Dostoevsky. She lifted her gaze, stared at him and, almost imperceptibly, shook her head, compelling him to stay where he was. At the next stop, Elektrozavodskaya, she got off the train and walked across to the opposite platform. Following her path, he kept a good fifty feet away from her. She got out at Kurskaya; so did he.

He was getting good at the game now, trusting her that she would never completely lose him. She walked slowly out of the Metro station into a pool of light. Thick snow drifted down, softening the hardness of the city. She walked off into the darkness and, after a suitable interval, he followed, stumbling on the rough ground. Some time later, he reached a street corner and feared he was lost – when, to his right, from a basement, he saw a match flare and then die. Heading towards that light, he worked his way around a three-quarters closed door and felt a hand on his chest, drawing him in. The door closed tight shut.

There was straw underfoot, a thick bed of it, dampening all sound. As his eyes adapted to the darkness, he became aware of a feeble light, diffused, from a candle far away. Now he could just make her face out. She was beguilingly beautiful, with the blackest of black eyes. Close by, he heard a horse whinny and hooves shuffle on straw. From the sounds and smells, he guessed they were in a basement stable for droshky horses.

"Pa gêm yw hyn?" – *What game is this?* he whispered. "Pam ydych chi'n chwarae gyda mi?" – *Why are you playing with me?*

"Pam wnaethoch chi ddilyn fi?" – *Why did you follow me?* The conversation, as quietly spoken as humanly possible, continued in Welsh.

"I want to kiss you." He held her face in his hands.

"No," she said. His hands went to her waist and suddenly he realised that she was shivering, perhaps not from the cold.

"You're afraid?"

"Of course I'm afraid. Aren't you?"

"I don't know what this is about. It's hard to be afraid when you don't know what you're afraid of. All I do know is what you told me in Dnipro."

"Daliwch eich tafod, ffwl," she repeated. "Gwelodd rhywun arall hi hefyd. Daliwch eich tafod neu byddwch yn difetha popeth."

"Hold your tongue, fool. Others saw it too. Hold your tongue or you will ruin everything. Then you said, 'everything they show you is a lie. Everything.'"

She lifted his hands from her waist but turned to him, her lips pressing against his ear, her body leaning into his. "That is all true," she said.

"Did you see it, the mother leaving her dead child by Lenin?"

"I did."

"So what do you mean, you will ruin everything?"

She sighed. "Mr Jones, please wait a few minutes. Someone is coming who will explain everything to the poor ffwl."

"Where have you been? You vanished."

"I was out of Moscow working on a special project with the Party's permission."

"Where did a Ukrainian learn to speak Welsh so beautifully?"

"In Wales. I was born in Machynlleth."

"You're from Mongomeryshire?"

"I am."

"How did a Welshwoman end up a Ukrainian in Moscow?"

"My grandfathers and father were Welsh, born in Stalino. Before the revolution, it was called Hughesova, named after John Hughes, a Welsh engineer who built it in the 1860s. They used oxen to drag the furnaces across the steppe. Hughes built the coalmines and the iron foundries. To help him, hundreds of Welsh workers came too. My father and mother came home to Wales shortly before I was born. Then we all returned to Russia." She paused before going on. "They were both killed during the revolution."

"Killed by which side?"

"Some things are best left unsaid."

"The Reds?"

Evgenia said nothing.

"I'm a ffwl."

"We were trapped in Russia."

"We?"

"My grandmother and I. She brought me up. I owe her everything."

"Your name is Evgenia?"

"I was born Eugenia Owen. My grandmother paid a fortune for fresh baptism papers. In the chaos of the revolution, it worked. No-one knows that I am foreign-born."

"These are secrets."

"Dangerous ones, to me."

"Why are you telling them to me, then?"

"Because I trust you."

"Why?"

"Because you're in love with me, ffwl."

Now it was Jones' turn to say nothing. The need to whisper meant that the two of them were, for him, unbearably close. The sweetness of her scent, mixed with her perfume and the smell of wet wool from the thawing snow on her coat, drove him to lose his natural caution.

"Yes."

"You won't betray us?"

"Us?" The word shocked him. "Us? Who is we?"

"A friend, some friends."

"Your lover?"

She said nothing.

"Duranty?"

She slapped him, once.

"Don't be a fool, ffwl." The repetition of the same word, the same sound in English and Welsh, hit home. His hands dropped to his sides and he stepped away from her, his head bowed.

"Was it you?"

"With him on the train? Yes."

"Why? How could you?"

A whistle out in the street, ringing out a tune that Jones couldn't quite recall. She whistled back, answering him, two notes, if that. The door to the stables opened and a figure solidified in the gloom.

"He wasn't followed?" asked Evgenia, pulling further away from Jones.

"No." Jones recognised the melancholy in his voice but couldn't make out the face for sure.

"Max? Max Borodin?" asked Jones in English.

"At your service, Mr Jones."

Borodin kissed Evgenia, once. Jones' eyes flicked away.

"What's this about, Max?" Jones asked, studying the floor. "Why all the skullduggery?"

"Forgive me. Forgive us. We want to ask you a favour, Mr Jones.

You may say yes, you may say no. But before we ask this favour, we ask that you promise us, on your life, never to speak a word about this meeting. Will you so promise?"

A muffled knock startled them, then a horse in the stalls gave a soft whinny.

"I promise," said Jones.

"On your life?"

"Isn't this all a bit amateur dramatic?"

"Do you promise on your life?" asked Borodin, insistent.

Jones nodded.

"Say it."

"I promise on my life," said Jones irritably.

"We have something precious we wish to deliver to London. For the moment, I am being watched. Evgenia is a Soviet citizen and cannot help. Our other friends here are either compromised or watched. I'm told you can be trusted, that you understand what is happening here. Your value to us is simple. As far as the Soviet authorities are concerned, they consider you to be a useful idiot."

"Thank you very much," said Jones.

"Ah, English irony."

"I'm Welsh."

"It's possible," continued Borodin, "that our package could simply be delivered via diplomatic bag through the good offices of the British embassy. All we ask is that you try."

Jones immediately thought of Ilver. "What's in the package?"

Outside, a car wheeled past in the snow. Borodin said nothing until the sound of its engine had quite died away.

"Documentary evidence. A little bulky."

"What is the documentary evidence?"

"Jones, it's best you don't know."

"Then the answer is no."

The wheels in the snow returned, coming to a halt close by. Doors opened, then came footsteps, then someone pounding on a door, insistent, demanding. A door opened, and Jones heard the sound of yet more steps, ascending. After that, there was silence. In the stable, no-one moved, no-one spoke.

Somewhere out there, in the night, a woman screamed, "Don't take him, he's done nothing!" Then came the rough bark of a man's voice: "Shut up you bitch!" After that, the steps returned to street level. From up above there came the sound of some kind of commotion, then the wheels of the car crunching through the freshly fallen snow, heading away until nobody in the cellar could hear anything at all.

Jones was the first to speak. "If I don't know what exactly I'm smuggling, then I'm not going to help you."

Borodin sighed. "I'd been told that you were sympathetic, Jones, but clearly there's been some misunderstanding. Thank you for your time. Please honour your promise to us. Do not speak of this meeting."

"Not a word."

"Goodnight, then."

"Goodnight Borodin, goodnight Evgenia."

Jones made for the door.

"Tell him, Max," urged Evgenia, "tell him."

"Goodnight Jones," said Borodin flatly.

Jones was reaching for the handle when Evgenia seized his wrist. "For God's sake, Max, this may be our last chance."

"Evgenia, we need to talk. This isn't just a decision for us. Jones, thank you for coming. Perhaps we can figure something out with Mr Jones at a later date."

"That's not going to happen. I'm leaving Russia."

"What?" said Evgenia, astonished. "What are you talking about?"

Jones let out a long sigh. "Today I went to the show trial of the coal wreckers. It was one of the darkest things I've seen, a travesty of justice. At the end, one of the accused said he had been asked to wreck his coalmine by a British engineer, Harold Attercliffe. I know this Attercliffe, he's a friend of mine. They put him in the dock and he said, 'Not bloody guilty'. I believe that he's innocent and the accused man was tortured to implicate him. So, for the first time, I wrote the truth. I filed the truth. I gave my copy to Duranty to give to the censors. The moment they read it, my days in Russia are over."

Silence.

"This is what I wrote at the end of the piece: 'The truth is that the Soviet Union is a monstrous tyranny where the innocent are framed, where the state tells lies and where hunger is rampant. This useful idiot is one no more.'"

"We're finished, then," said Borodin, softly.

"You are Mr Jones, I think, our last best hope," said Evgenia. Her tone was pleading. "Tell him, Max, tell him."

"No. Not tonight," said Borodin. "We must simply observe that Mr Jones' potential usefulness to us has gone."

"It's not too late..." Evgenia's voice was urgent. "Duranty's lazy and he doesn't need to file for the *New York Times* till past midnight. Who is the censor tonight?"

"Oumansky," said Jones.

"Duranty most often prefers the Metropol to traipsing through the snow," said Evgenia. "Most nights he gets someone else to deliver his copy to Oumansky's flat. It's not far from the Lubyanka."

She said something to Borodin in Russian, so fast that Jones had no hope of understanding it. Turning back to Jones, she said, "Find Duranty. Get your copy back. It's worth a try."

"What about Attercliffe? To withdraw my article would be a betrayal."

"You break with them openly, and you'll never be able to help your friend in any practical way," Evgenia said, her dark eyes focussed entirely on Jones. "You continue to play the useful idiot, you might be able to help him. Or his family. And us."

Jones saw her logic instantly, and nodded his assent.

"Duranty will be at the Metropol, won't he?"

Jones nodded for a second time. The Metropol was Duranty's lair. "What about these documents?"

"Get your copy back first," said Evgenia. "Then we'll be in touch."

"One last thing, Jones," said Borodin. "For this to work, the less you have to do with Evgenia and me the better. If you see either Evgenia or I in the street, walk on by."

"Got it," said Jones.

Borodin led the way back up into the stable and to the door that led out onto the street. As Borodin busied himself unbolting the door, Evgenia kissed Jones, once, on his lips, hurriedly. The secret complicity of the kiss electrified him. Then, tumbling out onto the street, he headed for the Metropol where he had his single best chance of finding Duranty. Up above, the night sky was dulled by low cloud. There was no moon. He got to the first street corner and, before he turned into it, he looked behind him. No-one was following him. He started to walk, fast, through the snow.

The tune that Borodin had whistled and Evgenia had taken up? Suddenly it came to him. *Let My People Go*.

Chapter Nine

Duranty was in heaven, or the nearest thing to it on this side of paradise, perched upon a bar stool in the Metropol, Morgan to his left and Natasha to his right, a glass of vermouth in his hand. Jones sauntered in, cocky, snowflakes in his hair, his glasses lightly steaming from coming in from the cold.

"Dear boy!" said Duranty. His voice was slurred but there was no hiding his pleasure in seeing the younger man. Duranty's success with women troubled Jones more than he would like to admit. The older man was no Adonis. His features were middling, if that. Too many late nights had given him hooded eyelids; too much alcohol a fern of red capillaries on his nose. Yet he had some lizard-like animality that women wanted and, no matter how much he tried not to, Jones envied that. But Jones also observed something else, too: sometimes it seemed that Duranty had become bored by his extraordinary success with women and liked, possibly even preferred, male conversation. Whatever the logic, Duranty's good mood appeared to make the job in hand all the easier.

"May I buy everybody a drink?" asked Jones.

There were cheers all around.

"I've had a very good day," said Jones. "Can't tell you about it, but I've got a bit of a scoop. Which means, Duranty old chap, I want that copy I gave to you earlier at the House of Nobles. I want it back so I can polish it a bit."

Duranty nodded and said, "Absolutely, old boy. Here it is."

But, when he went to fetch the envelope from his inside jacket pocket, he found only air. He studied his empty hand, perplexed, while the two women looked irked. This minor bureaucratic issue was dampening the party mood.

"Forget about your boring work for one minute, baby," said Natasha, her fingers running along Jones' jaw.

"Workers need to relax sometimes, comrade," advised Morgan, "or else they do a disservice to the revolution." She said it with such deadpan seriousness that he could not quite work out whether she was mocking him or not.

"Hell, damn," said Duranty, apologetically, "I remember. I gave it to Colonel Zakovsky to give to Oumansky. The colonel has an appointment to see him at home."

Jones beamed. From the look of him, he could not have been more delighted to make contact with the Cheka colonel.

"He's on his way there now. If you get your skates on, you might be able to catch him."

"What's Oumansky's address?"

"Not far from the Lubyanka, old boy, but ssssh, don't tell anyone."

Duranty wrote, "Oumansky, Top Flat, 7 Little Lubyanka Street" in English and Russian on a scrap of paper and gave it to Jones.

"Where is it?"

"Get to the Lubyanka and dive round the back. You can't miss it."

Jones nodded.

"You still buy everyone drinkies darlink?" implored Natasha.

"Later," said Jones, backing away – and, once outside, he started to run.

The moment Jones left the bar, Duranty made his excuses and hurried to the lobby where he made a brief telephone call.

The Lubyanka sat like a great grey and yellow toad at the heart of Moscow, due north of the Kremlin. Jones had heard dark things about what happened in its basement but, as with so much else in Russia, you couldn't buy the truth in a shop.

Running at night in Moscow through the January snow wasn't the done thing, he realised, when three police officers took overmuch interest in him. From that moment on, he slowed down to a fast walk and made it to the Lubyanka within ten minutes, then curved to the right-hand side and started asking people for directions. As usual, Muscovites bolted the moment he – an obvious foreigner – tried to engage them in conversation. But, after searching for some time, he found the street himself, his brain clumsily decoding the Cyrillic in the dim pool of light thrown by a streetlamp.

Number 7 was, as luck would have it, at the far end of the street. He hurried along. Two hundred feet ahead of him, a man was heading in the same direction.

Could it be Zakovsky? The man twisted around and there was something about his gait, the way he held himself, that made Jones confident he'd found his target.

As Jones sought to close the gap between them, he wondered what on earth he was going to say to Zakovsky when he caught up with him. But he had not yet reached the figure when a noise behind him made him turn around – and he saw, coming along the street, the box on wheels with the shark's teeth grille.

As it swept past, he saw that the passenger window was down and through that Lyushkov's face. The Kapitan waved happily at Jones, like a schoolboy on a day trip to the seaside. The limo was moving fast, churning up slush as it passed. As it caught up with the man ahead, the limo slowed to his pace. Then there was a shout. Two shots rang out and the man fell to the ground, the limo accelerating away into the night.

Jones hurried to the fallen man, but it was already too late. Zakovsky was lying in a pool of blood, face upright, his black fur hat still sitting in place. Kneeling down at his side, Jones lowered his head to his chest, listening for the breath of life. In the distance a tram clanged its bell; close by, a dog barked monotonously.

From Zakovsky, nothing.

Jones studied the corpse and thought of his poor boy, Marlen, staring woodenly at the camera. One bullet had gone to the heart, a second to the head. The widening pool of blood came from his chest; his left temple had been pierced by a neat hole.

Above him, he heard shouts, windows being opened. Bending low, he unbuttoned the dead man's coat, felt in his inside pocket and found two envelopes, both addressed to "Comrade Oumansky", one in Duranty's handwriting, one in his own. Fishing out his own envelope, he stashed it in his pocket.

A police siren sounded, the klaxon becoming louder. Jones hesitated, uncertain what to do: should he stay, seek to explain why he had robbed the corpse of a Chekist colonel murdered in cold blood? In the end, it was impulse that drove him. Standing up, Jones saw an alley leading to a dim courtyard and hurried towards the darkness. Behind him, a fan of light was cast on the snow as someone above opened a window and started shouting in Russian, "Hey you! Why are you running away?"

The alley opened out into a courtyard. On the far side of it there was a brick wall, so high that it rose up into the night. He moved crabwise to his left. Feeling his way rather than seeing, he tripped over a low chain fence and came crashing to the ground, his trilby flying, his cheekbone bashing against the asphalt, his head smashing into a raised stone pavement. When his hand went to his scalp, his palm came away thick with blood; blood was dripping down the front of his coat; blood was pattering onto the snow beneath him.

Jones looked desperately around, but there seemed no possible exit. In the far left corner a drainpipe climbed to a balcony. Beyond that, he couldn't see. Behind him, he heard shouts. Then, a thin pencil of light from a torch lanced through the darkness.

The police were in the courtyard.

Jones grabbed the drainpipe and started shinning up it. When he got to the top, his hands clawed at the balcony and he edged sideways, until he came to a brick wall at a ninety degree angle. Straddling the wall, he saw only darkness ahead.

Behind him: three torches now, probing the dark. One shaft of light lifted high and caught him.

For a moment, Jones hung there, dazzled by the light.

Four shots rang out, one bullet cracking past his ear.
There was nowhere else to go.
He pitched forwards and fell into blackness.

Chapter Ten

The stage-set for the trial of the coal saboteurs had been removed temporarily for the night's event and the Hall of Columns transformed into a lecture hall. Comrade Oumansky was the master of ceremonies. Twitching nervously, he spoke some words of praise – and then Professor Aubyn trotted up to the dais and blinked in the glare of the spotlights, taking in an audience of a thousand workers who were all on their feet, clapping and cheering and stomping their boots. Aubyn, who had not yet said a word, smiled apologetically, then held up a hand. The applause softened, people sat down and he let out a thin, dry cough. His subject was the reality of the Soviet economic achievement and brevity did not become it. Or him.

"Errm... In many ways... ermm..." There were to be a lot of hesitations. "...the task of accurately assessing the scale and achievement of the Soviet economic revolution is... ermm... beyond the scale of one man..."

The professor paused for a beat, then another. If it was for laughter, it did not come.

"...but it behoves me, in the absence of others, to step into the epistemic breach... ermm..." Momentarily, he lost his flow; then a new spasm of energy jerked fresh life into him and he was off again.

For ten minutes, the professor talked in his high-pitched academic English. Aware of the importance of evidence, of the purity of facts, he set out the details of the progress made thus far in the electrification of the Soviet Union. The truth was in the detail, he intoned. So it was necessary to articulate the output in kilowatts of all Soviet hydro-electric-powered, oil-powered and coal-powered power stations. As he listed their names, their type and the megawatts produced and projected, he occasionally lost his way in the maze of figures.

"And now... ermm... pig-iron."

Evgenia, sitting on the stage to his right, coughed twice. Professor Aubyn jerked to a halt, eyed the interruption querulously, then continued.

"... Soviet pig-iron production is, in many ways..."

Evgenia coughed for a third time.

"Have you a chill, young woman?"

"The translation, Professor Aubyn?"

"Ermm... what?" He did a near-perfect impression of a toddler forbidden cake.

"I have been asked to translate your speech so that the comrades whose English is not fluent may gather the meaning of your important lecture," said Evgenia.

"Ermm."

"This was explained to you earlier."

"What about pig-iron?"

"First, I must translate what you said about electricity output. So translation of electricity output, then, pig-iron."

"Errm."

If it was a concession, it was gracelessly done. Evgenia rattled through the electricity marvel in Russian at a frenzied pace and, when she was done, she turned to Aubyn and said, "Professor, pig-iron."

The name fitted him just right.

"Pig-iron..."

Jones sat three rows from the front, wrestling with the statistics the Professor Pig-iron was regurgitating. At last, unable to keep up, he went back instead to what had happened two nights ago. His joints still ached from the fall. He'd discovered rabbit droppings in the turn-ups of his trousers so he guessed that he'd landed on somebody's rabbit hutch. Bruised and bloodied, he'd hurried out onto the street, parallel to the one where Zakovsky had been shot, and from there staggered back to the Hotel Lux.

He feared arrest at every step. What had been striking was that everyone out that night, civilians, police, militia and GPU men, ignored him. It took a while before the answer came to him: that bloodied drunks in the new Soviet civilisation were not an uncommon sight.

When he finally reached the Hotel Lux, the concierge was sitting in her usual place on his landing, half-asleep. He tip-toed past her, not waking her.

It was only when he turned the key in the lock of his room and crept across the threshold that he knew something was wrong.

On the dead centre of his bed was his hat.

Going to the sink, he filled the basin with cold water and washed the blood – Zakovsky's and his own – from his hands and face. Wincing in pain, he stripped off his bloodied shirt and vest, and resolved to throw them away. But what was the point of trying to hide the fact that he'd been at the murder scene when Zakovsky had been shot?

Jones had been stupid enough to have left his hat in the courtyard. That made it all the more easier for the Cheka. But instead of being arrested, someone had gone to the bother of leaving it on his bed.

The Cheka could have him arrested at any moment – not for the ordinary wrongs foreigners committed, like changing money on the black market, but for something far darker, as an accessory to the murder of an agent of the state.

Jones wracked his brain, trying to work this thing through. He'd been on a mission to retrieve his show trial copy from the Chekist officer. Duranty knew that and he was their creature. But something was wrong here – because, if the Cheka had found his hat and examined it, they would have found his initials, G.J., in the band. Had that been the case, then he would have been their guest right now, sweating in a Lubyanka hot room. But he wasn't.

Duranty swanned into the hall, stood at the side of the audience and listened to the professor's bone-dry incantations for half a minute. Catching Jones' eye, he stifled a yawn so long and protracted Jones had last seen the like of it at the ape house at London Zoo.

Jones' right hand started to shake so much that he put it in his pocket to hide it from sight. The last person he wanted to talk to, to mess around with, was the man from the *New York Times* – but he also knew that it was absolutely essential for him to act as normally as possible. The memory of being bullied at his primary school came back to haunt him: a much bigger boy with freckles lurking in the shadows, waiting to hurt him. The thing that Jones had learnt more than anything was that he must not show fear, not cry, not shy away from an invitation to come out to play.

Jones arranged a grin on his face, and Duranty signalled for him to join him outside. Together, they moved out of the shadows of the Hall of Unions. The day was gin-sharp, the sun bouncing daggers of light off the brilliant snow. Duranty hobbled along by Jones' side, lit a cigarette and sucked on it hungrily, all the while studying Jones with a sceptical air.

Duranty studied his black eye. "Angry husband?"

"I'm sorry?"

"Who beat you up?"

"I tripped on the pavement."

"Enjoying the professor?"

"Professor Pig-iron? Enjoyment and him are two words that don't sit well together. That man bores for America."

Duranty nodded. "He'll be droning for two hours, more. Let's go see Lenin. There's something about queue-jumping all those Commies waiting for hours in the cold that does wonders for my appetite."

"No guilty pleasure better than bunking off a boring lecture," said Jones, his right hand twitching in his pocket. They crossed the main road and headed towards Red Square, climbing uphill on the frozen cobbles.

"Heard about Zakovsky?" Duranty asked.

"Yes," said Jones flatly. "Awful news."

"May his immortal soul rest in peace." Ordinarily Jones would have savoured Duranty's command of irony but today his wordplay was not to his taste.

"Are you going to report on his death?" asked Jones.

"Don't be silly. Did you manage to get your copy back from him, old boy? Before he passed away, that is?"

"Yes. I was walking up to Oumansky's place when I caught up with him. I got my envelope from him, thanked him and turned away. Then I heard a couple of shots from a car. By the time I hurried up, people were already gathered around the dead man. He was lying on the ground in a pool of blood." Jones paused, for effect. "I thought there was no point in getting involved."

Duranty took a drag on his cigarette and exhaled, watching the smoke rise into the chill air. They were through now onto the Red Square, the slab of Lenin's tomb dead ahead.

"Zakovsky died in a car accident. Do keep up."

The high windows in the turrets of the Kremlin glinted in the sunlight. Jones said nothing.

By the side of the road, a babushka in rags was shovelling an enormous pile of brown slush from one heap to another. The arthiritic slowness of her movement attracted Duranty's mockery.

"Look at that useless cow. It's as if she's calibrating just how little effort she can make and still claim that she's working. The liberals say New Soviet Man is too brutal. Sometimes I think he's not brutal enough. She'd be better off dead. So many of them would."

Duranty shook his head, dropped the remains of his cigarette and stubbed it out with his shoe. His nihilism was dark, darker than Jones could take. And yet swallowing it and smiling was his challenge, for the greater good. They strolled past the queue of peasants waiting to pay their respects to the father of the revolution.

"It's their devotion to unholiness that's so amusing," said Duranty. Approaching the militia post at the head of the queue, he took out his letter of credentials from the Foreign Ministry. The officer read it twice, slowly, then ushered them into the Mausoleum. Inside, Lenin lay in warmth in a glass box, four GPU soldiers at each corner of the raised dais. Red spotlights lit up the living-dead god from below.

"Looks like he's just arrived from hell, eh?" Duranty said through the side of his mouth, causing Jones to laugh out loud. A plain-clothes GPU man – Jones felt he could now recognise them rather easily – turned and scowled at him. Jones bowed his head by way of apology.

"No giggling in the tomb, thank you," said Duranty, but he was off again, using, abusing his protected status as an important for-eigner, knowing that it would be a brave GPU soldier to order them out of the Mausoleum.

"So the latest joke is that Stalin has a dream, meets Lenin, and Stalin tells him all about the five-year-plan and how successful col-lectivisation is going. 'Look, Comrade,' said Stalin, 'the masses are with me.' 'No, Comrade,' says Lenin, who suddenly reeks of the grave, 'I think you'll find the masses are with me.'"

Their turn came to approach the glass box. Inside, the skin was puffy, strawberry pink, unreal.

"One of the diplomats told me that they removed his brain and are forever dicing it up to work out the secret of why he ended up so clever. To no avail, I'm told. What you've got left is rubbish, frankly. They bleached the dark spots, sewed up all the holes and pumped him full of some embalming fluid. He's more paraffin than human. Behold their waxwork god." One of the GPU soldiers stared at him, disturbed as much by the sardonic tone as the alien tongue in which it was expressed. The embalming process had somehow heightened Lenin's Asiatic features, evidence of his family's high-born status going back to the old aristocracy under the Tartars.

"Looks like Fu Manchu in a suit, poor dear," said Duranty.

"Shhh," said Jones.

"Don't worry. If we get thrown out, the Cheka will cover it up."

They followed an old man and his woman, slowly tottering out from the gloom of the mausoleum into the sunlight.

"How many people did Lenin have killed?" asked Jones.

"Tens of thousands."

"So much adoration for a mass murderer," said Jones. "Something wrong about this, surely?"

"I like bad people. They make the world go round. They do stuff. Good people, with their pathetic kindnesses, their little acts of humanity, they don't get embalmed, they don't merit soldiers standing at attention for years on end, the veneration. There may be a few sentimental tears but no devotion. For that, you need to have done something truly terrible. Good on the bad, I say."

Their stroll had led them to the front of St Basil's.

"Look at this. Built by Ivan The Terrible to mark his victory over the Tartars. Word is he had the architect blinded so that he could never build anything comparable ever again. Another bad man, Ivan The Terrible. Yet he broke the Tartar and won Siberia. Bad men do stuff."

Jones stared up at the cathedral, its fantastic multi-coloured onion domes towering above them.

"No better expression of the sugary make-believe that is the love of God," said Duranty.

A shadow crossed Jones' face.

"They've padlocked the gates. So this sugary make-believe must be kept under lock and key lest it cause trouble?"

Duranty, quick to spot a weakness, a non-Soviet sensibility, pounced. "You're not a believer in the magic baby, are you?"

Jones shook his head.

"Explain that look on your face."

"In a packed church I'm an atheist. In an empty church I confess that, sometimes, I am touched by the presence of God."

"Pathetic. I'm LMG."

"What's that?"

"League of the Militant Godless. The league is making good the

106

Party's five-year-plan, launched by Stalin – who, let's remember trained to be a priest – to make this country godless in five years. It's working. Russia used to have 30,000 priests. Now they're rarer than a black swan. The believers in the magic baby are dying out."

"But if the League of the Militant Godless is so sure that it's in the right, why use force to kill off the old ways?"

"Sentimental tosh."

"I believe in human goodness," said Jones. Even to his own ears, he sounded stuffy.

"Then you're in the wrong town." He gestured to the Kremlin. "In there, they work for the other side."

"No argument about that," replied Jones.

Duranty turned his head away from the cathedral to study Jones amiably. "My favourite Bolshevik is Radek," said Duranty. "Always got a joke on his lips. Heard his latest?"

"No," said Jones.

"So Stalin tells Radek to stop cracking jokes against the government. 'OK,' says Radek, 'but the latest one, that you are our Vozhd, that's not one of mine.'"

Jones said nothing.

"You know what the GPU call the peasants in transit out east?"

"I don't know."

"White coal."

"Is that supposed to be amusing?"

"You've gone off the great Soviet experiment, haven't you, old man? Think it's all a big lie, eh?"

Jones did his utmost not to give away what both of them knew was the truth.

"You with the bourgeoisie, Jonesy? Come on, you can come clean with me. New Soviet Man is a bit of a fraud, that's what you think, eh?"

Jones shook his head.

"Zakovsky was shot, you say. Where did you get that nonsense from?"

Jones stayed silent, watching his sly interrogator like a dumb animal his abusive master, waiting patiently, helplessly for the next blow.

"Oumansky broke the news to us at a little not-for-publication soirée yesterday. Road accident. Tragic loss. Greatly mourned, etc. No mention of him being shot. Perhaps he was shot, then he had the car accident. Or perhaps," Duranty smiled to himself, "it was the other way round."

Deep inside his pocket, Jones' right hand jerked in spasm. He was not sure if Duranty had clocked it, but then Duranty clocked everything.

"If Zakovsky was shot as you say," Duranty continued, "you've got to wonder who might have done it."

"The Cheka?" Jones said at length. Remaining silent for too long would risk Duranty concluding that his accusations of Jones' anti-Soviet sympathies had merit. "I've heard they're not against killing their own if they transgress from the chosen path."

"Perhaps the Cheka did turn on him," Duranty continued, "but his killing – if he was killed – doesn't have their handwriting on it. If one of their own fails, they handle it discreetly. A quickie trial in the bowels of the Lubyanka and then nine grammes of lead in the back of the neck. To kill a Chekist officer in the street, by bullet, that's not their style. It's bad for business. So one has to look for other possibilities."

"Such as?"

"Opposition forces."

"Come on, Duranty. The opposition to Soviet Communism was snuffed out long ago. Now Stalin is going round picking off all his opponents inside the party itself."

Duranty's eyes lost their amusement.

"Did you work them out, those two? Zakovsky and Lyushkov?"

"I don't quite know what you mean."

"Zakovsky was an idealist, a true believer in the Communist ideal. Oh, he killed people, lots of people, 'former people', Trotskyists, rightists, White Army, Boy Scouts, tennis players, whatever – but he did so because that was the correct path. Lyushkov is different, Lyushkov is..." Duranty hunted for the correct word, a rare break in his usual fluency. "... a mere technician of killing. The end of the idealist, by accident or by design, and the promotion of the technician tells you everything you need to know about where things are going here. So what you're doing is playing with molten lead."

"I beg your pardon?"

"A word of advice, from a man with a gammy leg to an acrobat. Take care who you join up there on the high wire. If you make a mistake and hang out with the wrong kind of acrobat, here in Russia, you will have a very long way to fall."

"Are you actually saying that there's some kind of effective opposition to Stalin that's going around killing the Cheka?" Jones' voice was high-pitched with incredulity. His hand twitched once more.

"No. I'm not saying anything. I'm just passing on what I'm hearing."

"Hearing from whom?"

Duranty shrugged and waved a hand in goodbye. That was the strangest thing about this extraordinary man, thought Jones, as he watched him hobble diagonally across Red Square towards the Metropol. Clever, smart, and sensitive too, he understood every angle of the dark geometry dissecting this country. He was no Communist, no believer. No-one who could crack jokes in Lenin's tomb could possibly believe in the higher call of Marxism-Leninism. Duranty knew full well that what was carried out in the name of the great theory was nonsense. He understood the appalling cost of Communism in human life completely. He just didn't care. It was like someone working out a piece of algebra: if x meant seven million dead, who cared? What mattered to Duranty was understanding power and, better, being close to it, so that power valued him. If millions perished, so what? They were only numbers.

At the Hall of Columns, Professor Aubyn was still going strong. "By which I mean... one means... the extraordinary rise in food production in the Soviet Union. Under the helmsmanship of Comrade Stalin... ermm... bread production..."

One moment, Evgenia was sitting on a wooden chair writing notes in pencil. The next, she had keeled over and was out cold. The physics of it were simple enough. Take a mass of a thousand people and the thermal product of that mass would be no small thing. Heat rises. Heat and exhaustion can lead to a fainting fit. The professor stopped in mid-sentence, irritated at this fresh distraction, and froze where he was. Oumansky wandered off-stage in order to get help.

No-one was attending to the victim, so it would have to be Jones.

Walking down the aisle, Jones used his hands to vault up to the dais. Hurrying over to the stand where the professor stood, immobile, puzzled, he stole the glass of water on it and hurried back to Evgenia. Then, kneeling beside her, he dipped the index finger of his right hand in it and, as tenderly as he could, ran that along her lips. After a moment, she came to and, as she did so, there was a roar of applause from the workers. Bored to distraction by the professor's dreary nonsense, they knew the score, that booing or catcalling the honoured guest could lead to big trouble. But when an honest citizen did a simple thing like bring back a lady who had fainted, no penalty would ensue. So they cheered and cheered and cheered.

Jones huddled closer to her and whispered, "Nid oedd marwolaeth Zakovsky yn ddamwain. Gwelais rhywun yn saethu iddo" – *Zakovsky's death wasn't an accident. I saw who shot him.*

She replied, "Ddim yma, nid yn awr, ffwl. Mae'n rhaid i chi gerdded ymlaen" – *Not here, not now, fool. You're supposed to walk on by.*

Jones winced. While Professor Aubyn looked on, disturbed but still immobile, Oumansky returned to the stage, armed with a glass of water, to discover Jones ministering to Evgenia, gently encouraging her to sip from the glass. The official gestured to Jones to leave the stage in an imperious manner. That's when the booing started. The workers in the audience were unlit, hard to identify in the gloom. They gave Oumansky the raspberry and then the subversion started: "Get off!" "Leave her be!" and "No wonder she fainted, she had to translate all that rubbish!"

Twitching, Oumansky closed the event due to unforeseen circumstances, thanked the professor for his illuminating contribution and the workers for their interest and the hall lights went on.

In whispered Welsh, Evgenia told him to get away, fast. She would find him when it was safe to do so. Jones nodded, wiped her lips once more with a brush of water and walked off the stage – only to find Dr Limner blocking his path.

"You ruined the professor's speech," said Dr Limner, his lips so thin as if they had been drawn by a ruler. "You make a fetish out of democracy while you seek to block progress with every action. You did that deliberately. You and that hussy."

Jones smiled at Dr Limner. "No, Dr Limner. The professor ruined his speech all by himself."

He walked off, knowing that he had just made one more enemy in Moscow.

Chapter Eleven

His typewriter was clacking out the necessary lie, Professor Aubyn's lecture on the great increase in electricity output across the Soviet Union, when darkness fell as suddenly as the blow of an axe. Sometimes, the power-cuts would be momentary, sometimes they would last all night – but the bewildering fickleness in electricity supply was, officially, a lie. Officially, the lights in his room at the Hotel Lux were still on.

Snow crystals on the neighbouring roofs glittered under a full moon, its ghost-light rendering Moscow's shadows all the darker. From one deep pool of blackness, immediately across the street from Jones' hotel window, a figure stepped out and looked up. Jones went to his chest of drawers, found his bottle of vodka and poured himself a thick slug, then returned to the window and raised the glass to his lips.

"Damn you," said Jones and drained the glass in one. They still hadn't arrested him. They might never, of course. Zakovsky's life had officially ended in Oumansky's fictional car accident. That was another lie. Duranty was suggesting that he was killed by the oppositionists. That, too, was a lie. Or was it?

His right hand jerked in spasm. Out of habit he plunged it into his pocket. He knew that Zakovsky had been murdered and he knew who had done it – and he was certain that, sooner or later, he would pay a price for that knowledge. It was one thing to be in the basement of the Lyubianka, under the third degree, to face his tormentors head on, to try to come up with some plausible explanation as to why he had taken an envelope from the still warm corpse of their own officer and not report the murder to the police. But to sit in the waiting room of his own fear was worse. He'd read about how the Spanish Inquisition used to show their instruments of torture to the poor wretch in their hands before they started on him. It was a clever policy. Jones was stretched out on the rack of his own imagination and his nerves were shot.

The moonlight silvered his room. Feeling the vodka burn its way down his throat, he shivered at the terrible mistake he had made. He should never have followed Evgenia across Moscow to the horse stables. He should never have indulged their strange conspiracy, whatever it was Evgenia and Borodin were up to. He should never have tried to retrieve his story from Zakovsky. He should have stayed with the dead man and explained everything to the authorities. Sooner or later, the Cheka would kill him. He wondered how they might do it. Nine grammes of lead in the back of the head was the most likely method. A fall from a window? A car crash on a lonely country road? Poison? He shook his head. Poison was for high value enemies of the state, for someone it was necessary to project a judgment to the wider world. Jones would just merit the ordinary murder of a useful idiot, one who had outlived his usefulness.

Studying his glass of vodka, he swirled around the last bead of alcohol. Someone had left his hat on his bed to show that they knew he was there when Zakovsky had been shot.

Who would do that? As a foreign journalist, he was under some degree of surveillance the whole time. No-one else other than the Cheka would dare risk to plonk his hat back on his bed. So why wasn't he with Attercliffe in some hellhole in the Lubyanka right now? They were toying with him, of that he had no doubt.

He held his head in his hands, his mind faltering, and drained the last of his vodka.

There was no electricity but, by the light of the moon, he finished his piece on Professor Aubyn's lecture. He didn't include Evgenia's collapse or the heckles from the workers or the nickname "Professor Pig-iron" in his reporting. That wasn't what was expected of him. When he had done, he took out the original and the under-copy from the typewriter, placed the original in an envelope and addressed it to Oumansky. The copy he filed in a drawer. Out on the street, there was no sign of the watcher. He had either gone home or retreated back into the shadows. Squaring the copy with the Foreign Ministry would pose no problem, but that could wait until the morning. He put on his coat and trilby and headed out into the moonlight.

Nobody followed him. The watcher had been called off. Out of habit he headed towards the Metropol, but the idea of making light banter with Duranty and his women that night made his head ache. He'd gone two hundred yards when he passed a small park, trees etched in silver, shadows painted in black, and heard the softest of whistles. A few bars from *Let My People Go* and then silence. Stooping down, he affected to tie his shoe laces, then looked behind him. There was no-one in sight. Standing up, he headed towards the park, keeping to the shadows as best he could. To one corner there was a child's playground, a swing in motion. Someone had left the seat just moment's before.

A cloud passed in front of the moon, dulling the light. Then, once more, there came a soft whistle: that tune, coming this time from a stand of pine trees some distance ahead. Walking onwards, he ducked his head under a branch, and a sliver of snow off-set his trilby, sending ice-water trickling down his back.

He smelt her before he saw her: a hint of perfume, the scent of wet wool. A touch on the small of his back, and he spun round to face her. He longed to hold her but, more, he longed to know the truth.

"So, Evgenia, what's happening?" His voice was over-wrought, racked with tension. "I saw Lyuskov shoot Zakovsky."

"Zakovsky passed away in a car accident." Her tone was that of a schoolchild reciting the seven times table.

His breath ballooned out. "Evgenia, I was there. Lyushkov drove past me in his ZIS. Then two shots and Zakovsky falls down dead. I took the envelope from the corpse. I did that to help you. What game are you playing with me?"

"A game where the winner gets to tell the truth to the world about a great crime."

"The truth may get us all killed. Duranty says that the opposition may have killed Zakovsky. He's warned me to stay away from dangerous friends. Is Lyushkov with you?"

"Do you seriously think that?"

He fell silent.

"Believe Duranty, if you want. Run, Welshman, run. This is a volunteer army. We don't seek cowards."

"Whore."

She slapped him.

He gripped her wrists with his hands so harshly that she cried out. "Don't do that again, Evgenia because, firstly, we're not supposed to draw attention to ourselves and, secondly, because I object to being called a coward simply because I have foolishly allowed myself to get into a situation where I am an accessory to murder. Where I come from, we don't go around murdering people we don't like. You and Max, you could well be with Lyushkov for all I know. I want nothing more to do with you and your games."

"Then run. We will never contact you again. Run. By the way, a whore is a woman who sleeps with a man for money. A woman who sleeps with a man to stay alive is not a whore. A woman who sleeps with a man so that a wider truth can be told is not a whore. Run, coward, run."

He released her wrists.

"I'm not sure that in Moscow in 1933 running is an option."

"Oh very good, ffwl. You're paying attention."

"Duranty..." He hesitated. "Duranty says that 'the opposition' could have killed Zakovsky. Did you and Max have anything to do with the killing?"

She breathed out a long deep sigh and angled her body so that she was tantalisingly close to him. Moonlight cascaded through the pines trees and lit her features, her brow deathly pale, her eyes obsidian, her full lips red. The moonlight shone on Jones, too.

"What happened to your face?" she asked, a tenderness in her voice he had never heard from her before.

"I fell off a wall."

"Like Humpty Dumpty."

"Exactly. And all the Kremlin's horses and all the Kremlin's men couldn't put me back together again."

"They didn't catch you."

"No." He paused. "Not yet. You haven't answered my question. Did you and Max have anything to do with Zakovsky's murder?"

"If you become a guest of the Lubyanka, you will tell them everything. So it would be better for you if I do not answer your questions. Walk away now. Leave Russia. Go back to England. Play golf."

"I hate golf. Spoils a good walk."

"Then write about the cricket and the weather. Rain stops play."

"It's cricket. Not 'the' cricket."

"Imperialist."

"I'm not an Imperialist. Evgenia, if you cannot answer a fair question then I will not help you do the thing you want me to do."

She gave out a second sigh, her breath ballooning in front of her in the frozen air. "You know what the Cheka is, don't you, ffwl?"

"It's the armed fist of the revolution," Jones replied.

"And do you know what it does?"

"It does what armed fists do," said Jones, feebly.

"Under Lenin's command, the Cheka was created in 1917 by Felix Dzerzhinsky, a Polish noble, psychotic, twisted. The Communists knew they could not win an election, so the mass murders started. From the very start, this whole thing wasn't about the people. It was about gaining and keeping power by spilling blood. They killed by list. In 1919, the Cheka had all Moscow's Boy Scouts shot. In 1920, every single member of Moscow's Lawn Tennis Club, shot. Once the revolution was secure, the killing slowed down. Stalin bided his time, for a time. But now a new terror is being unleashed. No-one knows why. A neuro-pathologist diagnosed Stalin as paranoid. Two days later, he died of poison. They're very imaginative when it comes to killing. When I was seven, not long after the revolution, the Cheka came to my home town in the very depth of winter..."

"Stalino?"

"Yes, Stalino. They came to a big house in the main street and they arrested a man. He'd been protesting about the lack of safety for the workers at the iron foundry he ran. There was a great pile of wood in our garden and I had a secret hiding place under it, so I was able to see everything. They took the man out of his house in his shirtsleeves and chained him to a wooden post so that he couldn't move. It was minus thirty. Then they poured bucket after bucket of water over him until he was frozen solid, a pillar of ice. That man was my father." She paused. "So, if I answer your questions, will you be strong enough to handle the Cheka if they come for you?"

"I'm sorry about your father," Jones began, "but please stop trying to frighten me."

"Ffwl, I'm not trying to frighten you. I just want you to know what you're dealing with."

"I'm not going to help you unless I know the facts. Did you have anything to do with killing Zakovsky?"

She whistled two bars of *Let My People Go*.

"That's no explanation."

"Some things are best left unsaid."

"Zakovsky was Cheka," said Jones. "I remember that time on the way to the Lenin Dam when he said that, if anyone got in the way of the revolution, they would be smashed to a pulp by the GPU, the armed fist. I remember it because he meant me. And you hate the Cheka. "

"You're suggesting I shot Zakovsky now?"

"No."

"And by the way, not everyone in the Cheka thinks this New Soviet famine is a good thing. If you're in the Cheka, you're better placed than most in our society to understand what is really going on. You see how the men in power feast, how the wretches are shot or starved. Some of them are with us."

"Lyushkov?"

She said nothing.

Jones could feel the cold gnawing at his bones. He started a sentence, then stopped and asked a quite different question.

"When I fled from the police, I left my hat at the scene. It made its own way back to my hotel room."

"So black magic exists."

"Stop playing with me, Evgenia."

"I am not playing with you. Someone found your hat and put it on your bed. For the moment, you are not in the Lubyanka. That's good for you and good for us."

"Who told you the hat was left on my bed?"

She bowed her head a fraction, and the half-memory of a smile played on her lips. Evgenia so rarely smiled that, when she did, Jones found it almost unbearably erotic. With a struggle, he remembered he needed to stay angry with her.

"You and your friends work your black magic so I can carry on playing useful idiot for you?"

"Exactly."

"So that you can use me?"

"Yes."

Defeated by her honesty, he fell silent. Then his jealousy got the better of him.

"Like you use Max? Or is it Max using you?"

"Both, I think. Max is my lover. In the new civilisation, a woman can have as many lovers as she wants. It is the only real improvement from the time before."

"Why do you sleep with Duranty?"

"I have no choice. He holds the power of life and death over all of us translators."

"That night on the train?"

"He planned it, all of it, deliberately to enrage you, to make you seethe with jealousy. He knew you were attracted to me. He was angry with you, jealous that you'd interviewed Hitler. He hated it that you won his cigarette lighter, the one he'd been given by Aleister Crowley."

"That's pathetic."

"He is pathetic. He did it to break you. He takes obscene pleasure in sleeping with a woman once he knows another man wants her. More than anything else, it excites him."

"And you?"

"I had no choice, ffwl."

"But you like him, yes?"

The shaft of moonlight died and her face was shrouded once more.

"Walter Duranty is the darkest human being I have ever met, worse than any Chekist, worse, perhaps, than Stalin. He is not a believer, not a Communist, not a fanatic. He can be extraordinarily amusing. He's always sharp, brutally so sometimes. But he believes in nothing. He is the most immoral human being I have ever met. It's no surprise that he was a friend of Crowley, this Satanist."

"Anyone with any sense in Britain knows that Crowley was a silly old ham. Pentacles and Beelzebub and a load of old rot."

"Maybe. But for me, for us Russians and Ukrainians, Duranty is a living evil."

He bowed his head. "I'm sorry. I am a ffwl."

"Ssssh." She lifted his jaw with a caress of her fingers and kissed him lightly. There was no helping it: he kissed her back with all the pent-up desire he had felt since the first moment he'd seen her. Within seconds, they were lost in each other's passion. In the distance, a steam engine whistled and its melancholy sound travelled through a ghost world.

Later, they walked through the moonlit streets, arm in arm. "We might be seen together, no?" he asked, anxiously.

"For a translator to take a Western reporter as a lover is expected."

"I already have a translator. Madame Koloshny."

"Is she a good worker?"

119

He shook his head.

"Does she sleep with you?"

"Certainly not."

"Do you want to sleep with her?"

"No."

"Then fire her and hire me."

"You're quite the capitalist, aren't you?"

She smiled to herself.

"All right."

"I will have to spy on you, of course."

"Of course. What will you tell them?"

"I will tell them everything." She paused. "Everything that is appropriate."

"Which is?"

"That you are a useful idiot. That you are sympathetic to the workers' state and admire the heroism of the Soviet Union – but that, from time to time, you wonder about food shortages and things that don't seem right. Nothing too alarming. That you like girls. Not boys. You are a reasonable catch for them and for me. It is only a pity that your newspaper is not a major organ of Western propaganda like the *New York Times* but a provincial voice. Tolstoy, I think, once wrote: 'there is nothing worse than a provincial celebrity'. That is you, yes, Mr Jones?"

He pinched her on the arm and she laughed.

"Evgenia, may I ask, what does Duranty think of me?"

"The provincial celebrity wants to know what the national celebrity thinks of him now?"

"Steady on."

"He says that you are dull, something of a nobody, neither a capitalist nor a Communist, with no real passion for anything much. But secretly?"

"Yes?"

"He hates you."

"What? At Kurskaya station that day, he saved my life."

"He saved the face of Soviet power, he saved Lyushkov from, how shall I say, embarrassment. It would have been a terrible thing for them if the opening of their precious Lenin Dam had been marred by the killing of a foreign journalist."

"OK, but why do you say he hates me?"

"Never underestimate the loathing ambition holds for talent."

"Ha!" He kissed her out of delight, then asked, "Where are we going?"

"To the stables. When we get close, I will go ahead and you follow me, two hundred feet behind. If you see anyone following us, just walk on by and go home and I will find you another time."

No-one was about. As he ducked down, the small door into the basement opened inwards. The brilliance of the moon and the darkness within blind-sided him, making him stumble down the steps – but a woman's hands steadied him.

"Steady, Mr Jones..." The voice was the smokiest in the whole of Moscow.

"Winnie?"

"Sssh. You didn't see me here. I'm singing cabaret in a tractor factory right now and you best remember that."

Winnie moved past him, bolted the door and led him by the hand down the passageway. At the end, Evgenia appeared out of the gloom, the light from a candle dancing in her eyes. Jones looked at her too longingly and, with the most subtle of gestures, she turned her gaze from him to Borodin, standing on the edge of the light.

In the far corner, a third figure stirred. It was far too dark for Jones to make out who it was.

"Howdy, friend." The voice, gravel on moonshine, belonged to Big Bill Haywood.

"We've agreed we can show you the documents we'd like you to ship out for us," said Borodin. He fell to his knees and cleared some of the straw underfoot, lifting up a latch and dropping down to a hidden room below. Jones followed, then Evgenia and Winnie, with Haywood coming last. The ceiling was so low they had to crouch.

Borodin led the way in the near-complete darkness. Twenty feet further on, a thick black blanket lay ahead. Feeling with his hands, Borodin found a switch and a film projector clicked into life. The screen was a white sheet, pinned to a brick wall.

Three... Two... One...

And the film flickered into life.

A corpse, skeletally thin, on a mortuary slab. The camera pans left and finds eight, nine, ten corpses, more bone than flesh, lying on slabs. The cut jumps again. A railway wagon in a siding. The tarpaulin is lifted and the camera sees a jumble of stick-limbs, giant heads, swollen bellies, thirty, maybe forty corpses in all. The cut jumps for the last time. The camera sees the Lenin statue in Dnipro. A woman hurries in black towards Lenin, carrying an object which she lays down before him. The camera closes in and sees that it is a baby and the baby is dead. There is no sound but it's clear that the woman starts screaming. A GPU truck arrives and the woman and the baby are removed. The film fades to black.

"It's the famine," said Evgenia. "One reel and every second shows our people, men, women and children, dying of hunger. The best shot, you saw it yourself, with your own eyes."

"Daliwch eich tafod, ffwl," said Jones. "Gwelodd rhywun arall hi hefyd. Daliwch eich tafod neu byddwch yn difetha popeth."

"What are you talking about?" asked Haywood.

Jones stayed silent for a time.

"How many dead?" he asked.

"Five million," said Evgenia. "Six million. Seven million. No-one knows for sure because no-one is counting. But millions, no doubting it. Stalin's collectivisation is killing the peasants. The Cheka go in, shoot their horses, butcher their cattle and sheep, leave them with nothing. Anyone who fights back is shot. Anyone who doesn't, starves. The famine is raging across the whole of Russia but it's worst in the Ukraine."

Jones was silent for a long time. Then he spoke. "You do realise that this is some kind of collective suicide mission, don't you? The

Cheka will kill you all. Why are you doing this? Why are you fighting them, this system?"

"I am Ukrainian, Mr Jones," said Evgenia, stiffly, "and this system, as you call it, is murdering my people."

"You were born in Wales."

"But I am Ukrainian now."

"I am half-Russian," said Borodin, "but all human being and this a monstrous crime against humanity."

"And you, Haywood, why should an American dare touch this live wire?"

Haywood hesitated, thinking it over. "I am an American. The Cheka may have taken our passports but, so long as Stalin wants diplomatic recognition from the USA, we Americans in this, we have an insurance policy. They're killers but they're subtle. They don't want bad headlines in the American papers about us disappearing or going missing. For now. So we're protected. The Russians have a word for it, 'krysha'. It means 'roof' or cover. We've got roof."

"Come on. That's not a real insurance policy and that's no answer."

Haywood laughed. "This, my friend," said Haywood, "is the Wobblies' last stand. The International Workers of the World have always stood for the rights of the working man. Our last great battle, Moscow, 1933, is to get the truth out about the famine that's killing the workers in the fields here. Better die fighting than be a slave. What about you, Mr Jones?"

"Mr Jones?" asked Evgenia, softly.

"I'll do it," said Jones. "I will try and smuggle your 'documents' out. I will deliver the film to the British embassy Monday morning. I already have an appointment with them."

"I knew you would," said Evgenia, startling him by kissing him on the lips.

Winnie came up and said, "Move over, sister, he's mine", and the two women competed to hold him close.

As pacts with death go, Jones mused, this one was starting nicely. Perhaps pacts with death always did.

"Mr Jones, welcome to the International Workers of the World," growled Haywood. A bottle was uncorked and Borodin poured vodka into six glasses.

"The sixth glass?" asked Jones.

"We're waiting for someone."

On cue came the sound of shoes scuffling overhead and a soft tap-tap. Borodin answered the tapping and the trapdoor was opened, revealing Fred Beal.

"You sure throw a mean punch, Mr Jones," said Beal.

"Last time I saw this man, he was supping with the Cheka," replied Jones hotly, his knuckles tightening into fists.

Haywood rested a hand on Jones' arm. "Garry, Fred is one of us. Suits us to stage a fracas between ourselves every now and then to keep the Cheka on their toes."

Beal smiled at Jones while Haywood made a toast. "To the Wobblies' last stand. We're going to tell the truth about the famine." They clinked their glasses and emptied them.

Borodin's mournful voice cut in. "I've heard that London is sick with worry about the rise of Hitler. They don't want to offend him lest he create a pretext for a war. But they don't want to offend Stalin either, if a war with Germany does break out. How confident are you that the British won't sit on the fence?"

Borodin's pessimism could always be relied upon.

"I am British," said Jones. "I am confident that my government will do the right thing."

"If they don't accept the film reel," said Borodin, "take your hat off. We will be watching the embassy. Hat on, the British are with us; hat off, they're with Stalin." Borodin paused, gravely. "And one more thing. You were right: if the Cheka catch you helping us, they will kill you…"

"There are times, Max," said Jones, "when you are just too bloody gloomy for your own good."

"In Russia, the truth is bleak."

There was nothing to add to that, nothing at all.

Chapter Twelve

At ten o'clock sharp, Jones stood before the wrought iron gates of the British Embassy. Despite his hat, overcoat, scarf and suit, he shivered – and not just from the cold. The embassy stood directly across the Moskva river from the Kremlin. It had been the home of a fabulously wealthy Russian industrialist in the Nineteenth Century, seized during the Revolution and given to the British in the '20s to succour their good will. From this distance and this angle, mused Jones, you could be forgiven for thinking that the Kremlin was more fairy castle than seat of pitiless power. The forbidding walls and turrets seemed less oppressive from across the river, the white-walled palace within easier to see and more welcoming. Jones marked his observation down as an optical illusion. Immediately in front of him, the Moskva river was a field of ice, inching along and growling. That was more like it.

A Royal Marine in full dress uniform opened a side gate and Jones explained who he was and that he had an appointment with Ilver. In Jones' briefcase was a selection of Evgenia's lingerie and, beneath that, a round metal tin containing the film reel. The marine opened the gate, thought briefly about searching his briefcase, but decided against it; Jones' spectacles conveyed an air of harmlessness, so in the end he didn't bother. Jones followed the marine to the main door of the embassy proper. The door opened and behind it stood a preposterously young diplomat in an Oxford shirt, tie and sleeveless pullover.

"Good morning. Mr Jones?" The boy introduced himself as a Mr Plumley.

An ancient butler, a native Russian in a frock coat with skin as translucent as tracing paper, took Jones' hat, scarf and overcoat and wandered off. Then, Plumley led Jones up a marble staircase and into a library populated with books no-one read. Once he was seated, Plumley offered Jones tea with milk, his voice squeaking as he did so. This was a very British luxury, unheard of in Russia, and Jones readily accepted.

A fire of two or three logs crackled in the hearth, throwing out not enough heat to warm the room. Jones wanted his coat back but the butler had disappeared. In one corner, a grandfather clock ticked; in another, a full length portrait of George V scowled down at the riff-raff. Paintings depicted soldiers in red defeating sundry foreigners: Blenheim, Waterloo, Agincourt.

Sipping his tea, Jones wondered how long his luck might last, how long it might be before the Cheka pounced and Borodin's melancholic prediction came true. His thoughts moved to Attercliffe and his anxious wife. Attercliffe would be in the Lubyanka right now.

Then, yet again, he saw, in his mind's eye, the woman in black laying her dead infant down in the snow in front of Lenin.

His teacup rattled in its saucer.

It was chilly in the room, true, but not that cold. Jones put cup and saucer to one side and studied his hands. They were trembling. Now that he knew something of the reality of Stalin's Russia, now that he was carrying proof of the monstrous crime happening in the countryside in the briefcase by his feet, nothing seemed safe. In this country, you could get killed for that. In the Soviet Union you could get killed for nothing at all.

The grandfather clock ticked on. After a time, he glanced at his watch and realised that he had been left in the library for half an hour. The door to the library opened out onto the staircase and occasionally he heard voices, always muted, some speaking Russian, some English, wafting his way. After an hour and a half, he got up and went to the open door, coughing rhetorically. That drew no response – so, next, he coughed operatically. This time, Plumley opened a second door along from the library and peeked at Jones.

"Will Mr Ilver be long?" asked Jones.

"I'm afraid there's rather a lot going on today. Mr Ilver is very pressed. If you're not in a hurry, perhaps you should come back another day?"

"No, I'll wait," said Jones.

Embassies, visa offices, borders, police stations, banks: power, thought Jones, always treats its supplicants the same. Power eats other people's time. He could have been a lowly petitioner at the Sublime Court, hoping to catch the eye of a vizier to Abdul the Damned. That he was a reporter in Stalin's Russia in late January 1933, trying to smuggle a film out about the famine, made no difference. You could wait. Or you could leave. If you left, you lost.

It was one o'clock when Ilver entered the library, pipe in his mouth. "Listen, sorry Jones. God, what a day you've picked!"

"I'm sorry. What?"

"You're a reporter, aren't you? You haven't heard?"

"No."

Ilver's laugh was mocking. "On this day, the 30th January 1933, Anno Domini, President Hindenburg has held a brief ceremony in his office. There is a new cabinet in Germany and the National Socialist German Workers Party have gained three posts. Herr Wilhelm Frick was sworn in as Interior Minister, Herr Hermann Göring is both Minister Without Portfolio and Minister of the Interior for Prussia and Herr Adolf Hitler is now the Chancellor of Germany."

"Bloody hell," said Jones.

"Exactly. So this isn't a good day for small talk, I'm afraid."

Jones bristled. "The envelope I gave you contained a photograph of Soviet and German officers next to a tank, almost certainly taken in Russia. That is a breach of the Treaty of Versailles. The British subject, Mr Attercliffe, who entrusted that photograph to me, has ended up in the dock of a show trial as a co-conspirator in wrecking the Soviet economy. He faces a death sentence."

"We are aware that Mr Attercliffe has been charged and has appeared in court."

"What are you doing to help him?"

Ilver let out a long, exasperated sigh. "Mr Jones, we are doing our level best, but you have to understand that this isn't the Home Counties."

"Have you been able to see him yet?"

"No. As I said, we will do our very best to secure consular access to Mr Attercliffe."

"Attercliffe told me that, five days after he gave me the photograph, the Cheka started following him. That is one day after I gave it to you."

Ilver stared at Jones in silence. A log in the grate dropped, causing a little flurry of sparks to rise up in the hearth. Then, "What are you implying, Mr Jones?"

"I am implying nothing. I am just reporting to you what he told me."

"Well, that's good to hear." Ilver stood up, marking that the meeting would be ending imminently. Jones stood up too.

"Listen, Mr Jones. King Charles Street is rather interested in the Soviet reaction to the latest developments in Germany. Not only that, but I have an important meeting with our Russian colleagues and..."

"I'm also here to talk about the famine."

"What famine?" Ilver's face grew paler, heightening the impression of his skin drawn back over his skull.

"The famine in the countryside, the famine which is causing the deaths of millions of Russians and Ukrainians right here and now. It's coming to the city. I stumbled across three beggars who'd frozen to death only the other day."

"There are beggars in London and Paris too, Mr Jones."

"But there is no famine. There is here and it's happening under your very nose."

"The Soviet side admit there's some malnutrition but deny these reports of famine and say they are fanciful propaganda dreamt up by far right fanatics. I understand that you yourself were granted a flight with Herr Hitler."

Jones held in his anger as best he could.

"Mr Ilver, I'm a reporter. That I managed to get a ride on Hitler's plane does not mean that I am sympathetic to the National Socialist party in Germany. Far from it. I called Herr Hitler as I found him: unimpressive and flabby. But that, sir, is a distraction from the point. I am fully aware of what the Soviet side says about the famine." He picked up the suitcase. "It's a lie. It's a lie from a lie factory."

"Perhaps you're losing your objectivity."

Jones motioned to his suitcase. "We have evidence to prove the famine. In here is a reel of film showing dead men, women and children being transported from the famine area to some mass grave. I can't speak to the veracity of those images but I do not think they have been fabricated. But the last image I can verify. It is of a mother leaving her dead infant by a Lenin statue in Dnipropetrovsk. I saw this happen with my own eyes. I ask only that you ship this suitcase to my office in London by diplomatic bag."

Ilver's eyes darted through the windows to the citadel across the frozen Moskva, then down to the boulevard below. Jones' eyes followed Ilver's but he couldn't make out what he'd been looking at. It was starting to snow.

Ilver turned back to Jones. "Take your film and get out."

Jones picked up the briefcase and walked down the marble steps, Ilver following him at a distance. The butler appeared with his hat, scarf and overcoat and helped Jones put them on. When the butler opened the front door, Jones stood on the threshold and looked back at Ilver who was standing halfway down the staircase. Jones said nothing and walked out, the embassy door slamming behind him.

Outside, the snow was thickening. Jones took his hat off and carried it in one hand, the briefcase in the other.

Chapter Thirteen

The snow came in thick from the north, sweeping across the Moskva river, driving into Jones' face, half-blinding him. To be accused of being pro-Hitler – his eyes smarted at the thought of it.

Without the protection of his hat, soon his spectacles were matted with snow. Stopping, he put down the suitcase and wiped his glasses with his handkerchief. While he was about it, he wiped his eyes too. Once he could see properly, he could make out, about two hundred yards ahead of him, the limo with the shark's teeth grille. The opening of the Lenin Dam in Dnipro felt like a thousand years ago – and yet, here it was again, parked by the side of the road, waiting for him. He squinted, slowed down but kept on walking.

His left hand, the one carrying the briefcase, began to burn with the cold. No matter how hard he tried, the thought would not leave him alone: inside that briefcase lay the evidence that could have him shot. Pathetic to carry on walking towards the ZIS – and yet it felt silly, somehow, to turn round and head in the opposite direction.

This was how the nobles of France had met their death during the time of the Revolution, of loftily being carried along in the tumbril, rather than do something to avoid the inevitable. Step by step, he began to slow down.

A rear door of the ZIS opened – and there was Lyushkov, in a black leather coat, cigarette in hand.

A fish truck slid to a stop on the opposite side of the road. Stepping out of the ZIS, Lyushkov studied Jones patiently, cigarette now to his lips.

The driver's window of the fish truck opened, revealing Fred

Beal, and from inside came a low whistle, *Let My People Go*. Beal lifted his hands from the wheel of the truck, a gesture of impatience.

Jones looked round. There was a wooden barrier down the middle of the road, preventing the ZIS from doing a U-turn. If he ran for the truck, he still had a chance.

A line of limousines was moving fast towards Jones, a police car with a blue flashing light heading the procession. Seizing his opportunity, Jones hurried across the road and ran to the back of the truck, where someone pulled up the tarpaulin just enough for Jones to see through. Flinging his hat and suitcase in first, he vaulted in. As soon as he had landed, a big man in black workers' overalls banged his fist on the back of the cab and the truck surged forwards before it could be overtaken by the convoy of VIPs.

The back of the truck stank of fish. Jones had landed in a narrow aisle, between stacks of wooden boxes filled with fish and ice.

Big Bill Haywood studied him with his one good eye.

"The British, they didn't take the reel?"

"No. I was thrown out on my ear."

"Goddamn limeys."

"Quite."

"Who gave you the cold shoulder?"

"Ilver, the commercial attaché."

"Ilver, eh? We'll ask around."

The truck slogged through the traffic, the stacks of fish boxes straining against their tethers.

"Give me the reel. We'll find another way."

Jones opened his briefcase, rifled through Evgenia's lingerie and produced the metal tin. When the truck came to a standstill in traffic, Haywood wrapped it in a sack, then put it in an empty fish box, then unloaded fish and ice from another box on top of it. As he was finishing off, the truck lurched into motion and a huge cod, its mouth gaping open, surfed on the ice towards Jones. His hands now covered in fish slime, Jones picked it up and returned it to the fish box. Haywood then reorganised the stack so that the fish box with the film was at the bottom. Not even the Cheka would think of looking for a film reel in a fish box.

"Nice work," said Jones, admiringly. "But it's hopeless, isn't it?"

"What are you doing in a fish truck, Mr Jones?" Haywood's tone hardened. As mock-interrogators went, he was good.

"I needed a lift."

"In a fish truck?"

"It was snowing."

Haywood grinned. "Not bad. There's a party tonight at Winnie's. You're invited."

"You've heard about Hitler, haven't you? Why are you having a party on the day that hopes for peace in Europe just died?"

"To cheer us up. And because we're not dead yet. Bring vodka, sausage, whatever you can spare."

"Where's Winnie's place?"

"She's got a room in the attic in the Red Star Hotel on Lenin Prospekt. We kind of spill over onto the roof. From ten o'clock."

The truck ground to a sudden halt and Beal banged on the metal wall, dividing the cab from the back of the truck.

"Time for you to get out," Haywood said.

The truck had stopped, ludicrously, directly outside the Metropol. Jones jumped out of the back, Haywood passed him his hat and briefcase, and he walked directly through the doors. The doorman, Dmitry, nodded as he passed, then wrinkled his nose in distaste. So, thought Jones, the stink of fish was still all over him. Hurrying to the cloakroom, he spent a good five minutes washing his hands over and over again. Cleaner than before, but still feeling fish slime on his fingers, he made his way to the bar where he ordered a vodka, then another.

After the second, he held out his hand in front of his face. The trembling had stopped, somehow.

*

132

The Red Star Hotel was a dowdy copy of the Hotel Lux. The lobby's seating area had been done up in red velour some time in the last century and, over the decades, the colour had degenerated to a brownish stain. It smelt as if a creature had died under the floorboards. As in the Lux, a concierge played prison warder, his eyes patrolling the lobby from behind a gloomy desk. Automatically, Jones handed over a copy of his passport, and the concierge opened a thick black book to start copying down the details with an ink pen.

Oils of Stalin and Lenin stared down on the joylessness. A telephone rang in a back office but no-one answered it. On a sofa sat two men in ill-fitting suits. They didn't pretend not to stare at Jones as the forms were filled in, his name and passport number copied, twice. After an ice age of time, Jones made towards the lift shift and pressed the oval ceramic call button. It had once been a pale cream but it had aged over time, and now had the look of a cracked brown egg.

The elevator car descended arthritically and an old babushka within swung the inner scissor gate to one side, then opened the outer door. Once, it had been a wonder of delicate cast iron filigree. Now, it was a spider's web spun in metal, trapping dust and decay in its rusting coils. Jones indicated the seventh floor and the old grandma clanged the cast iron outer cage door shut, then heaved the scissor gate closed and stabbed the button for the seventh. As the lift rose, Jones saw one of the two thugs take out a notebook and start jotting something in it.

The melancholy notes of a tenor saxophone drifted down the elevator shaft from above. On the seventh floor, another babushka sat behind a schoolchild's desk. She held out her hand and Jones handed over his passport so that she could scratch the details all over again in a thick book. When she had finished, she returned the passport to Jones and her eyes followed him as he made his way to the room from which the music was coming. He knocked on a stout wooden door and, while he waited, he counted up in his head, just for the fun of it, that five people had witnessed his entry to the hotel.

Then a hidden hand swung open the door.

Stepping across the threshold, he entered another Moscow, another world.

Swirls of thick cigarette smoke hung in a red spotlight. It was Beal who was playing the sax, Winnie to his side, beating her thigh with her hand. The negress was sporting her trademark boiler suit, red handkerchief tumbling out of a pocket, and bowler hat. It was a ridiculous ensemble, New Soviet Man meets English Banker, and all the more subversive for that. She smiled delightedly at Jones and he grinned back. The room was some kind of suite, unusually spacious for Moscow in these times, its walls crowded with old American radicals, some Russians, and no other reporters that he could see. Before he could move further, he was accosted by Haywood, gripping a beer. Haywood gestured to a door which opened out on to a roof, beyond which lay the whole of the Moscow skyline. To the south lay the Kremlin, a red star atop its highest tower, a drop of blood in a pool of ink.

"Drink?" asked Haywood.

"Yes, please."

Haywood produced a bottle of vodka from his overcoat pocket, uncorked it with his teeth and passed the bottle to Jones. Outside, they leaned against a stack of chimneys, warming their backs – while, from inside, came the strains of Winnie singing a German lullaby.

"Guten Abend, gute Nacht..."

"Winnie sings so beautifully," said Jones.

"Like an angel. Not that she is an angel," Haywood corrected himself with a mocking grin. "Far from it."

"Cheers."

"Cheers," returned Haywood. "Too much alcohol, they say, is bad for your health."

"With Herr Hitler in power, I don't think any of us need to worry too much about that."

Haywood allowed himself the tightest of smiles, then turned away to consider the red star above the Kremlin.

"He" – Jones knew exactly who Haywood meant – "helped Hitler do this. That's what makes no sense to me, none at all. The KPD, the German Communists, they worked with the Nazis. Their boss, Ernst Thälmann, he smashed the Social Democrats. Social Fascists? No, sir. Now the real fascists are in power in Berlin. And that man in his fancy palace," Haywood was still staring remorselessly at the Kremlin, "made this nightmare come about. I reckon purity matters to him. Better have total purity, total loyalty to the Party, than ally with people who are less sure about the certainty of Communism. You run with that logic, you get Hitler."

Jones nodded but said nothing.

"Back in my day, we Wobblies, we felt we were on the cusp of history, that if we tried a little bit harder, capitalism in the United States would crash and burn. We got that wrong. Boy, did we get that wrong! But I never dreamt that we – or, at least, the people supposedly on our side – would end up helping the likes of Adolf Hitler to power. Today is the darkest moment of my long life, no question."

"Mine too," said Jones.

"You've met Hitler, people say. That true?"

"They gave me a lift on his plane. I had a few words with him, nothing deep."

"And?"

"More than anything, Hitler's banal." Jones eyed the sleeping city underneath the snow, the Kremlin's towers dully lit by the half-moon. "Not magical, not uplifting, not clever, not to me, anyway. Whey-faced, flabby. But... there's a certain magnetism in his eyes. His voice electrifies his supporters. They're so unquestioning it's terrifying and toxic. You have the worshippers who may have been good people, once, locked in adoration of their strange blue-eyed God. He hates, with a passion. He hates the Jews, above all, but it's the hate that drives him more than anything. His *volk*, they feed off him. He feeds off them. It's a kind of madness, a mad larva grown, mutated into a monstrous insect. And that insect now controls a nation in thrall to a political religion."

"And this? What's this, here?" Haywood gestured to the great city lying beyond the red star.

"It's the same show."

"God help us. Not that I believe in God, of course."

Jones smiled and shivered, both at the same time.

"We've been asking around about your friend at the British Embassy, Mr Ilver."

"And?"

"He's no Communist. Hates this place, hates Russia, hates New Soviet Man."

"So he's safe?"

"I didn't say that."

Jones studied Haywood's one good eye.

"Winnie makes extra money singing this and that at parties and the like. She tells me she did a gig, that's what them jazz singers call an engagement these days, about a year back at a dacha not far from Moscow for the German military attaché, Verbling. Lots of beautiful girls there, as usual for Russia. Lots of beautiful boys, too. Lots and lots of beautiful boys."

"So?"

"Now Winnie, she likes boys."

Jones said nothing.

"So Winnie ends up going to bed with a boy at Verbling's party and he makes some pillow talk. Winnie's boy says that Verbling doesn't just like boys, he loves them. As in, he loves going to bed with them. The Cheka are very happy to cater for his tastes. Word is that the Germans are paying the Russians a lot of money so that they can test their new tanks without any of the western powers knowing anything about it. So Verbling and his friends get the pick of all the Russian boys they want."

"What's this to do with Ilver?"

"Winnie's boy, he swings both ways. Winnie keeps on seeing him. Turns out Winnie ends up sharing her boy with Verbling."

"Not at the same time?"

"No, leastways, I don't think so. And Winnie also finds out that he is sharing the boy with an Englishman who works at the embassy."

"Ilver?"

"Uh-huh."

"That doesn't mean that Ilver informs for the Cheka."

"No, it sure doesn't. But Verbling has something on him. If Ilver doesn't share what he knows with Verbling, he might get into trouble."

"Attercliffe gave me a photograph of a German-Soviet tank research programme. I told Ilver."

"You told Ilver you got the photo from Attercliffe?"

"Attercliffe didn't tell me not to. Not when he handed it over to me. I didn't know."

"Attercliffe is in the Lubyanka."

Jones bowed his head. "I know. I feel so..." He searched for the right phrase "...so wretchedly guilty."

"Red and Brown, they keep it quiet but they stick together."

Jones sighed. "I told Ilver about the film, that I had a film reel shot in Ukraine of famine victims. I asked him to get it to London."

"To Verbling, that information is worth ten boys. The Cheka will be pleased."

"Ilver works for the British embassy, for Christ's sake. I had no idea."

Low cloud scudded across a half-moon, casting their world into a greater darkness.

"You didn't know," said Haywood. "We didn't know about Ilver until we started asking around. But it's not good news about the film. They'll want to know who shot it. They'll suspect Max."

"Where is he?"

"He should be here."

"Is there anything I can do to make amends?"

"Nothing. We know the risks, Max most of all. It's a volunteer army we've got here."

On the other side of the flat roof, a worker, soot on his face, tumbled through a gap in the chimneys and dropped down lightly. Both men started – but Jones was quicker, his right hand open, his left curled into a hard fist, closing in on the intruder.

"V chem delo?" Jones demanded *What's going on?* His voice was tight, requiring an explanation, and a quick one too. He raised his fist. The answer had better be good.

The worker lifted off his hat, revealing a great lick of glossy black hair.

"Evgenia?"

"I hated the thought of missing one of Winnie's parties. Too many watchers out tonight, so I made my way here through a different entrance."

"Over the roof?"

"A true English gentleman would give the newly arrived lady at a party a drink, not question her about how she got here."

"I've told you a thousand times, I'm Welsh."

"The drink?"

"Let's go inside," suggested Haywood.

"Wait," said Evgenia. "Something bad's happened."

"We know about Hitler becoming Chancellor," said Jones. "That's old news."

There was ice in her dark eyes. "I know that, idiot." She hesitated, before going on, "The Americans are going to recognise the Soviet Union."

"But Roosevelt isn't going to be inaugurated until March," said Jones. "No change until then."

"Professor Pig-iron has written his report for the State Department. It heavily recommends that the American transition team take urgent steps to recognise."

"Who told you that?"

"Duranty, of course. He got it from Dr Limner. This means our 'roof' has gone."

Jones didn't get it.

"Roof, sonny," Haywood explained. "Krysha. I told you. It means protection, cover, insurance policy. And it's just been torn up."

Inside, the party was getting into full swing. They went in from the cold and Jones found Evgenia a glass and poured two fingers of vodka which she knocked back in one. Wiping her mouth with the back of her hand, she said, "Climbing over roofs is thirsty work. More." He poured another while Winnie started to hum, soft and low. Soon the hum had turned into a whistle, and soon after that her whistling had turned into song. Winnie's voice lifted the room: husky, sensual, bitter-sweet.

"Und der Haifisch, der hat Zähne..."

Jones knew the tune well enough. Back home, they called it Mack The Knife. No sooner had he made the connection, Winnie switched from German to English, and the song of a clever murderer who hid his crimes held the room in rapt attention:

"Oh, the shark, babe, has such teeth, dear..."

Evgenia sat down on a chair, her head to one side, the vodka in her glass turning by a trick of the red spotlight into blood. As the song continued, she raised her glass to Jones, who nodded back as coolly as he could pretend.

There was no better audience in the world, perhaps, to understand the heft of those words, the clever, unstated implication that lay behind them. When Winnie finished, there was a long, wistful silence, one which broke into a storm of applause, the stamping of feet and catcalls. Moments later, Beal lifted his sax, and couples hit the dance floor as a buzz of conversation took off.

This party was far, far poorer than the spectaculars thrown by the Soviets or the wild nihilism at the Metropol – but all the better for it. There was some awful urgency about it, too, for the people gathered here had all heard the news from Berlin. They knew the context, the intricate threads that had led to this knot being tied between the German people and the man with the small moustache, and they feared its consequence. They knew, too, that Herr Hitler had been helped to power by the man here in the Kremlin, the one with the bigger moustache, and that bode well for none of them. More than anything, they needed release, in alcohol, in the easy lie of each other's bodies.

Haywood raised a hand and called for silence. "I'm a country boy from out West, born in Salt Lake City, back in '69. My old pa, he was a rider for the Pony Express. He died when I was only three, sick as a dog from being worked too hard. So I never had that much education. But I've always loved poetry, man and boy. Here's a new poem, by one of Russia's best, Osip Mandelstam. He's kind of an honorary Wobblie. It's called... never mind what's it's called. I'm going to read it out and then all of you are going to forget this ever happened."

Holding a piece of flimsy typewritten paper in his hand, the one-eyed man recited the poem in his beautiful gravelly tones. Its subject was a man in the Kremlin, a killer. It closed:

He pokes out a sausage-shaped finger,
And he alone goes boom."

The poem was received in silence.

Beal was the first to recover. Soon he began to lift the room by playing a Cab Calloway number. Beal was very good with his sax and Jones fleetingly regretted hitting him quite so hard on the jaw that time he had started a fight in the Metropol. With the music soaring around him, Jones asked Evgenia for a dance with an awkwardness just this side of pitiable. She smiled, mockingly, but did not say no. Soon they were locked in a slow dance.

"The poem. What's it called?" asked Jones, softly, into her ear.

"The Stalin Epigram."

"It's on the nail."

"You never heard it."

"Liar."

Evgenia's fingernails dug into his back, a pain Jones found unbearably erotic. Closing his eyes, he inhaled her scent – and later, elsewhere, he remembered thinking that this was the most perfect moment in his whole life.

A telephone rang somewhere. It rang and rang and eventually the ringing stopped. Shortly afterwards, so too did the sax.

Jones felt a tap on his shoulder. He opened his eyes and saw Winnie, her eyes wide, frightened. Evgenia sensed her alarm and, quickly, they stood apart.

"I'm sorry," said Winnie. "I'm so sorry."

"What is it, Winnie?" asked Evgenia.

Winnie paused, as if she could not bear to say what came next.

"They're coming."

Chapter Fourteen

Evgenia kissed Jones on the lips and whispered into his ear: "I told you, we lost our roof."

"Run, Evgenia, run!" Jones cried out.

Evegenia did not need telling twice. While Big Bill and Jones hurried to barricade the door, she scrambled outside and away across the rooftops. The rest of the party stood still, eyes on the door, waiting for the knock.

Haltingly, Winnie began to sing – quietly, without accompaniment:

"When Israel was in Egypt's land..."

The first knock was soft, beguilingly gentle. The second was much louder, an imperious demand. Winnie stopped, hesitated, then carried on singing. Tears were running down her face but her voice showed no strain.

The third knock didn't come. Instead, a bullet went through the lock, splintering the wood around the door.

The sound of the shot was deafeningly loud. Someone screamed – and then the scream died, as suddenly as it had begun. Magically, the shot didn't hurt anyone in the room. Winnie fell silent. Haywood and Jones backed off, hands in the air as the GPU entered the room, a dozen of them, more, including Klachov and Lintz. Lyushkov was last to come through, his eyes bright. Once they landed on Jones, he started rumbling at him in Russian. In spite of his dread, Jones affected to smile affably, scarcely understanding a word. Then, Lyushkov called out "Yacob" and one of the Chekists – grey-faced and hesitant, with intelligence written on his face – came forward. Lyushkov spoke once more and Yacob translated.

"Colonel Lyushkov says that you, Mr Jones, are a hard man to find. But the armed fist of the revolution has tracked you down to this den of bourgeois sentiment."

The other Chekists were flipping open their notebooks, taking down the details of everyone at the party. No-one argued; no-one raised their voice. The partygoers' submission in the face of the power of the secret policemen was total.

Jones stuck a smile on his face and addressed Lyushkov directly. "Please pass on my congratulations to the colonel on his promotion. I am sure it was richly deserved."

Lyushkov rumbled again. Jones might have been wrong but he got a sense that Yacob wasn't translating every single phrase.

"The colonel would like you to know that it has come to the attention of the armed fist of the revolution that you, or people close to you, have been heard spreading false rumours, that Colonel Zakovsky died by bullet, not in a tragic car accident. In this regard, Colonel Lyushkov asks you to come with him to answer a small number of questions. He hopes that this will not be an inconvenience for you."

"Where would this conversation take place?" asked Jones.

Without waiting for Yacob, Lyushkov replied, "Lubyanka, konechno" – *The Lubyanka, of course.*

*

Jones left Winnie's party escorted by Klachov, Lintz, Lyushkov and Yacob. As they passed the floor concierge, she took up a pen and hastily ruled a line through his name in her book.

Outside the Red Star, the street was carpeted with a fresh fall of snow. Lintz drove the ZIS, Jones sandwiched between Lyushkov and Yacob. The car was warm – the engine had been kept running – and its leather soft, Moscow at night surreally beautiful.

Jones said, "Please may I telephone the British embassy, to let them know I have been detained?"

Silence.

"It's cold for this time of year, no?"

Nothing.

"Someone shot Colonel Zakovsky. You've got to ask, who did his removal benefit?"

Jones turned, theatrically, to gaze at Lyushkov. The latter ignored him. Nothing more was said.

At the back of the Lubyanka, GPU guards opened steel doors and the ZIS came to a stop by a concrete ramp. Lyushkov snapped a few words out and Yacob said, "The Colonel will see you when his work permits." Then Lintz and Klachov led Jones into the building.

To the left was a long line of prisoners, queuing so that their personal effects could be logged, then taken. To the right was a service lift. The three of them turned to the right and entered the lift. Beneath them, the floor was stained with splotches of brown, dried blood. Lintz pressed the button for the fourth floor.

They weren't taking him to the basement. Things could be worse.

Soon, Jones was shown into a small room with white-washed walls, bare apart from a single chair. The room, decorated with photographs of Lenin and Stalin, had a high ceiling and was well lit by three overhead lamps. The window may have overlooked the main square out front but its glass was frosted, whether by design or by snow Jones could not be sure.

Inside, Lintz and Klachov waited until Jones had sat down and then left, closing and locking the door behind him. Shortly after, Klachov returned with a cup of black tea. Then he closed and locked the door again.

Jones looked at his watch: half past three in the morning. He took a sip of the tea. It was heavily sugared, too sweet for Jones' taste. He tried to sleep, but the combination of the room's bright lights, the lack of somewhere to lie down and the uncertainty of the interrogation to come made that impossible. After a time, he got up, folded his overcoat into a pillow, lay down on the floor and closed his eyes.

The moment he did that, he heard the sound of a key in the door. When he opened his eyes, he saw the door already ajar and three GPU guards coming in. He clambered to his feet. They turned him round, mimed for him to take off his jacket. Then, putting handcuffs on his wrists, they led him gently to the chair where they sat him down.

Soon, Lintz and Yacob came in, Yacob carrying a cardboard box.

While the three guards looked on, Lintz unfastened Jones' watch from his wrist and, from his jacket, removed his wallet, keys, notebook and fountain pen. He read out a description of each object to Yacob who laboriously filled in a docket. Lintz then took off Jones' jacket, tie and belt from his trousers and took away his shoes, taking out the laces and returning the shoes to him. Jacket, tie, belt and laces went into the box, and were logged in the docket along with everything else. Lastly, Lintz went to take off Jones' glasses. Jones swung his head to one side, refusing permission. One of the guards, a huge Uzbek, was summoned. He held out his hands politely, signalling that he needed to take the glasses. Once more, Jones shook his head. The Uzbek turned to Lintz, who nodded. With little anger, the Uzbek placed Jones in a choke-hold. Lintz took off his glasses and placed them in the box. Jones' world was reduced to a fuzzy blur.

"Listen, give me my glasses back now. When I'm out of here, I'm going to complain in the strongest possible terms to the British Embassy. I'm a British reporter."

A blow to the back of the head knocked him clean off the chair. As he lay on the ground, the Uzbek guard kicked him in the neck once – but Lintz said, "nyet", and after that the kicking stopped. The Uzbek picked Jones up and, together the five of them left the room. With no belt and no laces in his shoes, his glasses removed, his hands cuffed behind his back, he shuffled along the corridor, blinking in the light, uncertain and afraid.

They got to the lift, but this time, almost as blind as a freshly-born mole, Jones couldn't make out which button was punched. His stomach lurched as they went down. He counted the floors they passed. Six in all. They were at minus-two, the under basement. Down here, the Lubyanka was unheated and his breath ballooned in front of his face. In his shirt, he began to shiver. They pushed him along a dark, dank corridor. Then, stopping in front of a cell, they unlocked the door, unlocked his handcuffs and thrust him forward. The cell door clanged shut behind him and he heard the key turn in the lock.

It was the stench that hit him first. The only illumination came from a slit of light underneath the door. As his eyes grew accustomed to the darkness, he made out a dark hole in the far corner. That would be the source of the stink. He sat down with his back against the door and closed his eyes. Not so far away, a scream, intense, animal, pierced the silence.

The scream grew louder and louder; then it lost its force, and soon the Lubyanka basement returned to silence.

Chapter Fifteen

Time had no meaning down here. With his watch gone, no light worthy of the name, Jones was entombed. Hours treacled by. He was broken, finished and he tasted salt as tears ran down his cheeks.

Then he remembered that last kiss from Evgenia and her warning that their roof had run out, and he yearned for her sweetness and beauty and savoured the memory, etched in his mind's eye, of that last dance with her, while Winnie sang so beautifully. He remembered, too, the moments after Evgenia had fled, all of them waiting for the knock on the door – and Winnie singing the song that the Wobblies who'd ended up trapped in Stalin's enormous prison camp so loved. Here in the darkness, he started to sing it too.

"When Israel was in Egypt's land..."

The silence of the basement was not only broken by his singing. There was something else: footfalls coming his way. They stopped outside his cell and a key turned in the lock. Jones stood up and blinked in the harsh light from the corridor. Lintz and the Uzbek guard were standing there. The Uzbek stepped behind him and snapped handcuffs onto his wrists. Then he followed them out of the cell into the corridor, back towards the lift.

Robbed of his glasses Jones couldn't make out anything with clarity but coming the other way was a group, two dark blobs either side, a white blob in the middle, a prisoner escorted by two guards. The two groups closed within a few feet of each other and that was when Jones could make out detail. The prisoner was dressed in a white shirt above the waist; below he was naked, his groin dripping with blood. Only when they were virtually face to face did he recognise the prisoner. As he passed Jones, Attercliffe spat in his face.

Jones was too shocked to react and couldn't wipe his face because of his handcuffs. This time, when they got into the service lift, they ascended seven floors. Lintz took Jones to a large bathroom, airy and spacious. Here his handcuffs were unlocked and removed and Lintz made his exit.

Alone in the bathroom, Jones washed Attercliffe's spittle off his face – but the memory of it stayed with him, and always would. On a chair was the box containing his possessions, on some hooks his jacket, overcoat, belt, tie, hat and a large towel. Jones studied himself in the bathroom mirror and realised that both his hands were shaking uncontrollably.

"Get a grip man," he said out loud. The Cheka were playing with him, of course. But to see Attercliffe in that hideous state had unmanned him, far more than the spell in the under-basement. The sight of the poor man, untouched from the waist up, tortured from the waist down, explained the confessions in the show trial succinctly.

Jones studied himself in the mirror and said out loud, "Behold, the useful idiot."

Drying himself, he dressed and went to open the door of the bathroom. It was locked. He knocked, once, and almost instantly it was opened by Yacob, Lintz and the Uzbek standing a few steps behind him. They took him along a wide corridor with a wooden parquet to a door. Yacob knocked, a voice said "enter" in Russian and soon Jones was taken through. A clear view of the office ahead was blocked by a large wooden screen, effectively making a kind of internal lobby. Beyond that, Jones could hear someone working, breathing rather heavily and the scratch-scratch-scratch of a fountain pen.

After a time, the man within cleared his throat and asked, "Cigareta?" It was Lyushkov. No mistaking that rumble.

"No, thank you," said Jones. "I don't smoke."

Still unseen, Lyushkov could be heard lighting a cigarette, giving out a satisfied puff of smoke and returning to scratching his nib across the page. More minutes passed. Then the sound of the colonel writing stopped and he snapped his fingers. At this command, Yacob urged Jones around the partition, and Lyushkov finally came into view, his pink jowls wobbling behind a large mahogany desk. To his side, the last of the day's sunlight poured in through the window. To Jones' right was a second wooden screen, masking a corner of the room.

"Ah, Mr Jones. I'm sorry that you've been kept waiting." Yacob translated so professionally, neutrally, almost as if he wasn't in the room at all; then he bowed to Jones and sat to one side. Lintz and the Uzbek stood behind Jones, arms akimbo.

Lyushkov paused for Jones to accept the apology. Jones said nothing. Lyushkov said something in Russian, mentioning the words Hitler and Mein Fuhrer.

"Ya ne ponimayu," said Jones. "I don't understand."

Lyushkov added something. From behind the screen in the far corner, an unseen woman's voice delivered the translation: "You've met Hitler, they say. Tell us about the man the Germans call My Fuhrer."

The sunlight ended as suddenly as if someone had pulled a giant switch. Slabs of black cloud were banking up in the sky.

"Hitler, Stalin?" replied Jones without thinking, "It's the same show, the same faces."

From behind the screen again came a women's cough: light, discreet – even, you might say, bourgeois. The unseen woman duly translated.

Once more, a controlled, elegant cough. Evgenia.

Pieces of an appalling puzzle fell into place. Shadows receded, fresh horrors revealed themselves.

She worked for them. Evgenia worked for the Cheka.

A sickening impotence washed over him. In all their conversations, in everything she'd said about the Cheka, its cruelty, how it had turned her own father into a pillar of ice, how it would treat Jones most terribly if he ever ended up in the basement of the Lubyanka, she had not once found it necessary to mention that she was their creature.

The hated secret police? She was one of them.

Yet, at that very moment, his mind started to fret at another possibility: that she was both one of them and also, at the same time, their prisoner too. Jones himself could do what he liked. If he wanted, he could leave Russia far behind. He was, after all, a British subject. But the Cheka held power over the woman he loved. They could destroy her for their pleasure and his agony and do so in a twinkling of an eye.

They had him.

A fresh cough brought him back to the surface.

"Hitler was banal," gabbled Jones, "a grey figure, flabby and insignificant. I should tell you that I was given a ride in his plane to Berlin but that I had only a few words with him. In fact, I spent more time in the company of his praetorian guard, the SS."

Evgenia translated that at a gallop. Out of the corner of his eye, he watched Yacob jot everything down in a notebook. If Evgenia mistranslated a word, Yacob would pick up on it. They would know.

"The SS, what are they like?" asked Lyushkov.

"The SS remind me of you, the Cheka." This time the translation came slowly, almost stumbling. Lyushkov broke into a smile, snuffed out his cigarette and immediately lit a fresh one.

"How so?"

"You both..." he searched for the right word, "...share commitment."

"What do you mean by that?"

"I mean that," Jones paused while Evgenia translated the half-phrase, "if you or the SS had a snake in the grass, you would throttle it with your bare hands."

"Snake?" asked Lyushkov.

"Zmeya," Evgenia hissed.

"Zmeya," Jones repeated her hiss.

"Kakaya zmeya?" asked Lyushkov – "what snake?"

"There are always snakes seeking to undermine the cause. The issue for both the SS in Hitler's New Germany or the New Soviet Man is faith."

Jones could tell from Evgenia's tone as she translated that she thought what he was saying wasn't helping.

"Faith?"

"Sorry, I meant not faith but fidelity to the cause."

Lyushkov drew on his cigarette and leaned back in his chair. "The Hitlerite experiment in Germany is a return to barbarism. What we are trying to do here, under the guidance of Joseph Stalin, is to create a new future. Do you agree with that, Mr Jones?"

"Yes," said Jones, "very much so."

Through the window, the chimneys on the roofs of the buildings opposite the Lubyanka had been transformed into towers of white. A mass of snow had fallen in the time Jones had been the Cheka's guest in the basement.

"Tell me about the poem."

"What poem?"

"Come on, Mr Jones, I'm not an idiot."

"I don't know what you're talking about."

"*He pokes out a sausage-shaped finger, And he alone goes boom,*" Lyushkov quoted. "That poem."

"Not heard of it. Is it about a butcher?" Jones' expression was deadpan.

Lyushkov snorted, then moved on. "In the car on the way here, you said Colonel Lyushkov had been shot. Tell me more."

"He died in a car accident."

"Did he?"

In the corner, a radiator bubbled to itself.

"Oumansky held a conference at which it was made clear that Colonel Zakovsky had been killed in a car accident."

"Oumansky is a functionary of a lower organ of the state. What he says is of no serious merit."

Jones could not help but smile.

"Mr Jones, this is not a laughing matter. Explain your theory that Zakovsky was shot."

Jones hesitated.

"Can you answer the question, Mr Jones?"

He cast his mind back and lived those moments again. In his mind, the limo with the shark teeth grille was overtaking him, Lyushkov waving at him. Then it slowed down, the bullets were fired, the man gunned down...

"Please answer the question, Mr Jones."

It was Evgenia speaking. To ensure that he understood the dark majesty of their power over him, they were using her to torture him. If he got the answer to the question wrong, it would end in her execution, not his.

"The vehicle from which Zakovsky was shot," asked Lyushkov, "was it a fish truck?"

Jones smiled and shook his head. "My theory that Zakovsky was shot was based solely on a paranoid alcoholic delusion."

"Meaning what?" snapped Lyushkov.

"Meaning I have a problem with alcohol. The night before I had too much to drink. Meaning I got so drunk I had a nightmare soused in alcohol and I mistakenly thought that my nightmare was the truth."

"Surely someone must have put that thought into your head?"

"Only Madame Vodka. And her friends: fine red wine, brandy, flaming sambucas, limoncello."

Lyushkov roared with laughter, his jowls a-wobble with glee, his fit of merriment all the more striking because the other five people in the room – Jones, Evgenia, Lintz, the Uzbek and Yacob – remained stony-faced.

"Very good, Mr Jones, very good. You are a close friend, are you not, of Mr Harold Attercliffe?"

"What of it?"

"He is an enemy of the Soviet Union."

"No, Colonel, you are mistaken. He is accused of being a wrecker. An accusation is not the same as a verdict. The People's Court has yet to deliberate and he has indicated that he is not guilty."

Lyushkov said nothing but held his cigarette to his lips, a finger of ash growing longer in the silence. He stubbed it out, smiled, and said, "We are minded to release you from our care."

"May I go?"

Lyushkov looked down at his notes. "One last question, Mr Jones. This talk of famine in the bourgeois capitalist press in Berlin, New York?"

He leaned forward in his chair, the finger of ash dropping onto his precious desk unregarded. He was taut, engaged, his former pretence of joviality forgotten. This was the real meat, Jones realised. The rest had just been softening him up.

"There is no famine. Perhaps some isolated cases of malnutrition."

"You're sure?"

"There is no famine, Colonel."

"Very good. It has been a pleasure and an honour talking to you, Mr Jones. Please go carefully. The revolution faces a thousand snakes, as you like to put it."

Jones stood up. The Uzbek handed him his overcoat and hat.

"Good day to you, Mr Jones."

"Good day to you, Colonel – and congratulations, once again, on your promotion."

Lyushkov bowed, acknowledging both the compliment and its falseness at the same time.

Jones was led by the Uzbek and Lintz out of the room, down into the lift and out through the front door of the Lubyanka. Standing on the front step, the great grey and yellow toad of the Lubyanka behind him, he gasped for air.

In front of him, the snow lifted and spiralled, creating a little tornado of swirling flakes. He headed straight into it.

Chapter Sixteen

The snow that had fallen whilst he had been a guest of the Cheka was the deepest in living memory. In the outside world, roads tunnelled through banks of snow as high as a house; the boughs of trees barely punched through the blanket of white. Jones hurried, dismal and alone, through the great white canyons to the Metropol. In the short walk, his cheekbones developed a dull ache, his fingers and toes lost their feeling, his throat burned with cold.

The bar was empty apart from a well-dressed foreigner, middle-aged, crumpled and ugly, with a beautiful Russian woman half his age. They studied each other intensely. They could have been discussing poetry; they could have been negotiating a price. Jones ordered a bottle of one of the very best red wines the Metropol had to offer, drank it, ordered a second, drank that too and was on his third when Evgenia came in.

Jones had a full glass of red in his hand, on the table a bottle embossed with two crossed keys.

"Is the wine French?" she asked.

"Yes. Chateauneuf du Pape."

"Expensive?"

"Very." He did not ask her join him but took a hefty slug of the wine. His rudeness was so out of character that it could only be deliberate. He was drunk, vilely so, but he hated her for her betrayal – and there was a certain satisfaction in knowing that she was the most worthless human being he had ever met.

Then she did something that burned through the alcohol he'd had, the thing he found so adorable in her. She turned her head away, suggesting that she would rather be anywhere else than where she was right now.

"You told them about that bloody poem?" Jones' voice was slurred, his tone solemn, stating a fact.

She shook her head.

"Well, somebody ratted us out and it wasn't bloody me. You work for them so logic suggests that you are the rat, sweetie."

Her dark eyes were cast down at the floor. In a trembling voice, she whispered, "Something dreadful has happened. I need to talk to you."

"I'm sorry, I'm working on my alcohol-fuelled delusions," said Jones. "Lyushkov didn't shoot Zakovsky. There is no famine and," he raised his voice, "you don't work for the bloody Ch-Ch-Cheka."

The couple on the far side of the bar turned their heads, then went back to their haggling. If there was one word you didn't overhear in the Soviet Union, it was "Cheka".

Evgenia said, "Gareth, please, you must listen to me."

It was the first time she had ever used his first name.

"I don't see what the problem is about anyone knowing you work for the Ch-Ch-Ch-Cheka." His stammer drew even more attention to the taboo word. "The Ch-Ch-Cheka know you work for them. And the Cheka is the only thing that matters in this town."

She whispered something.

"What? What's that you say?" His parody of an old and deaf man was all too accurate.

"I had," she lifted her voice, "I had and have no choice. But you must listen to me. Something terrible..."

His mind, dulled by the buckets of alcohol he'd consumed, suddenly cleared. "Enough! You could have told me you worked for the killers. It would have been nice to know. It's too late now to come up with some new sob story. I've heard enough fairy stories from you."

She turned and fled.

Putting his wine glass down, he thought hard about what he had witnessed, strove to process it as rationally as he could. What was so extraordinary about the Cheka was its subtle calibration of human pain, how it managed to be so cruel and yet so cunning.

With a sudden insight which made his head spin – as if he had been lifted up by a giant's hand to the top of a thousand-foot cliff – he realised that what he had endured was a specific edition of a general cruelty which spanned nine time zones, from the old borders of what had been the Austro-Hungarian Empire to the icy wastes overlooking Alaska.

But as far as the rest of the world was concerned, this empire of cruelty did not exist. Fear had smudged out terror. Perhaps even better calibrated than the Cheka's masking of torture by torture was the castration of the reporters in Moscow. This was, for him, the Cheka's greatest triumph. From the perspective of the reader in London, New York, Berlin, the Soviet Union was not only an economic miracle but also an admirable social revolution.

Every single reporter in Moscow knew that to be a lie – but the Cheka had managed, through a subtle combination of carrot and stick, to make that lie unsayable. When the Cheka had offered him the carrot, Jones had declined. Money, access to power, sex – no carrot was good enough. He could not be bought. Tonight, he had experienced the stick: the fear, the initimdation of a spell in the basement of the Lubyanka. Well, it had had an effect on him – his hands were still shaking – but it wasn't absolute. Yet... refashion the stick, whittle it down to the shape of a dagger and point it directly at Evgenia's heart? They had him.

Jones was still lost in these thoughts when Duranty appeared at the bar, his hair oil gleaming in the Metropol's chandeliers. Joining Jones for a drink, he prattled on about the snow, the cold and then said, "Pity about Max."

Jones spilt his drink.

"What?"

"Haven't you heard?"

Jones was becoming sick of that phrase.

"Suicide, it says here." He waved a copy of Komsomolskaya Pravda in the air. It was the least theoretical of the Soviet newspapers, running scandalous stories about the party's enemies, real and imagined. "Jumped out of the window of his flat, poor soul. Upset about Hitler gaining power, naturally, poor fellow. And showing signs of heavy intoxication. Depressed, drunk, he falls from the window. That's what it says here."

"What floor did he live on?" Even to his own ears, Jones' voice sounded slurry.

"The fifth, old boy, it says here."

"Does it give the address?"

"24 Tverskaya Street. Excuse me for asking, old boy, but have you been on the sauce again?"

Max's "suicide" must have been the news that Evgenia had been trying to break to him, had he given her the courtesy of listening.

"Word of advice, old boy," said Duranty. "You seem to be hitting the sauce overmuch these days. Worse, you're making enemies in all the wrong places. Perhaps it's time for you to say goodbye to Moscow. Move somewhere more forgiving of your foibles. The revolution is not a very charitable place at the best of times and these are not the best of times. You could do worse than Paris. Or Rome. Berlin, even?"

Jones studied the glass of red wine in his hand, holding it up to the light.

"Berlin, " repeated Jones, solemnly.

"Sex and blood and gold, old boy," Duranty said, "that's what the readers want from you. But it doesn't matter where, does it? You can do sex and blood and gold anywhere, any old how. It's only newspapers. Front page news today. Tomorrow's wrapping paper for fish and chips. What does it matter?"

"Do you think Max killed himself?"

"Obviously, for a Jew, Hitler as Chancellor would have been a terrible blow. He jumped out of the window, dead drunk and mightily unhappy because the big Jew-hater with the little moustache is now ruling the roost in Berlin. Maybe the Cheka gave him a push. Who knows? Who cares how he died? I'm sorry about Max, God rest his soul if there is a God, but I'm worrying about you

Jones. Sex and blood and gold, old boy. Reporting's the game but remember it's only a game. Don't take any of it too seriously. That way, you become boring –and there's nothing worse under the sun than a boring reporter."

"Berlin, then," said Jones. He smiled queasily at Duranty, got up, paid the bill and set off into the Moscow night.

Tverskaya wasn't too far from the Metropol. His head became clearer with every step in the freezing air. Jones knew one thing with an absolute certainty, that Max's brother Ralf had killed himself by throwing himself out of a window in Berlin and that he, Max, would never have chosen that way to die. He hadn't shared that thought with Duranty because he wasn't too keen to share it with the Cheka.

When Jones got to 24 Tverskaya Street, an old woman was leaving by the front door. Galloping up the steps, he held the door open for her, slipped inside and was vaulting up the stairwell before the concierge started shouting at him. There was no lift shaft, at least none that he could see. That gave him some time.

Max's fifth floor flat was easily identified. A black ribbon had been tied to the door knob and the lock had been shot out, the Cheka's calling card.

The door opened inwards under a light touch, so Jones stole inside and closed the door softly behind him. The flat was almost completely dark, apart from a few edges of light seeping out underneath the shutters. Once again, he cursed himself for not smoking. All he needed was a match but he didn't have one, and, yet again, he'd forgotten Crowley's lighter. His fingers scrabbled around on the wall hunting for a light switch. No luck.

He took a step forwards and tripped over a piece of furniture, crashing to the ground. On the floor, his fingers traced out what was closest to him: an overturned chair, books, shards of broken glass or crockery, something sticky.

He raised his fingers to his lips and tasted blood.

Crawling on his hands and knees, his breathing heavy, he moved three, four feet towards the shutters, and there he crashed into a tower of pots and pans which fell with enough noise to wake up a cemetery. Not caring now, he half-stumbled, half-ran to the shutters and pulled one open. The street lights streaming in lit up a scene of chaos. Bookcases overturned, a sofa upended, a mahogany table splintered and broken, a hatstand smashed into pieces, pots, pans, plates, knives, forks and spoons and even a kettle from Borodin's tiny kitchen littered the floor.

Under attack, Borodin must have thrown everything he had at the intruders, and then some. Against one wall, a bloodstained handprint. And in the middle of the wreckage, on the floor: a film reel, yards and yards of it. Unique footage of the famine, hard evidence of Stalin's monstrous crime, destroyed.

"You put up a bloody good fight, Max," Jones said out loud. As funeral orations went it was short, honest and the only one the dead man would get.

From outside the flat, he heard a voice, frail yet angry. The concierge had made it to the fifth floor. Jones had been pretty confident that the concierge hadn't got a proper look at him when he'd entered the building but being trapped inside the flat was different. There was a soft knock at the door, then it swung open.

Jones fully opened the shutters and stepped out onto the small balcony overlooking the street sixty feet below. In the snow on the balcony there was blood, and lots of it. He tried not to think about that now. If the concierge got a look at him, he would be able to give the Cheka a description, and that would not end well for him.

Down on the street a figure stepped into a pool of light from a lamppost. A woman in brown.

The concierge's voice was stronger now, more assertive, calling on him to come back into the room from the balcony. Jones was boxed in, with nowhere to go. The only way of ensuring that the concierge didn't give the Cheka his description was to silence him – and Jones wasn't that man.

A fresh flurry of snow started to fall. Jones leant over the balcony, looked down and made his decision. Inside the room came the sounds of the concierge picking his way through the chaos.

Jones straddled the balcony, gripped onto his hat with one hand. Then he jumped.

Chapter Seventeen

They had come for Evgenia shortly after dawn that morning, two polite knocks on the door, then a third, insistent. She was hurrying to get herself organised when the knocking intensified. Terrified of what might happen if she didn't open the door, she flung it open. She was wearing a satin nightdress, a gift from Duranty.

The Cheka came in threes. This visit was no exception.

"Ah, Colonel Lyushkov."

"Miss Miranova, I'm sorry to disturb you but the Extraordinary Commission needs your services at short notice."

Behind the Colonel stood an Uzbek Cheka soldier, a giant of a man, and Lintz. His hair dye was absurd.

"Can you give me a moment?" She gestured to her lingerie.

"We'll wait inside."

"That's not convenient, Colonel. I'm always happy to work for the Cheka but my flat is tiny and I'm afraid I cannot change my clothes without making an unfortunate exhibition of myself."

Lyushkov relented. Then, closing the door, she put the small icon of the Virgin Mary by her bed under a pillow and proceeded to dress for "over there" – code for the gulag. It took time and Lyushkov knocked again.

Opening the door, she put on a cheery smile and said, "Patience, Colonel, is an art to master."

"Listen, bitch, we've got work to do."

She had pushed her luck too far and it wasn't even seven o'clock in the morning. After that, they rode in the ZIS to the Lubyanka in silence. Once there, they took the lift to Lyushkov's office, a grand affair occupying a corner room. Lyushkov went to his desk, sat behind it and ordered Lintz to sit in the prisoner's chair. Then, waving his fingers at Evgenia, he ordered her to sit to one side.

"The trick to any interrogation is not to give the prisoner the slightest advantage," Lyushkov announced. "I'm worried that, if he can see your face, Miss Mironova, he might pick up some intelligence."

"Colonel, let me assure you that I would not dream of alerting a prisoner to anything. It would be unprofessional."

"You're a whore with a smart tongue inside you, woman, that's all. Shut up or the Cheka will find someone else to carry out your services, someone who has a bit more nous." He told Lintz to find two wooden screens. Lintz and the Uzbek hurried off while Lyushkov sat at his desk and started reading reports from a stack of folders in his in-tray.

After a time, Lintz and the Uzbek returned, out of breath, with two screens. They spent a few minutes arranging them, one to block whoever was standing at the door from seeing Lyushkov at his desk, the other to screen off Evgenia from the prisoner. This interrogation was going to be performance art.

They were still fussing over the exact positioning of the second screen when there was a gentle knock at the door and in walked a man in a peaked cap, pale tunic, black belt, and wide black breeches. He wore a leather holster holding a revolver on one shoulder and a brown satchel on the other. The most striking thing about him was his toothbrush moustache, directly under his nostrils. You could have mistaken him for a disciple of Herr Hitler. The skull was shaven, the face forbiddingly pale, as if it had never seen sunshine. The moment he appeared, Evgenia felt the temperature in the room drop.

Lyushkov shot out of his chair and saluted the newcomer. "Comrade Yagoda. It's a great pleasure to see you here, as always. Is there anything we can assist you with, Comrade?"

Evgenia recognised him from the famous photograph of Stalin at the opening of the White Sea Canal: Genrikh Grigoryevich

Yagoda, the deputy head of the Cheka. The nominal head, Vyacheslav Menzhinsky, was a permanent invalid and rarely seen or spoken of. Yagoda was the boss and everyone knew it.

"Settling in very nicely in your new office, I see, Comrade Lyushkov," said Yagoda. His voice was dry, ascetic, prickly. Sitting down opposite Lyushkov, he threw his cap onto his desk. "Wooden screens just so, a beautiful assistant, some of the GPU's best men to play butler for you."

Lyushkov gulped, a fish on a hook.

"This was Colonel Zakovsky's office until his death?"

Lyushkov's jowls wobbled yes.

"And now the new tenant has moved in and everything is nice as pie."

Lyushkov said nothing.

"Girl, go to the Registry."

"She's not..." Lyushkov interrupted.

Yagoda lifted his palm and stared at Lyushkov. The colonel fell silent.

Yagoda studied him coldly. "Colonel, Comrade Stalin has appointed me to be the deputy head of the Cheka, not you. You are not my superior. Please do not countermand my orders. Girl, go to the Registry and tell them that Comrade Yagoda wishes to see the file on Zakovsky, his death and any other files pertaining to it. Do that now."

"Yes, Comrade," said Evgenia.

"The colonel and I are going to have a chat about the unfortunate demise of his predecessor. The files will help refresh our memories of the..." he paused, theatrically "...tragedy."

She turned to go, then hesitated.

"Yes, what is it, girl?"

She bowed her head and stared at the floor. "Sir, I fear that without written authorisation from you, the Registry will not release such important files to someone, such as me, who lacks seniority."

The edges of Yagoda's lips curved upwards. It could have been mistaken for a smile. "Good observation," he said.

Unbuckling his satchel, he took out a piece of paper with the red OGPU shield and some sentences already typewritten on it.

"Name?"

"Evgenia Davidovich Miranova, Comrade Yagoda."

"Pen?"

Lyushkov scrambled to offer Yagoda his pen. Yagoda laid the paper out on Lyushkov's desk and scratched his name underneath the typewritten words. He then took out a silver box from his satchel, opened it and removed a rubber stamp. He stamped the paper, then countersigned it. The whole rigmarole was carried out with a time-eating fastidiousness.

Duly authorised, Evgenia hurried out of Lyushkov's office, curbing her instinct to run off down the corridor. At the central staircase, she halted. Officers strutted to and fro. Clerks, mainly women, walked hurriedly this way and that. Evgenia waited until a woman clerk roughly her own age walked past her and she asked, "Excuse me, I'm new here. Could you tell me where the Registry is?"

The woman explained that it was on the first floor. She took the stairs. The Registry was a cavern of a room, with files in metal stacks climbing to a ceiling. Wheeled ladders helped the clerks, mostly women, access files above head height. A long queue of clerks and Chekist officers, some of them colonels, waited patiently in line to have their request served. Evgenia bit her lip and hurried to the very front of the queue.

"Have you gone blind? Can't you see there's a queue?" said a middle-aged clerk, a pin on her breast proclaiming that she was the Chief Registry Clerk.

"Comrade Yagoda has asked for the file on Colonel Zakovsky's death and all files pertaining to it."

"Authorisation?"

Evgenia handed over the stamped letter. The chief clerk read it twice, buckled in fear, and then returned the letter, saying, quietly, "At once, Comrade."

Yagoda's letter did its dark magic. The chief clerk shouted for clerks to assist her. Three came running. The chief clerk rattled out her commands, nodded to Evgenia and said the dread word, Yagoda. While she waited, Evgenia read Yagoda's letter properly for the first time. It read:

"To whom it may concern, Comrade Genrikh Yagoda, deputy head of the OGPU, states that Evegenia Mironova is carrying out work of the utmost urgency for the armed fist of the revolution and that every help and assistance must be given to this person."

She handed it back to the chief clerk. "Please make one copy of this letter and do that now."

"Certainly, Comrade."

The copying took two minutes. Evgenia had no idea how it was done but it was a perfect copy of the original, down to an exact replica of Yagoda's signature. She placed both the original and the copy in one pocket of her jacket. The files took longer. After an ocean of time, thirteen files were slammed down on the desk in front of her.

Before she could touch them, the chief clerk pushed across a type-written master list detailing all the files, starting with Zakovsky's post mortem. Only after she had signed the master list would she be given the files. Her eyes scanned down the list. The last one, the thirteenth, was for "Mironova, E". For a fraction of a second she blanched. It was a kiss in time but the chief clerk noted Evgenia's fear. In the Lubyanka, smelling other people's terror was commonplace, like the buttering of bread. Evgenia, recovering, smiled and signed the list.

The chief clerk smiled sourly. "Is there a difficulty, Comrade?"

"None," said Evgenia, curtly.

She counter-signed for the thirteen files.

"You're new here," the chief clerk said, stating a fact.

"Yes, very," said Evgenia.

"Watch your step, girl."

Evgenia hurried off, thirteen files in her hands, including her own – which might, or might not, contain evidence sufficient for her own death sentence. Every human instinct told her to open and start reading her own file but she dared not do that in the Registry. The whole country from the Finnish border to the Bering Sea was cobwebbed with spies, but this room in this building was at the dead centre of all the threads. If she stopped to read, she would be seen, and that would be the end of her.

Walking out of the Registry, as slowly as she dared, she mounted the steps of the great staircase. Every step was a kind of death. She dared not open her file. But if she didn't she would never get this opportunity ever again.

Trembling, at the fifth floor landing she turned right and headed to the women's toilets, then hurried past critical eyes into the nearest cubicle. Locking the door behind her, she sat on the closed toilet seat, untied the file and opened it. Hers was the thinnest of all. Mironova, E was, in the Cheka's terms, something of a nobody. She leafed through her photographs and the closely typed pages, detailing her date of birth, the social position of her parents, her university grades, homes, love affairs, work, attitude to the party, attitude to the "widespread malnutrition" in the countryside. It was a make-believe world she herself had helped create. To her intense relief, the central lies that she had told about herself – that she was born in Ukraine, not Wales, that her mother and father were ordinary peasants, both killed in the war – had been swallowed.

Her fingers scrabbled, turning page after page. Time was against her. But it was all right. The Cheka had nothing bad on her. That is, until she came to the very last page in the file, a report written by an unidentified Cheka officer following a conversation with Duranty. One sentence jumped out at her:

"Duranty noted that Mironova, E has certain irreddemably bourgeois traits. As a translator, she is second to none. Her

mastery of the English language is extraordinary, down to intonation and a command of nuance and irony that makes him suspect that her story that her parents were workers from Stalino who died during the civil war is a fabrication. RECOMMENDATION: At some future point, the armed fist should interrogate Mironova, E harshly to establish the correct facts."

Evgenia ripped out the page from the string bindings and ate it. It would do no good, of course, because eventually the bureaucracy would discover the missing page. But it might buy her some time. A week? A month? She closed the file, put it at the bottom of the stack, and hurried out of the cubicle. On the stairwell corner she cannoned into the Uzbek guard.

"I'm so sorry," she said to the Uzbek.

He grunted that he had been sent to fetch her because she had been gone too long. The way he had grunted it suggested he didn't really care, but the bosses might and you don't want to mess with them. Together, they walked to Lyushkov's office, the Uzbek just behind her.

The moment she opened the door, Yagoda pounced.

"What kept you so long, girl?"

"There was a delay at the Registry. I'm so sorry that I have kept you waiting."

Yagoda's dry voice repeated her phrase in a high-pitched girlish falsetto.

"A file was being updated, Comrade Yagoda," said Evgenia, coolly. "That was the cause of the delay. If there was any fault, it was mine alone." She handed over the thirteen files and the original of Yagoda's letter, bowed her head and held her hands behind her back, waiting for the verdict from the man who had power over the life and death of every person in the Soviet Union.

Yagoda said nothing.

"You were too slow," said Lyushkov.

"Hold your tongue, Colonel, or someone will cut it out. Girl, what is your speciality?"

"I work for Special Services, sir. I'm a translator for the party, the armed fist, when required, foreign dignitaries and from day to day foreign reporters. Such as Walter Duranty of the *New York Times*."

Yagoda's eyes twinkled. "Ah, yes. Duranty is a good friend of New Soviet Man."

She bowed her head. And New Soviet Woman, she thought.

"You may sit, child."

Yagoda lined the files up, opened the master file on Zakovsky and started reading, using Lyushkov's pen to make a crisp note in the margins. It was as thick as a bible.

Sitting on the edge of his seat, Lyushkov's pink tongue kept darting out and wetting his lips. You could smell his fear.

Twenty minutes later, there was a knock on the door. Yagoda said, "Enter" and the Chief Clerk came in, bearing a file.

"One more file that we thought relevant for you to examine, sir," she said.

"Name of said file?" asked Yagoda, without looking up.

"Borodin, M."

"Status?"

"WRC."

WRC was shortform for a ten-year sentence "Without the Right of Correspondence". It was the bureaucracy's fondest lie, the phrase suggesting that the guilty citizen was denied the right to send and receive letters. In reality, it meant Max had been shot.

"Legend?"

"Suicide."

"Significance?"

"Borodin was a Jew," said the Chief Clerk, "half-Russian, half-German, suspected of working with the left-wing deviatonists and a known sentimentalist about the fascist wreckers in the agriculture sector. Well known to Zakovsky."

Yagoda grunted, then opened the file. Flicking through its pages in a hurried fashion, he soon came across a photograph, which he laid out flat on the desk in front of him. In the image, Borodin was lying flat on a mortuary slab, a bullet through this forehead.

Yagoda yawned, then returned to reading the file on Zakovsky. Behind him, the Chief Clerk left the room.

At length, Yagoda closed this file too. He looked briefly at the stack of others, yawned once more, and used his right thumb to stroke his toothbrush moustache. Then he spoke: "The rest of you, get out. Colonel Lyushkov and I need to have a private conversation."

Evgenia, Lintz and the Uzbek walked out of the room and along the corridor, coming to a stop halfway between Lyushkov's office and the central stairwell. Even from this distance, they could hear raised voices: Lyushkov's rumble, Yagoda's dry jabs. Eventually, Lyushkov appeared, his trademark smile on his face. The private conversation had gone well for him, it seemed.

Yagoda left the office and, as he passed, he nodded pleasantly to Evgenia. "I do hope we meet again, Comrade?"

"That would be a pleasure, Comrade Yagoda."

She turned to watch him go, his breeches swishing against each other as he plodded along the corridor, his satchel swaying this way and that, making him look like nothing more than an enormous schoolboy.

Chapter Eighteen

After Evgenia had typed up her notes of Jones' translation, she and Lyushkov had had a long conversation; then, she had been free to leave. She had gone to the Metropol to find Jones and tell him the grim news about Max but he had been both drunk and obnoxious. After that, she found herself drawn to Max's flat, not quite believing the evidence of her own eyes: the photograph of a corpse lying on the slab in the morgue with a bullet through his brains. Though she got close, she had not dared enter the apartment block herself. Instead, she had watched from a distance, astonished and afraid, as Jones ran up the steps and inveigled his way in.

But her bemusement and fear were nothing compared to her feelings when, looking up, she saw Jones appear on the balcony, then climb onto the balustrade and jump.

Jones vanished into a great bank of snow, his fall creating an avalanche which cannoned out into the road. After the balls of snow, big and small, stopped rolling and the cloud of billowing snow dust settled, the whiteness lay thick and deep and even.

Evgenia hurried to the core of the avalanche, scrabbling around in the snow, calling out, "Jones! Jones!"

Nothing moved.

"You stupid bloody Englishman, where are you?"

Sitting bolt upright in front of her, caked in snow, more ghost than man, and said, "Not a bad cure for a hangover, I'd say. But, personally, I wouldn't recommend it. One more thing. I'm not Engli..."

She hit him, not at all tenderly, pummeling him on the shoulders and chest. Grappling out for her, he dragged her down into the snow and kissed her with the passion of a man who should by rights be dead.

From the balcony, the concierge yelled something, appalled at this fresh outrage. They got up, both coated in snow, and, laughing uncontrollably, disappeared into the night.

*

They held each other close in his bed in the Hotel Lux, in awe at the tender savagery of the sex they had just had: guilty that Max was dead, full of joy that they were still alive.

"Mae'n ddrwg gen" – "I'm sorry..." they both said.

Here, where perhaps nobody was listening, they felt free to speak in Welsh.

"You first," said Jones.

"No, you first, Mr Jones."

"I'm sorry that I was so drunk and angry with you that I ignored you at the Metropol."

Evgenia kissed him on the forehead, then began, "I'm sorry that I didn't tell you that I work for them from time to time. You cannot think for a second that I have any choice in the matter. They call me up, sometimes just send a car, and whatever I'm doing I have to drop and attend to them. Sometimes, they send for me in the middle of the night. But most of the time it's for VIPs, such as yourself."

"I'm honoured to be a VIP in the eyes of a Chekist." She squeezed his balls, hard, and he yelped with pain. "But you are a Chekist," he said, doggedly.

She studied him along the side of her eyes. There was something determined about him which made her both afraid of and for him. "Nyet, idiot. I work for them but I am not one of them. Nor will I ever be."

Jones picked his words carefully, lest she hurt him again. "But to work for them, that's the same as being one, isn't it?"

"No." She shook her head, rubbing her nose against his. "They can use and dispose of me whenever it suits. It gives me some protection, a little roof perhaps, against party big shots or others who get too big for their boots. I mention I do some work for the Cheka and they go away with their tails between their legs."

"Why didn't you tell me? Didn't you trust me?"

She fell silent. He listened to the soft murmur of her breathing.

"I read somewhere that, when a thunderbolt strikes, it has the force of a billion volts. It can heat the air around the strike five times hotter than the surface of the sun. The Cheka is like a thunderbolt. Fear, suspicion of it, is so strong. For me to say that I touch this thing, that I have been close to it, that, from time to time, I work in the Lubyanka, it's too frightening. So I didn't tell you and for that I am truly sorry."

"You are forgiven."

She kissed him, softly, gently.

"Stalin's Epigram," said Jones. "Who told the Cheka about the bloody poem?"

"I don't know," she said. "Bill should never have read it out loud."

"One of us is an informer."

"Welcome to Russia."

His eyes challenged her.

"Not me," she said.

"Not me, either. But one of us, one of the Moscow Wobblies, is an informer."

"I don't know. There were too many people at the party. You must remember, they have such power over us, our families and friends, our loved ones. They can break any one of us whenever they want. The pressure..."

"...it's as if you're excusing the person who betrayed us."

"I'm just stating a fact of life."

They lay side by side, not wanting to deepen the gap between them.

"I have a present for you," she said.

"What kind of present?"

"It's a letter, a magic one."

"Show it to me."

Easing out of bed, she began searching for something in her jacket, her naked curves and angles turned to a flickering golden yellow by the light of a candle. The image was extraordinarily erotic, burning into his mind's eye. He gave out an animal sigh.

"You are sad?"

"No, I'm full of joy... I'm so intensely happy it's a kind of sadness."

"You're beginning to sound like one of us. Time to leave Russia?"

He leapt out of bed, aroused and took her from behind with a demonic energy until they were both sated. When they were finished and lay on the bed, gasping, she whispered into his ear, "Under my express authority, you may stay in Moscow for a while yet."

"Under whose authority?"

"Mine."

"Evgenia, you were born in Machynlleth. You are Welsh-Ukrainian, bourgeois and a known enemy of the revolution. You have no authority here."

"I have a letter signed and counter-stamped by Comrade Genrikh Yagoda himself, affording me all assistance on urgent Cheka business."

"Fuck off."

She had never heard Jones swear before, and the sound of him doing so startled her. Finding Yagoda's letter, she waved it in his face. He read it but the Cyrillic letters danced in front of his eyes. Then she translated the letter in her quiet, official voice. The evil behind the power of it caused the two lovers to cuddle more closely.

"What are you thinking, Mr Jones?" Her voice was small, not a little afraid.

"I'm thinking about Max."

She held him more closely still.

"It was never suicide," said Jones. "His brother..."

"...fell from a window in Berlin and Max would never have done the same." She completed his sentence. "In the Lubyanka they had a file on him. He was sentenced to ten years without the right of correspondence. That means he was shot."

"You have the free run of the files in the Lubyanka, do you? So you're very well connected indeed."

"It was a one-off opportunity. Yagoda was playing with Lyushkov, testing his loyalty, so it suited him to place me higher than my station, just to taunt Lyushkov. Yagoda doesn't believe that Zakovsky died in a road accident. No-one does. But that's how I got the magical letter."

"How powerful is it?"

She hesitated, frightened that articulating its power might break a spell.

"Go on, Evgenia, tell me."

"With this letter, I could get out."

He stiffened. "No?"

"Yes."

"Then let's both go. Where shall we go?"

"Paris. I want to go to the Eiffel Tower and fly a paper airplane from the very top."

"Yes, that can be arranged."

"I want to go to London and have tea with your Queen."

"Done."

"Then I want to settle in Machynlleth with a black hat, a broom and a cat and become a Welsh witch and cast a spell on you that you should never, ever leave me."

She laughed slowly at first, just a merry gurgle. Then the comedy of her ambition and the tension and the fear that had gripped her for so long melted away. Every second she laughed made her longing to live an ordinary life unmolested by the powers that held sway in Moscow somehow more possible, somehow more true.

A moment later, the laughter turned suddenly to weeping –and Jones watched her with dread, knowing that this woman who was so unutterably beautiful and that he loved so deeply was more than a little mad.

Chapter Nineteen

Laddered by a half-open set of blinds, slashes of sunlight found Jones in suit and tie bent over his typewriter, tapping away furiously. Evgenia woke up, sat up on one elbow and studied him with amused contempt.

"Come here, Englishman."

Ignoring her, he continued pounding on his typewriter – until, tired of waiting, she threw the bedclothes aside and walked over to perch upon his lap. Her hair was up. She undid it slowly, its blackness contrasting with the paleness of her skin.

Leaning forward, she read his letter of resignation to the *Western Mail*, telling them that he was quitting Moscow as soon as humanly possible. She hit the shift-key and typed: "IDIOT."

Doing his best to ignore the distraction, he typed, "As I was typing before I was so rudely interrupted..."

She lifted his hands away from the keyboard and replied, "COME BACK TO BED, IDIOT."

He struggled to find the correct typewriter keys but managed to tap out, "Hwo can I get any worf done if there is a naked woman pestering me?"

She ripped the letter out of the typewriter, popped it into her mouth and started to chew.

"I know there is a famine," he said, "but eating my resignation letter doesn't help."

"You write that, the Cheka will read it and detain me."

Standing up, she walked over to the window and pulled up the blind, exposing her nakedness to anyone who cared to glance at the window.

"Come away from there, Evgenia."

"If I am lucky I might find a real man, one who finds me attractive."

Goaded, Jones grabbed her and led her back to bed.

When they had done, he kissed her once, twice and then studied her thoughtfully. "If I let them know I'm leaving, they will come for you?"

She nodded, firmly.

"The letter from Yagoda?"

"Its magic will work on the lowly Commissar, a Cheka officer out in the middle of nowhere, a border guard, perhaps. But, once the Lubyanka knows you are leaving, they will act. They want to make sure that you will hold your tongue about the famine. They know you are in love with me."

"How do they know that?"

"I told them."

Dropping his jaw to his chest, he looked down and then, quietly, greatly troubled, asked, "Why in heaven's name did you do that, Evgenia?"

"They already know, idiot. Duranty smelt your lust for me the very first moment you saw me. That's why he made me do what I did on the train. I've told you this already."

After a time, he said, "I'm sorry. You must remember that I'm new to thinking like this. It's like playing a game in which the rules keep changing. But there is only one real rule. Against the Cheka, you lose."

"Welcome to Moscow, little one," she said this with relish, as if he were a rather dim pupil who had finally got something right.

"So you were saying... If I leave?"

"They will hold me here. I will be their hostage. You'll be in London, but you won't know whether I am alive or dead. If I'm alive, you are theirs. If I am dead, you will dare to tell the truth. Their solution will be to keep me alive in your mind for as long as possible, long after I am dead. Before they execute someone, they sometimes make them write ten, twenty love letters, each one dated another year in the future."

"How do you know that?"

"I've read files, read letters from the dead to lovers abroad dated many years into the future."

"So they kill you in a month's time?"

"And you get a love letter from me every year. The last one will be in 1953, saying wait for me, just wait for me. This way, the Cheka creates its very own time machine."

"That is evil."

"That is the Cheka."

He kissed her bare shoulder. "I have a dark question for you."

"We are lovers. There are no secrets between us."

"Have you translated while someone has been under torture?" His words came out too fast. Her eyes were cast down. He repeated his question. Her head dipped, once, infinitesimally. He paused for a time.

"Who?"

She said something so softly he couldn't hear her.

"Who?"

"Harold Attercliffe."

"No."

"Yes."

"But his Russian is perfect. There was no need for a translator."

"When the Cheka tortures someone, they believe that the subject will find it harder to resist if a woman is also present. It somehow makes it, in their view, worse, more humiliating. To have a woman present there for no purpose feels wrong. But a female translator, it works for them."

"How bad?"

"Unspeakable."

"What did they want from him?"

"He lived and worked in Kazan. Somehow he got hold of a photograph showing German tank specialists at a top secret tank proving ground near Kazan. This is a breach of the Treaty of Versailles. Somehow this photograph ended up in the hands of the British Embassy. The Cheka wanted to know how that happened."

"Did he tell them?"

"No."

He kissed her and said nothing. A few moments ago, she'd said that between lovers there should be no secrets. What had happened between Attercliffe and him at Kurskaya station, that would be an exception.

She ran her fingers through his hair, stroking his face. "There was something else, too. They wanted to know if he had heard about a document, some kind of protocol agreement between the German army and the Soviet side."

"Who was running the interrogation?"

"Lyushkov. He is the most brutal one they've got. Yagoda knows Lyushkov got rid of Zakovsky to advance his own career but they don't care. In their eyes, he's the best."

In the distance, a great thump sounded from an iron foundry. They held each other more tightly and, whispering even more quietly than before, they planned their exit. No bags, no preparation. Reporters often made the run to Helsinki from Moscow, to freshen up, to buy things you just couldn't get in Moscow: film, typewriter ribbons, fine wine. The magic paper from Yagoda might just do the trick. They would tell no-one and go north, to Finland. They would do so that very night.

"What happens if we..."

Jones' words faded away.

"...get caught?" asked Evgenia. "Then we're dead. We're dead anyway."

*

The hardest thing was behaving normally. They could take nothing out of the ordinary with them: just the clothes they stood up in, all his money, his passport, her ID card, her magic letter. Being normal also meant that they had to go to the Hall of Columns for Professor Aubyn's press conference on the findings of his research into Soviet society, and what that meant for the United States' policy of non-recognition of the Soviet government. On the way, they passed seventeen bodies in the snow. Before, when the famine had been raging just in the countryside, it had been easier to ignore. But now, in February 1933, it was claiming so many lives in the centre of Moscow that it was a fact of life, like the omnipresence of Stalin, like the fear scribbled so brutally in people's faces, like the endless cold.

All the boys were there: Duranty, with an Uzbek woman translator who looked a third of his age, Lyons, Fischer, the rest of the gang. Behind them sat some several hundred loyal workers from some Stalinist factory who had been corralled along to make up the numbers. Lyushkov prowled a side aisle, a smile on his lips, a revolver on his hip. Other uniformed guards strutted here and there. The plainclothes Cheka men were scattered on the benches, their look of self-confident boredom giving them away. Borodin's film crew was present for the great moment but there was, of course, no Max.

Jones and Evgenia were the last to enter. The two of them sat together at the far left of the second row from the front. Duranty, sitting at the far right, leaned forward and winked at both of them conspiratorially, as if they had been late for church – which, in a way, they had.

"I hate being the subject of gossip," said Jones.

"Get used to it," Evgenia whispered in his ear, "it will be far worse in Paris."

"No, Macynlleth." She squeezed his hand.

Dr Limner appeared first, followed onto the stage by Aubyn. This time there was no translator. Everything would go much more smoothly, more quickly if the workers did not understand a word.

In the side aisle, Lyushkov made a "get up" gesture with both hands and the workers stood up, en masse. The foreign reporters knew submission wasn't the proper form, but this was Stalin's Russia. They stood up too.

Aubyn cast his hands out, Christ-like, to still the sea of humanity. Down they all sat. His face lit up, ecstatic that so many had come to listen to his thoughts.

"Erm..."

What followed was a long list of wrong numbers, fake statistics fashioned by people in thrall to the Cheka, un-facts presented as power wanted them, not as they were. The biggest lie of all, as usual, was the "astonishing progress" made by the Soviet Union in the production of food. So much wheat, so much barley, so much meat of all kinds. If that were for a moment true, thought Jones, then why weren't the seventeen corpses they had seen that morning aware of it?

Eventually, Aubyn's drone came to a conclusion: "And so I hereby state that the considered view of the Aubyn Commission is to recommend that... erm... the United States should mark the very real progress made by the Soviet Union and note the fundamentally peaceful nature of Soviet ambition and so extend diplomatic recognition to the... erm... Soviet...erm..."

In the side aisle, Lyushkov rammed his great pink hams together and the workers rose up, cheering and applauding. The film crew captured the applause, the workers in a frenzy, their worship of the professor and their rapture at his words never to be doubted. In the end, it was Aubyn who stopped the demonstration and then asked for questions.

The reporters knew the nature of the farce they were taking part in. A month ago, Jones might have uttered a faltering half-challenge, suggesting – but not articulating clearly – the essential absurdity of Aubyn citing food statistics created by a police state while the corpses of the famine victims stacked up in the snow outside, horribly easy for all to see. But now he had a chance of a life and a future with Evgenia, and he dare not risk it. The others, too, had their reasons to acquiesce.

"No questions at all?" Aubyn's voice was high-pitched, querulous.

Duranty raised a languid hand. The film crew scuttled towards him, the sound recordist using his long boom to capture the reporter's question.

"Professor, thank you very much for a most stimulating talk. Some newspapers in the West have been airing stories that the Soviet Union, far from being the bread basket of Europe, is actually suffering a famine. Would you like to comment?"

"This story... erm... concocted by propagandists sympathetic to Herr Hitler... erm... is a monstrous lie. There is no famine here. On the contrary, there is so much food being produced that the Soviet Union is exporting more grain than ever before."

Once again, Lyushkov made the "stand up" gesture with his hands and, once again, the workers expressed joy unbound and rapture unconfined.

Jones' hand went up. "Professor, thank you very much for your most interesting talk. Having finished the work of your commission, what are your plans now?"

"Erm... I find the Soviet Union a most stimulating place... I plan to go on a cultural tour of the country before making my way back, slowly, reluctantly, to Washington DC."

The meeting was called to a close and the reporters drifted out into the fresh air. Outside, the sky was overcast, the cold less biting than before.

Duranty came up to Jones and Evgenia, his eyes lively, his voice warm. "Your question was a bit dull, old cock. But talk of famine is a monstrous lie, eh? Is the *Western Mail* going to report that? The *New York Times* most certainly will. Best angle of the day, no?"

"Yes, best angle of the day."

"Is anyone going to organise a send-off for old Max?"

The question cut both Jones and Evgenia to the quick. Their faces, pink with the cold, turned to grey.

"Not a funeral, I guess," said Duranty, "not the way he died. But something to mark his passing, surely?"

Jones recovered first. "Not sure that would be appropriate, Duranty. Officially, Max died of suicide."

"You don't believe that suicide nonsense, do you?" asked Duranty, all of the warmth gone from his eyes.

"No," said Jones, "I don't. And you? The other day it seemed you did."

"I never believe a word anyone says here on principle."

"Does that go for Aubyn's line on the famine being a monstrous lie?"

"Of course. But as I've said before, who cares? They're only Russians."

Duranty smiled, knowingly, at them both and walked off to join his new Uzbek woman. When he said something to her, she burst out laughing – and together they disappeared into a Mercedes. The doors closed softly and it slid quietly away.

Jones and Evgenia were still standing on the steps of the House of the Unions when they were approached by a small boy, pitifully thin, his face old before its time. Out of habit, Jones was about to delve into his pockets and fetch a kopek when the boy handed him an envelope.

He opened it. Inside was the shortest letter he had ever received. In hand-writing that crabbed across the page, it read, "Come see me. Bill." There was an address, somewhere nondescript, nothing more.

*

Haywood was dirt-poor so, out of necessity, he lived out in the sticks, seven long miles north of the Kremlin. They took a droshki, the driver a thing plucked out of some nightmare, an Egyptian mummy swaddled in black, only his eyes alive. The old nag that pulled the carriage was so pitifully thin that they could see her ribs move with every breath.

"Get a move on, kolkhoznik!" the cabbie called out..

Evgenia explained that it meant a collective farmer, who, according to the general party line, were all fabulously lazy. The droshki was beyond cold, agonisingly uncomfortable and horribly slow, so slow that it would be impossible for the Cheka to follow them by car without them knowing. That did not happen. Even so, they paid off the droshki half a mile from where Haywood lived, then tramped through the snow and frozen slush, clinging onto each other for support. Out here, on the edge of the city, the towering apartment blocks gave way to homes made of brick, then of wood. They called them *izba*, log cabins, the fancier ones with sizeable yards walled off from the world.

Soon, certain that they were not being followed, they reached Haywood's *izba* and knocked on the door. Very softly, Evgenia whistled *Let My People Go*. After a long time, the door swung open, a candle casting a flickering light on the face of Big Bill Haywood. He'd lost a lot of weight, his face haggard, his eyes dull, the spirit of the man broken.

"You folks had better come in."

It felt colder inside than out. The wooden stove had long gone out, icicles hung from the ceiling, and the water in the kitchen sink had frozen, locking in dishes and glasses in ice. Evgenia said that she would go and buy some wood for the fire.

"Get some vodka too," Haywood rumbled.

"Yes, boss," said Evgenia.

"I'm no-one's boss. I'm A Wobbly 'till the day I die... which is pretty damn soon." Haywood started to laugh but it turned into a battle for his next breath.

Now that Evgenia had gone, Jones took the candle from him and helped the old man to a chair. It was a poor house, no doubting it. There was a rough wooden table, a bed with a quilt, a tiny kitchen of sorts. One wall was lined with books: Marx, Lenin, Jack London, Mark Twain, Shakespeare, Keats, Shelley. Jones lingered over a copy of *Macbeth* and pulled it out. The book fell open and, by the feeble light from the candle, he found himself reading out loud:

"Thou liest, abhorred tyrant; with my sword I'll prove the lie thou speak'st."

Jones paused.

"Go on," said Haywood.

"It's just a stage instruction."

"Read it."

"They fight and Young Siward is slain."

"That's what's happened here. We thought that there was a great revolution taking place, that the bosses were being made to kneel before the workers. Got that wrong, big time. All that's happened is that the whole of Russia is the stage for a new version of Macbeth, one with lies and blood and a lying abhorred tyrant, name of Stalin." Then he started to cough, helpless, a man drowning in his own phlegm.

Jones sat on the arm of the chair, his hand patting Haywood on the back.

"You don't look good, old man."

The whites of his eyes rolled upwards in his head. "Sounds paranoid but..." Haywood reached up to his scalp and pulled out a chunk of hair which came out in his hand with no effort at all. He examined it with a mixture of disgust and wonderment. "I think the bastards are poisoning me. They heard about Stalin's Epigram. Fancy being killed for reading out a poem. What kind of country is this?"

Jones said nothing.

"Thing is, Garry, I think we have a traitor in our midst and I think they're trying to knock me off before I can prove my suspicion."

At that very moment, the door opened and Evgenia returned, clutching firewood, bread, sausage and vodka. Haywood fell silent, looked down and very deftly retched into a bucket.

Jones lit the fire while Evgenia broke open the bread and diced the sausage.

"In the shop they called the sausage Budenny's First Cavalry," she said.

"What's that mean?" asked Jones, puzzled.

"The sausage is not from a cow."

Uncorking the bottle of vodka, she found three dirty glasses and went out to clean them in the snow.

Haywood's use of the word "traitor" hung in the air, a challenge not taken up by Evgenia. Ordinarily Jones would have disregarded the idea, told the old man not to be so crazy. But in that time, in that place, fear of betrayal was a rational, logical response.

Jones could not endure the silence for long. "What are you talking about a traitor for?"

"The Cheka know everything. They know that I read out the poem. They've asked everyone else about it, just not me. They're rolling up our network, no question, and she's been seen going in and out of the Lubyanka like she owned the place."

"She translates for them, from time to time. She has no choice."

The dying man studied him coldly. "In this world, son, there is always a choice. It's only when you leave it that you have none."

The door opened again, revealing Evgenia, and the two men fell silent.

When Evgenia passed him some bread and sausage, Jones had forgotten how hungry he was. As he fell on the food savagely, Evgenia passed Haywood a glass of vodka. Raising his glass, he made the toast. "To Max."

The others echoed him and downed their vodkas in one – but, as she drank, Evgenia was glowering at Haywood, the big man returning her stare with something not far off loathing.

"What is it?" asked Jones.

Haywood picked up his bucket and retched into it, this time more noisily than before.

"He thinks I'm traitor," said Evgenia in her dry official voice.

"Nope," said Haywood, "I ain't saying that. I'm saying that you've been seen walking in and out of the Lubyanka like it's some fancy department store, like Macy's or whatever."

"Then someone has been dripping poison into your ear."

"Or someone's been telling the truth."

She slapped him hard. The old man, almost twice her size, fell like an oak in a thunderstorm, crashing to the ground with a great thunk. Jones hurried to tend to him, lifted him up. Only once Haywood was back on his chair did he turn to Evgenia.

"He's... he's... he's..." Jones' stammer always reappeared at the worst moments. "He's an old man. Sick too. You don't hit an old man like that. What are you doing?"

She stormed out of the izba. To Jones' amazement, Haywood started to laugh, a great fat belly laugh.

"What's so funny?"

The laughter subsided and the old man's eyes went to the bottle of vodka. Jones got the bottle and poured him a slug.

"You were about to explain what amused you so?"

"Back in the day, with the Wobblies, we were plagued by Pinkerton spies, company men who were out to bust strikes and break us. If they could get close, they'd see something or make something up, didn't matter to them, and then we'd all go to jail charged with murder or some such. After a time, we developed a sixth sense, who to trust, who to doubt. If you had doubts about someone, you hit them with it. If they smiled and said that's not true, if they tried to cajole you out of your suspicions, then, by experience and instinct, you probably had your traitor. On the other hand, if they hit you, straight out, you'd accused an innocent party."

Jones' mouth opened but he said nothing.

"Get her back in here, Mr Jones. It's cold out there."

Outside, the sky was a mackerel blue and grey. It took some time to find her. She'd walked to the end of the rough road where Haywood's izba stood and was standing with her back to him, in front of a stream that had iced over.

"Evgenia." The cold scarred his throat.

"Go away."

"He was testing you, that's all."

"He thinks I am a traitor."

"No, but he thinks someone is. So he tested you. The good news is that you passed the test."

Her shoulders became a little less bowed. "How did he work that out?"

"The test is how you respond to the accusation of treachery. If you sweet-talk him, you're guilty. You hit him, you're innocent."

"That's idiotic."

He paused, sighed and said, "It's not my test. In Great Britain we do things differently."

She hit him, hard, and he fell back into the snow, his sides bursting with laughter.

They returned to Haywood's izba, hand in hand, ready to make their departure to Finland and a new life.

Inside, the old Wobbly sat in his chair, a glass of liquor by his side, beaming at the two of them. Standing up stiffly, he went to a pile of wood by the stove and very slowly started taking it apart. They studied each other, puzzled and amused, sensing that he was going to give them something, some kind of present. The rigmarole of him hiding whatever it was in the woodpile made them expectant. This wasn't just a fancy bottle of wine or a book. It must be something special. At length, he turned and produced from a black leather bag Borodin's Kinamo camera and a cylindrical tin case. He set the bag, camera and tin case on the table.

"There's the camera. There's one roll of film. It's good for seven minutes. I am dying and this is my dying wish. I want you two to go to Ukraine and film the famine, then get the hell out and tell the world the truth about Stalin's evil." He started to choke, a hacking cough that consumed his attention so that he did not take in how his request went down with its executors.

Evgenia gasped, all colour drained from her already pale complexion. Jones said, "Fuck", then shook his head, stammered a little, recovered and smiled. "Thank you, Bill, thank you."

Evgenia stared at Jones, shaking her head, a tear running down her cheek. This dying man's last wish could not be ignored but there was only one way this ended, in the cells beneath the Lubyanka, a written confession and a sentence without the right of correspondence.

Chapter Twenty

They returned to the Hotel Lux and stayed the night, seeking but not quite finding comfort in each other's bodies. In the small hours, Jones woke up, cradled Evgenia's pale beauty in his arms and listened to the soft murmur of her breath. Still not being able to sleep, he got up and opened the curtain. Down on the street, underneath a lampost, a watcher in hat and overcoat was staring up at him.

It was like fighting a monster unafraid to bite the heads off people. Something like this would be happening in Berlin, right now, too. There and here, power could signal its displeasure as it pleased.

In the morning, the telephone rang and rang but they ignored it, dressed and walked out of the hotel into a cold grey day, carrying only the leather bag with the Kinamo in it, the film reel in the tin case and a change of clothes.

On the street they bumped into Winnie, wrapped in a mountain of fur. She kissed them both. "The poem," she said. "They're picking everyone up. I had to warn you..."

"Winnie," said Jones, "we know."

"Big Bill should have kept his trap shut."

"He's not well, Winnie. He thinks they've poisoned him."

Her face crumpled, her brown eyes filled with a film of liquid. "No..."

She seemed frozen to the spot.

"Winnie," said Evgenia, "we must go."

"Where you folks heading?"

"South, through the Ukraine," replied Jones. "People say it's worst there."

"What's worst?"

"The famine."

"And then back to Moscow?"

He shook his head.

"How are you going to get out? Via Poland?"

"Odessa, perhaps. The old smugglers' city may be our best chance."

"I dream of leaving this city of ice. You make it, you let me know, brother, sister, ahuh?"

They took turns to hold her tightly, kissing her on the lips and the eyes, then hurried off to the Metro.

The night train to Dnipro trundled through the snowy wastes, often at walking pace. There was far less comfort here than on the special train to the Lenin Dam, but at least there was anonymity. No banquets here, no champagne – only a press of ordinary people, nearly all thin, some terrifyingly so, human beings trying to stay alive and out of trouble in a dark time.

GPU guards and ticket inspectors checked their documents but not once did they have to use their magic letter from Yagoda. Their time in Dnipro was a disaster. At sunrise, having not slept properly the whole way, they had tried to check into the hotel they had stayed in during their previous official visit. The moment the sleepy clerk had demanded their passports and identity papers, Jones had realised that this was a very bad idea. On the move, they could lose themselves amongst their fellow travellers. When they stopped to rest, questions started to be asked and the clerk had hit them with three: "Where is the rest of the party? Are you on an official tour? Where are the Soviet partners?"

Not a bad euphemism for the GPU, thought Jones, whilst his mind raced for a good answer.

"This is not the hotel we booked," said Evgenia, brightly.

"This is the only hotel for foreigners in Dnipro," the clerk fired back.

"Mr Jones and I are on Cheka business," said Evgenia. It was a good answer in the moment, because the clerk froze and they took their opportunity to disappear from the hotel. But, over time, Jones began to wonder whether it was a bad answer, because it gave anyone who might be looking for them in the biggest country on earth a place to start looking. The truth was that they were amateurs; they didn't know what they were doing or how to do it.

What surprised then was not what happened in the end but how they managed to run and keep on running for so long.

*

They had tramped through the snow since dawn and, as they approached the next village, they came across a dead horse and a dead man in the middle of the road. The horse still lay harnessed to the wagon, the man frozen upright, still holding the reins in his bone-white hands. Jones took out the Kinamo and filmed the dead horse and the dead man for fifteen seconds.

The village had fallen to a silent evil. Through the window of one hovel they saw a dead man propped up by his stove. His back against the wall, he stared at them, his eyes wide open. Some bodies were decomposed. Others were fresh. At one house there was a sign printed on the door: "God bless those who enter here, may they never have to suffer as we have." Inside, two men and a child lay dead. An icon lay beside them. Jones filmed that too, for forty-five seconds. Now the reel had six minutes left.

They walked on in silence. At the next village, a man, skeletally thin, emerged from a wooden hovel and stared at them. The village was but twenty houses and the blackened shell of a burnt down church. No mooing of cattle, no bleating of sheep, no neighing of horses. A girl appeared from behind a second shack, stared at them, then ran away.

Jones walked cautiously up to the man. "How are things here, may we ask?"

"He looks like a foreigner," the man said, addressing Evgenia. "Is he an idiot, like all the other foreigners who come here?"

"He is a foreigner, from Great Britain, but no," said Evgenia, "he is not an idiot. Can you tell us how things are here?"

"Where is the Cheka? When foreigners come, the Cheka comes too."

"We are here on our own," said Evgenia. "No-one knows we are here. Please, can you tell us how things are here?"

The man bent down to remove something from the top of his boot, taking the opportunity to glance around. No-one could be seen.

"Has anyone died of the hunger?"

He laughed, contemptuously, turned his back on them and started to trudge off.

"I'm sorry," she cried out, "but we are trying to find out the truth..."

The man carried on, affecting not to hear her.

"We have food."

He stopped dead.

"It's not much, some sausage, bread, a few chocolate bars. We can share with you and your family."

"Food first and then I'll sing."

Soon, the man led them to a wooden shack. On the table lay a broken belfry wheel, blackened from the fire, which he had been sawing into pieces for firewood. A woman, his wife, sheltered nervously behind a curtain. The man went to lift the wheel on his own but lacked the strength to do so. Only with Jones, Evgenia and his wife helping were they able to shift it off the table. Two little girls hid behind their mother's skirts, a smaller boy eyeing them coldly from a second room. The children had puffed out stomachs.

When Jones took out a length of sausage and white bread, their eyes told the story all too powerfully. The little boy had never seen sausage. None of them had ever seen chocolate. The woman sliced the sausage wafer-thin and gave each child one slice before disappearing somewhere to hide the rest of it; behind her back, the children fell on the chocolate like wolves.

Banquet over, the man stood his half of the bargain. Staring at the table, not lifting his eyes once, he told them the story of his life. "My name is Sergei. My father was Russian, my mother Ukrainian and the story I have to tell is bleak beyond words. As a kid, I remember the days before before the Revolution, when the village was a good place. There was plenty of food, then. Makes me cry to think about it, how it is now. The old count drank too much and spent most of his time somewhere fancy, somewhere foreign. but he came back for the war. 1914. A sorry mess, the war. My daddy went off to fight burning with patriotism. He came back lame and blind in one eye, seething with contempt for the Tsar's generals and full of stories about how rich the lands were to the west. The revolutions? We all got excited by the first one in February. The second, in October? Well, I was ten years old and, by this time, we had all got a bit bored with revolutions. The Bolsheviks came and killed. Then the Whites came and killed. Then the Bolsheviks returned for good. They shot the count but also all his family and all his servants, one of them my uncle. They liked killing, the Bolsheviks. They liked killing too much. There was a famine after the war and people, especially the old and the little ones, suffered a lot. Then the Americans came with their beautiful Ford trucks." The man paused, eyeing Jones carefully. "Is this one American? They make beautiful trucks, the Americans."

Evgenia said no.

The man shrugged and went on. "Well, they brought wheat and grain and soon things were better. Not as good as they had been under the Tsar but better. Things were OK until Lenin died. Things were even OK for a few years after that. We could go into the towns, Dnipro even, and sell our pork and lamb and beef and get good prices for them. But then, two years ago, they started with the kolkhoz nonsense. Everybody had to join. The Young Pioneers took away our horses and instead they promised us a tractor. It came on the back of a horse and cart and it didn't work. Not once did it work.

"The next time the Young Pioneers came, my older brother, Ivan, he took his knout out and lashed the air with it – and these young idiots scarpered pretty damn fast and everyone in the village, we all laughed. Three days later, the Young Pioneers returned – but this time with the Cheka. They had machine guns. They didn't use them. They didn't have to. Ivan and all his family were put on a train with three other families. The train went east. No-one has heard a word from any of them since. That day, they took the rest of the horses and all the cows. The next time they took the sheep and the goats, all of them. That time, one of my neighbours – he was a drunk, he beat his woman too much, but he was a brave fellow – he told them where to go, and they shot him and left him in the middle of the village for all the children to see.

"Then the Young Pioneers came, again with the Cheka, and this time they had some foreigners with them. Suddenly we were given bread and pork and told to smile and clap and, when the foreigners went away, they took it all back.

"Last year they came for our grain. This was the cruellest thing yet. They'd taken our animals. Now they came for the grain. The Cheka put virtually everybody on the train east. There were only four families left in this village." He paused. "One day the police came, not the Cheka, and they took away a family. A child's arm had been in their pot on the stove."

Sergei stared directly at them for the first time in the entire soliloquy: "I saw that with my own eyes. There is no bread. Tell them we are starving."

"Can I film you saying that?" asked Jones.

"Film, you mean like Charlie Chaplin?"

"Yes."

Sergei shook his head. "No, of course not."

For a time, he stopped talking and sat in silence – until, finally, Jones and Evgenia stood up to leave. They had already stayed in one place for too long. Sergei escorted them to the door and nodded to a path that ran into the woods.

"Follow that path. There is a priest. He's trying to do his best."

"To his best with what?" asked Evgenia.

"The children," Sergei breathed. "The children who ran away when the Cheka put their mothers and fathers on the train east."

*

The makeshift orphanage had been set up in an abandoned church.

The first child's stomach was a balloon made of papery skin, bigger than its head. Its limbs were thin sticks, its face bird-like, its mouth some kind of beak. The second child's naked body was covered in a thin film of hair, a werewolf from the darkest nightmare imaginable. The third child had the same swollen belly, stick limbs but a frog's wide-mouthed face. There were about twenty of them sitting in their dung, shafts of sunlight illuminating the strange creatures. All were listless; none spoke. A few mewed pitifully. The air was freezing; icicles hung down from the rafters, and the baptismal font had frozen over.

Jones reached for the Kinamo from its leather bag while the young priest watched at the window, his right leg twitching anxiously upon the stone floor.

Evgenia appeared at the doorway into the next room. "It's worse here."

"Is it well-lit?" asked Jones.

"No."

"Father, have you got a candle?"

The priest, summoned back from his terror, scrabbled in the pockets of his cassock and produced the stub of a candle.

"A match, Father?"

Nodding, he scrabbled in his pockets again and produced a matchbox.

"How long are you going to film for?" Evgenia asked.

"I'll shoot in here for three minutes and then enter the second room. Six minutes," said Jones.

"That's all of the reel."

"Yes."

"OK," said Evgenia.

Walking backwards to the farthest corner of the barn, he started to record, his hand cranking the camera, his right eye taking in the Kinamo's world view, his body bent as low as he could get so that the camera took it all in. Each child stared back at him, their eyes unblinking, their enormous heads like foetuses in jars of alcohol.

He was almost done in the first room when a rifle shot sounded, not far off, causing a murder of crows to rise up into the cobalt blue sky.

The priest smiled to himself, his nervousness gone now. "That's my sacristan, a warning shot. It means they're coming."

"Who?"

"The Cheka."

"How did they know we're here?"

"Who did you speak to in the village?"

"Sergei."

The priest's face crumpled. "People say he talks too much. Maybe he is an informer. You must go."

"How long have we got?" asked Jones.

"Fifteen minutes, maybe ten."

"I'll film the second room, then we go."

In the second room, a dozen infants and babies, pale, dead or dying, were spread out upon filthy straw. Jones gasped, "Jesus Christ" but his left hand held steady, and his right kept on cranking until the reel stopped turning. When he finally switched it off, the Kinamo answered with a click.

Seven minutes of Stalin's inhumanity, all of it captured in the can.

"Run," whispered the priest.

"And you, Father?"

"I'll stay here."

Evgenia frowned. "But Father?"

"Someone has to stay with the children. Run. Tell the world what is happening here. Tell them what they are doing to us." He paused. "You must run!"

Jones threw the Kinamo in his bag, his fingers struggling to fix the buckle.

"Run, for Christ's sake!"

The buckle secure, Jones embraced the priest and bowed stiffly to the dying children. The priest made the sign of the cross, index finger straight, middle finger slightly crooked.

Evgenia followed Jones out of the church door and it was only on the porch that they started to move more quickly. Soon, they were charging through a thicket of birch trees, their branches laden with snow.

Some distance on, tiring already, they heard the sound they feared the most: the barking of dogs.

Evgenia led the way, plunging down a ravine to a small river. Ice had formed on the edges but there was still flowing water in the middle. They were both panting.

"In there?" asked Jones, not quite believing it.

Three shots rang out from the direction of the orphanage.

"The dogs will find it harder to follow our scent if we go in."

"My God!"

"Don't drop the Kinamo."

The water was so cold it made Jones want to roar at the top of his voice –but such was his fear of the Cheka that all he did was hiss like an angered swan. The current was strong and the bed of the stream rocky. Jones almost fell over, but Evgenia steadied him and led the way to the far bank, pulling herself out of the water by gripping a tree branch, then turning round to help him out too.

By now, both of them were gibbering with cold. A fourth shot rang out, then there was fresh outrage from the crows. Instants later, there came a burst of machine gun fire, then more of it, again and again.

After that, there was only silence.

"The priest?"

"Not just the priest," said Evgenia.

"The children too?"

She nodded.

"Christ. The savages."

"Not savages. The Cheka."

They scrabbled up the far side of the ravine, their breaths ballooning in front of them, their clothes stiffening with every passing minute. They both knew that if they didn't warm themselves in front of a fire soon, they would not survive the night.

The weather was changing, a slow milky fog forming in the low-lying gulleys and furrows of the land. Hurrying out of the growing murk, they climbed up to a bluff and were running madly through the birch trees, Jones in the lead, when suddenly he disappeared from Evgenia's view. Evgenia was a little way back and, as she crested the hill, she stopped, astonished. Ahead of her, the hillside had been chewed away, like a bite taken out of a giant apple. Great clumps of broken rock lay higgledy-piggledy and, a mile away, three trucks slogged along an earth road, downhill, disappearing into the endless, dense fog.

There was no sign of Jones.

Then, seemingly from a long way off, came a cry for help. Looking straight down, Evgenia made out a stark drop ending in a pool of whiteness, a frozen sump, the remains of an old quarry. Jones was hanging half way down, clinging onto the satchel carrying the precious Kinamo with one hand. With the other, he was hanging on to the bough of a tree, his legs dancing in the air.

To the right was a workman's stone hut, long abandoned. Hurrying over to it, she forced the wooden door. Inside was a muddle of junk, a splintered pick-handle, a broken axe, two wooden chairs set against a rough table. Nothing of any use. She cursed and was about to leave, when she glanced at the back of a door and there, on a hook, was a coil of rope: grimy, ancient, matted with cobwebs. Was it long enough, she wondered, to reach him? Would it snap the moment any weight was put on it?

There was no alternative, so she hoisted it up and hurried on.

Charging back to the top of the chasm, she scrambled down as far as she dared without tumbling into the pit, then secured the rope to a stout tree and let the free end fall down. The rope ran out a full yard above Jones.

"I can't reach it," he said, matter-of-factly.

In a frenzy, Evgenia pulled the rope back up, found a tough stick of birch two yards long, tied that to the free end of the rope and lowered it again, more carefully this time. The stick touched Jones on the shoulder but he didn't move, only cried out something that she couldn't catch.

The fog was coiling upwards, moving in, obscuring the white sump below, first masking Jones, then moving away in an eddy.

"I can't move!" cried Jones. "My muscles are frozen!"

There was nothing else for it. Evgenia took hold of the rope in her hands and lowered herself over the edge.

Descending hand over hand, her shoes sometimes losing their grip, took an age.

"Hurry!" he called out. "I can't hold on much longer!"

Accelerating down the wall of the pit, showering his head and shoulders with stones and earth as she came, she pleaded for him to hang on. Just above where he'd come to rest was a goat track, a thin lip of earth which edged along the pit and disappeared around a bend. It could be an escape route. It could be nothing. She steeled herself to look down. Beneath them, the frozen sump had entirely disappeared. All that could be seen were coils of fog, their tendrils climbing higher, closer to Jones with every passing minute.

Finally, she was at his level. Grabbing hold of him with her free hand, she heaved him to the pit wall so that, for the first time, his feet could get some purchase. Scrabbling up to the goat track, he lay on his belly, gasping for air, his face blue with cold, his eyes unfocussed.

The goat track followed the pit wall until, by some strange mercy, it led into a cavern as big as a house. Leading off from the cavern were three tunnels that disappeared off into three separates darknesses. She half-dragged him, half-carried him into one of the tunnels and there laid him down, using the film bag as a pillow.

Only a feeble echo of daylight reached their resting place – but, even in the dimness, she could tell that Jones was not right, his breathing jerky, his forehead white, his cheeks a faint, sickly blue. Hurrying back to the entrance of the cavern, she used the very last of her strength to rip the few saplings growing here out of the rock and hurried back to Jones. Reaching into her handbag, she found the priest's matchbox – but it was sodden from their forced swim and none of the matches would light.

Jones mouthed something out loud but it meant nothing, only the gibberish of delirium.

They had come so far, captured the reality of Stalin's famine in one seven minute film reel – and now the man who had made it happen was being taken from her for the lack of a matchstick. A light wind sucked through the tunnel, ruffling a tendril of hair that had fallen on her face. Her eyes welled up and she let out a single sob.

In her mind's eye she travelled back to the first moment she'd set eyes on him. Sitting in sumptuous luxury in the special train, watching the ordinary people struggling to board their miserable carriages, she'd been thinking that she was one of *them*, when suddenly she heard shouting, a guard yelling "Nyet!" – and then, out of the mass of people, this man rose up from nowhere to land on his feet, balancing on the very top of the railings like a circus acrobat. She had been taken with him from that very first moment, and Duranty had sensed that too. He'd played that silly game with Aleister Crowley's cigarette lighter, and then Jones had won and Duranty, furious, had forced her to...

The cigarette lighter!

She delved into the bag holding the Kinamo and there it was, glinting at the bottom. Closing her eyes, saying a prayer she could barely remember, she pressed her thumb down hard on the igniter and opened her eyes.

The flame held good and true.

The fire took some moments to get going but, once it did, its flames reflected in the tunnel's walls, its heat spreading its healing warmth. Jones wriggled a little, studied the inscription by the light of the fire and murmured, "All my darkness, eh? At last old Crowley ended up doing someone a bit of good."

Evgenia held his head in her lap, stroked his hair with a deep love she had never before experienced , and sang *Myfanwy* to him as he fell asleep. Here, in this remote cavern, by the light of her faltering fire, she wondered when their luck would run out.

It held, for a time.

Chapter Twenty-One

For three days and three nights, they eked out an existence of a kind in the quarry tunnel, drinking icicles Evgenia melted in the sunlight and eating rotten berries and scraps of moss she found on the tunnel floor. Jones was still weak from his fall and, with no real food to eat, getting weaker by the hour. Soon, they would have to move or otherwise he would die here. But if they moved too soon, then the Cheka would find and kill them both.

On the fourth night, Evgenia was dozing in front of the fire, Jones' head lolling in her lap, when a distant sound made her sit up. Startled, Jones murmured something. She told him to hush and listened intently. Yes, there it was again: the sound of stones being dislodged, then a scuffling. Footsteps? The sound went away, died completely – and she dared to believe that they might be safe. But then the sound – footsteps, certainly – came nearer.

Her eyes were focused on the tunnel. In the distance, a tiny pinpoint of light appeared, danced, disappeared and then danced once more.

It seemed pointless to move. She knew that she, too, was weak. She could barely carry him ten yards, let along shift him half a mile down a dark tunnel. And even then, if they were unbelievably lucky and managed to escape at this moment, the Cheka would surely find them. The Cheka were remorseless.

The light grew brighter and danced less, the footsteps growing louder and louder still. From the impenetrable darkness came the click of a revolver's safety catch; then there was silence, only the sussuration of the wind sucking through the tunnel.

"So here you are." The words came softly.

She couldn't see the man behind the torchlight. The man came nearer, crouched down – and was in touching distance when Jones threw the rock at him.

The man fell back with a heavy thunk, his torch spilling, lighting up a cylinder formed of brilliant stars of dust, his revolver falling away into the darkness. In spite of his weakness, Jones moved astonishingly fast and was on him in a second, his knees on his chest, his hands around his throat, throttling him with manic intensity.

The man had started to utter a sickening gurgle, was surely close to the moment of death, when Evgenia went for Jones, using all her strength to break his hold.

"Stopiwch ef, ffwl. Dim ond mewn trioedd y daeth y Cheka erioed. Stopiwch ef. Rydych chi'n lladd ffrind."

The Welsh punched through Jones' madness far better than English.

"Stop it, fool. The Cheka only ever come in threes. Stop it. You're killing a friend."

Jones released the grip on the man's throat and, as he did so, Evgenia found the torch and illuminated the stranger. Silver-haired and gaunt, he was indefinably old, a bloody gash on his temple where the rock had struck.

"She's right," he said thickly, blood in his mouth. "I'm no Chekist and if I was one then there would be three of us."

"Perhaps you're an informer," said Jones, still suspicious.

"Listen, everyone, all the villagers, all the workers around here, they all know who you are. We've all seen the smoke coming out of the tunnel mouth. We know the Cheka are after you. That's why I came, to warn you to move."

"So why bring a revolver?"

"Because," he coughed up some blood and spat it out into the darkness, "I am afraid."

"Who are you afraid of?"

"Of them." He paused. "Of you."

The man's accent was Muscovite, not Ukrainian, refined, not thuggish.

"How long have we got?"

"They'll come for you in the morning. At first light."

"How do you know?"

The man braced himself. "Because I'll be the one guiding them through the tunnels. I know them better than any man alive. With my workmates I dug most of them myself. I told the Cheka it was too dangerous to search the tunnels at night and, like fools, they believed me."

"So you *are* an informer," said Jones. "Only, you're informing on the Cheka."

"Yes, you could put it like that," said the man with an air of bemusement. "We are all informers now."

The man smiled a little, and put his hand to the gash on his temple. It was sticky with blood where the rock had hit him. Evgenia found a handkerchief and dabbed the wound, tutting at it and pulling a face at Jones.

"I've brought you some food."

Squatting down, he removed a knapsack from his back and opened it. Then he lay out a white cloth and laid upon it some cheese, two onions, two lengths of sausage and half a loaf of black bread.

"Where did you get this?" asked Jones, hotly. He'd found the revolver and it rested in his hands, its muzzle pointing at the man.

"You still think I work for the Cheka, don't you?"

"Where did you get this food?"

"My name is Ilya. I am the manager of the All Soviet Marble Works. The marble from my tunnels is shipped all around the world, especially to Germany and Italy. The fascists love marble more than gold, and our collective brings in millions of roubles every year. For the moment, that means the Cheka leaves me and my workers alone, more or less. It means that we get more money than most and so we eat. But I am all too well aware," his voice dropped an octave, "that others are starving and that it is vital that the world knows what is happening here. Everyone around here heard them machine-gunning the orphanage. Everyone around here loved the priest. So I'm risking my life and that of my family and my friends to help you. You already hit me over the head with a rock, then strangled me – and now, when I offer you my family's food, you suspect me."

"He is a fool," said Evgenia flatly.

"I am a fool," echoed Jones. "The paranoia, you end up losing your wits. I am most terribly sorry, Ilya. My name is Gareth Jones of the *Western Mail* and this is Evgenia Davidovich Miranova."

Ilya smiled to himself once more. "Delighted to meet you both. Mr Jones, you are, I think, a good fool. Otherwise you would not be here. Now, eat, because we don't have much time. Oh, I forgot." He produced a small bottle of clear liquid from his knapsack. "A little vodka?"

"Now you're talking," said Jones.

"Eat. Drink."

As they followed his commands to the letter, Ilya told them about the Cheka's net for them: house-to-house searches of all properties, farms and outhouses in the surrounding villages for the last two days, checks at every railway station for one hundred miles around, checks at every road bridge, hundreds of troops combing the fields and forests for miles around.

"So we have no hope," said Jones, his mouth half-full of bread and sausage.

"Not quite," said Ilya.

"How do we get out?"

He looked them up and down. "You will leave inside the marble."

"We would die."

"If you stay here, you will die."

"But we would surely suffocate."

"I would not be suggesting this route if it were untried. It isn't. It's worked before."

"How?"

"For that, you've got to trust me. It won't be comfortable. In fact it will be extremely uncomfortable. But you will have someone with you the whole way, by road and river and sea, someone who will look after you as best he can."

"The whole way where?"

"To Odessa."

"And then?"

"Mr Jones, I can smuggle you and Miss Miranova out of this Cheka-infested hole underneath ten tons of marble. But I am not a magician. When you are in Odessa, you must find a foreign ship all by yourself."

"Why can't you come with us?"

"The Cheka watch me the whole time. I am the guardian of the marble goose that lays golden eggs. I cannot move from here."

"So who's going to look after us on the journey?"

Ilya whistled, softly, and once again they heard footsteps over the sound of the wind in the tunnel. The boy who appeared was big-boned, sure of himself, unafraid – but only fifteen years old, if that.

"Ond dim ond plentyn ydyw," Jones said to Evgenia. He's just a child.

"Is there a problem?" asked Ilya.

"He's very young."

"Yuri is someone I trust absolutely."

"And why's that?"

"Because, Mr Jones, he's the son of the murdered priest. He's also my grandson."

"The priest was your son?"

"Yes."

"Do the Cheka know that?"

"Not yet. He changed the name on his identity card to protect us." Evgenia looked away.

"But the boy is very young," said Jones.

"You're going to have trust him."

"Why is that?"

"Because, Mr Jones, you have no choice."

Chapter Twenty-Two

Ilya led the way into the labyrinth of tunnels, stopping every now and then in silence to listen. Nothing, only the wind's murmur. Soon, a tunnel took them downhill for a time, and then the darkness grew less thick. Twenty yards ahead, Jones sensed the tunnel opening out into the lesser darkness of the night. He took a step forward and, beneath the arc of the rock, he saw the heavens, the stars glittering all the more brightly in the frozen air. Banished from seeing the sky for four nights, he moved forward again until Ilya, roughly, dragged him back.

"Stay deep inside the cave, idiot. Someone could be watching."

Yuri disappeared into the night.

"What's the plan?"

"The truck will come here, where no-one can see us. You will lie down between two long slabs of marble. We'll put wooden planks and straw on top of you, then drive off to the factory where we'll use the crane to lift more marble slabs, crossways, on top of you. You will be quite safe. The bad news is that the truck will be so heavily laden it goes pretty slowly. So the journey to the river will take the whole day. Once there, Yuri will find the right moment for you to get out of the truck and into the barge. That's the hardest part – but he's good at staging a distraction so no-one tricky spots you."

"What about the dogs?"

"This is one of ten trucks. We bait the others with dead mice and rats. The dogs will be too busy to care about you two."

"You're sure?"

"Yes. We bait the dog handlers, too, if needs be. Under Communism, foreign currency can buy pretty much anything."

"Even the Cheka?"

"Especially the Cheka. Unless Moscow is involved. Then it gets more difficult."

Jones hesitated, then asked Evgenia to translate the phrase, "Sometimes I get claustrophobia."

Ilya looked puzzled. "Claustro-what?"

"Fear of being confined in a small space," explained Jones.

"Tough," said Ilya.

Some time later, they heard the sound of a truck engine being started up, the dynamo whining, the exhaust clearing its throat, gears grating as the truck moved slowly, ponderously towards them, showing no lights. The way Yuri backed the truck deep into the cave, fifty feet from the entrance, it was clear that this wasn't the first time this operation had been carried out.

Yuri and Ilya helped them climb up onto the flatbed. Sitting side by side were two big rectangles of marble, seven yards long, a yard deep and a yard high. Between the two slabs was a gap of around two feet wide, filled with straw. Yuri led them to the gap and invited them to lie down as close to the cab as possible. Once they were inside the gap, Ilya gave Jones three bottles of water, a sausage and a half-loaf of bread. Jones opened his satchel to put them inside and the tin of the film reel glinted in the gloom.

"What's that?" asked Ilya.

"Nothing," said Jones.

Ilya wished them good luck and watched them bed down between the two great slabs. Grandfather and son covered them with more straw, then they heard the squeak of a pulley and tackle, and a narrow square of rock fitting almost exactly the gap between the two long slabs was swung into place, blocking out what dim light they had enjoyed. Next they heard the clatter of wooden planks pressing down on the straw and their tomb was half-complete.

"Bloody hell," whispered Jones, failing to suppress his fear.

"Don't be a baby," said Evgenia, her hand reaching out to stroke his face.

The engine started and the first part of the journey began. The truck crept along extraordinarily slowly, the lack of light rendering them blind but strangely heightening their other senses. They heard a trickle of water running through the ice-bound river. That would be the same river they had tramped through five days before. The truck slowed to a crawl and they heard the timbers of a wooden bridge creaking, the flowing water trilling softly underneath. It cleared the bridge, sped up a little, climbed a hill, the engine grunting against gravity; then it accelerated downhill, slowed down, and they entered what must have been the headquarters of the quarry. Out there, they could hear the sound of men's voices. Someone laughed out loud, and a small engine, not a truck, coughed into life.

Then the small engine erupted with yet more noise and they heard the working of a winch. Suddenly the axles beneath them sunk an inch, two, and the whole frame of the truck groaned under the weight of the marble slabs being placed on top of them. Their tomb was complete.

They heard steps on the marble on top of them, someone unhooking ropes perhaps. Then, in every direction, more truck engines burbled into life, and their own slipped into gear, as if ready to be off.

Then, out of nowhere: the sound of a gunshot, the low rumble of a man's voice as he issued a series of commands.

Even through the thick marble, Jones knew that voice. He would know it anywhere.

Lyushkov.

All of the truck engines were stilled. All of a sudden, every other sound was drowned out by the barking of dogs, some very close, some far away. Trapped in their marble cave in the dark, their panic grew as they could hear a dog, its paws pattering on the back of the truck. Lyushkov, his voice muffled by the marble, timber and straw, said something Jones could not decipher. Someone replied unenthusiastically. Lyushkov repeated his order.

"We will miss the barges if we off-load the marble from this truck, Comrade."

"So be it," Lyushkov's voice.

"That will cost the Soviet Union seven million roubles, Comrade." The unenthusiastic voice belonged to Ilya.

"I said, so be it."

"Very well, comrade," said Ilya.

Jones sensed steps, once more, on the marble on top of them. From up above, he heard the crane engine being coaxed into life, the sound of the winch working, the truck's axles lifting, lifting...

Then there came a vicious snap, a whiplash of rope torn in two, the crane engine screaming, a heavy thunk as machinery hit the ground.

"For fuck's sake!" shouted Ilya.

"Sorry Comrade," yelled Yuri.

"I want to see what's underneath this rock," said Lyushkov.

"It's not rock, Comrade," said Ilya, "but the very finest marble, destined for Berlin. You can see it."

"Good," said Lyushkov.

"But you're going to have to wait for delivery of a new crane."

"How long will that take?"

"It will take time, Comrade."

"What does that mean?"

"We have been promised one for seven years now. I can show you the paperwork to and fro."

"I've been in this shithole for far too long," snapped Lyushkov. "I'm needed back in Moscow urgently."

"We can't offload that truck without a crane. We've been waiting for a new crane for seven years. I can show you the-"

"Shut up about the fucking paperwork, you moron." Lyushkov paused, seething. "All right, go on, send your precious marble to Berlin."

"Thank you, Comrade."

The truck engines roared into life once more, the marble started its long journey to the Reich – and, inside their tomb, Evgenia put a finger to Jones' lips, then kissed him with a passion all the greater for having fooled the GPU.

Chapter Twenty-Three

It was a pig of a journey, tortoise-slow, unbearably uncomfortable, with the constant jeopardy at the back of their minds that, if one truck spring snapped and the load capsized, they could in an instant be crushed to pulp. During the day it had not been entirely dark in their tomb, the serrated edges of the marble allowing a few smudges of light to penetrate – but, in the late afternoon, the smudges started to grey, then redden. The loss of light as night closed in made their jeopardy seem even more grim. Then, at last, the truck came to a stop and they heard the hooting of a river barge and the grinding and splintering of ice.

Steps on the marble above them, then a crane engine was fired up and they heard a man's voice barking out a command: "Go!" Moments later, a winch was turning and the axles of the truck started to ease slowly upwards, one inch, two, as the marble cross-slabs were lifted off.

"Stop! That's all we're doing tonight" The voice was Yuri's. "It's dangerous to work with marble in the dark. We'll do the rest at daybreak. Right, let's go eat."

He took so long that they feared they'd been forgotten; they were shivering, blue with cold, when they heard someone climb onto the top of the planks covering the two long slabs. One single plank was lifted and, suddenly, their eyes were entranced by starlight. Yuri climbed down, held a hand out and lifted first Evgenia, then Jones out of their tomb. Relaying the plank, Yuri led them along a rough track away from the river towards a clump of trees. Jones and Evgenia, their legs stiff from lack of use, stumbled and slipped on the icy ground.

"Where are we going?" asked Jones.

"Ssssh!"

In a rough clearing in the trees they could just make out a wooden shack. Yuri told them to stay where they were and disappeared within. A conversation, low and soft; then, as someone gave out a hacking cough, Yuri emerged and beckoned them into the shack. Inside sat a babushka sucking on a pipe, her weatherbeaten face half-illuminated by a candle, a tabby cat sitting on her lap, purring malevolently.

"This is the captain of the barge," said Yuri.

She took one look at them and spat. "No," she said and sucked on her pipe, puffing fresh life into its embers.

"Why no, Granma?" asked Evgenia.

"He stinks of foreign. Look at his glasses, the cut of his clothes, the weave of his coat. He's not one of us. Stands out like a mile. And you, love, you're obviously a lady of good family. 'A former person', that's what the Reds call your kind these days. I can tell from the way you hold yourself, the length of your hair. A working woman wouldn't have hair that long. They say you're here to make a film, like Charlie Chaplin."

"Not like Charlin Chaplin," said Evgenia. "Who told you about the film?"

"Word travels in these parts. You asked one of the villagers whether you could film here."

Yuri stood behind them, silent.

Evgenia glanced at Jones. He nodded, then Evgenia tried her best. "We are making a film. But it's about the hunger, the children starving, the dead villages. We need to get the film out, to tell the world what's happening. We have the proof on film. That's why, Granma. That's why we need to hide on your barge, to get out."

"The train would be faster."

"They're hunting for us. If we take the train..."

A sound came from the woods outside – something, perhaps an animal, bustling through the undergrowth. The cat stopped purring, its ears pricking up. The old woman listened intently. Then the cat stretched itself, licked a paw and started purring again. Granma sucked on her pipe and came to her decision.

"The hat? That's a giveaway, right there. His glasses? They have to go. His clothes, too. I can give him some good working men's clothes. And, you, my lady, you've got to look like a man. So the hair? It's got to be cut. Your fine clothes, you've got to throw them away. I've got a boiler suit that will fit you. When a barge comes along, or we're close to the bank or going through a town, you've got to hide, right down in the bilges, in the muck. Aye, both of your faces are bloody white, too. You need to look brown, common, like me."

"Thank you Granma," said Evgenia, "thank you with all our hearts." She translated the deal to Jones.

When he learnt that he could not wear his spectacles, he said: "Without them, I am blind."

"Tough," said Evgenia.

The old woman found some scissors and went to work on Evgenia's hair, great long tresses falling to the ground. Throughout it all, Evgenia wore a steely smile. Yuri disappeared for a time and came back with two sets of clothes, two pairs of boots. None of it was clean. From a jar, the old woman gave them each a dollop of molasses to make their faces less lily-white. When the transformation was finished, they looked into a mirror and saw two rough necks.

While the old woman headed off to the barge, to warn her crew, Evgenia, Yuri and Jones waited in the shack. Ten minutes later, they hurried through the dark, the eastern sky beginning to redden, heading towards a black hulk that lay in the ice-edged river. At the barge's stern, they could see a red dot, someone smoking a pipe. They waited in silence until the red dot was extinguished, then they hurried across a narrow, spindly gangplank and down a wooden ladder into the bowels of the ship. Down here, slabs of marble lay flat on a lattice of wooden railways sleepers. Yuri took out a hammer from a toolbox and headed for the largest slab and crawled underneath the overhang. In the gloom, all of the sleepers looked solid and immobile but with the hammer he knocked a wooden chock to one side to gain entry, opening up an access hole not much bigger than eighteen inches square. Jones had to wriggle sideways to get in. Rough wooden planks had been laid on a metal trellis above the bilges, the filthy oily water sucking and weeping beneath them. The gap between the planks and the bottom of the marble was but twelve inches.

"It's cold as iron," whispered Evgenia.

"The Cheka have never checked the barges before," replied Yuri, softly. "But Granma, she's worried. She says there's something especially dangerous about helping you two. Everyone on the river is talking about the two foreign spies with the camera." He hesitated. "This is the safest place on the boat. They'll never find you down here. Once we start moving, once we've made some headway, I'll come and get you out of here. I'm going the whole way, down this river, then joining the Dnieper, then hugging the coast of the Black Sea, then to Odessa. Once we've left this place, you'll be able to come up for air, to sit in the sun. For the moment, I'll try and find you some blankets, maybe a sheepskin. Suffer the cold for a night and then we'll see."

He came back with a huge fur. "Must be a bear," said Jones.

"It belongs to Granma," said Yuri, threading it through the gap.

"Did she kill it with her own fair hands?" asked Jones, trying to make light of the grimness of their hidey-hole. Yuri made no reply. They heard him hammer the wooden chock into place, sealing them in, and then his boots climbing the ladder out to the fresh night air and the stars without.

Water hissed and bubbled as the river's current played upon the ancient and very thin steel plate beneath them. Whenever the barge bumped against its moorings, the oily slop in the bilges licked against the underside of the planks. For Jones, his fear of enclosed places was far worse here than in the truck: if the barge hit a rock or a jagged ice-floe, then they would be trapped in a watery grave under ten tonnes of marble. Jones started to pant, his breathing irregular, jerky. It was only when he heard Evgenia hum a few bars from *"Let My People Go"* that he started to gain control again.

At length the engine came to life and, with bewildering slowness, the barge pushed through the river's newly-formed skin of ice. Soon, the noxious slop beneath Jones and Evgenia spouted between the gaps in the planks, soaking the bearskin and them in turn. Filled with oil as it was, the slop didn't freeze, just clung to their clothes, coating everything it touched.

For hours on end, the tension gnawed away at their nerves – until, finally, the scrape of boot steps on metal signalled an end to their torture. Yuri cursed as he hammered the wooden chock free and, suddenly, a dim light filtered through. Limbs cramped and half-frozen, it took Evgenia and Jones an age to scramble out through the hole, their hands and faces blackened by the slop. Yuri led them to the cargo ladder and allowed them to climb up so that their heads could peek out through an open hatch. Up above, sunrise. Pink fingers of light searched out the near-frozen river and the white steppe beyond, a steam engine pulling an endless succession of coal wagons running parallel with the river.

Soon, Yuri disappeared, only to reappear with two cups of "coffee", foul-smelling but hot, and with that chunks of freshly-caught carp, cooked in a metal tin. No more delicious a meal Jones had eaten his whole life.

"Bugger the Cheka," said Jones, "I'm not going down that hole ever again."

Evgenia studied him, unconvinced.

The barge had been built long before the revolution and was held together by rust and rivets, black smoke belching from its dwarfish smoke-stack. It moved arthritically, never faster than the current, lest its venerable hull be punctured by a big floe or its engine give out. But at least the tortoise pace had a soothing effect on both Jones and Evgenia. They were still being hunted and had to hide in the cargo hold disappear whenever the barge had to enter a lock or when they encountered river traffic coming upstream. But the hold was paradise compared to the darkness underneath the marble.

Later that morning, they met the two hands. Arkady was young, a bit simple, did everything Granma asked of him with a literalness that was both silly and touching. Arkady sensed that something was not quite right about the squinting man and the strange-looking boy but didn't know how to articulate his doubts and was afraid to cross Granma, so he ended up smiling at them slightly creepily, as he if he was a creature in a not very good horror movie. A little while later, the older hand, Pyotr, emerged from the engine room covered in coal dust. Looking Evgenia up and down, he half-smiled, half-grimaced and muttered something.

"What was that?" asked Evgenia.

"Trouble, more trouble than it's worth." He said this to himself, raising a flask to his lips and draining it, then wiping the back of his mouth. "The bilge pump. Built by the former people. It's knackered, keeps on getting blocked. When that happens, the bilges can rise a foot in an hour. Hate to think what might happen if it gets blocked when you two are hiding underneath the marble. Not a good way to go, eh?" Then he disappeared back to the engine room without saying another word. He had the same piercing blue eyes as Granma and had been handsome, once, before the drink had addled his looks.

Three days after they joined the barge, Granma allowed them up to the wheelhouse for the first time, Jones squinting at the fuzzy shapes in the near-distance, Evgenia – looking more like a boy than a woman in her boiler-suit and black cap – explaining what he was missing: the immensity of the Dnieper, at times so wide as to be an inland sea, snow on snow, ice-floes cracking and tumbling ahead. Granma said nothing but smoked her pipe. Small talk was not for her.

The one thing everybody on board did was fish, trailing lines in the barge's wake when it was moving, casting rods when the barge had to lay up to wait for oncoming traffic, or when a knot of ice blocked the channel until a ship with a specially hardened bow could pass through. During these enforced stops, Pyotr would walk off into the solid ice and drill a hole with an auger, then sit above the hole and wait. Jones would go to a porthole and, making sure that no-one would was looking, slip on his spectacles and spend hours watching nothing happen with sinful pleasure.

He made himself a promise, then: that, if they ever got out of the Soviet Union and he was done with journalism, he would take up fishing. Granma was the best of them: she simply had to cast a line over the stern to land a carp or pike or dace. The catch was always washed down by her moonshine, made from fermented potatoes – and old boots, Jones guessed – which she manufactured in a still in her cabin. Granma did her best to ignore them, day in, day out, but their very presence on her barge was an act, in those times, of extraordinary courage.

Or a kind of madness.

*

The wind saved them. Had it been in the wrong direction, they would never have heard the barking of dogs from a mile downstream, long before the lock came into view.

Granma hissed, "Get down under the stone and stay there until we come and get you!" Then she made the sign of the cross, index finger straight, middle finger slightly crooked. Jones couldn't remember the last time he'd seen an ordinary person make a show of religious belief. These days, they were for the doomed or the damned.

Yuri led the way, hurrying Jones and Evgenia down into the cargo hold and watching them wriggle into the hollow beneath the bottom slab of marble. It was grimmer down here than before, but there was no choice. Evgenia was the last one in, Jones clutching his bag with the Kinamo and reel of film to his side as she followed him through. In here, the bottom of the marble an inch from Jones' face, they held each other's hands and listened to the wooden chock being hammered home, then Yuri's steps on the ladder.

Nuzzling each other as tenderly they could, they did their best to close their minds to reality, the monolith above, the oily slop beneath. After a time Jones asked, "Evgenia, am I wrong or did Granma make the same sign of the cross as the priest?"

"Yes," she whispered. "I saw that too. I think they're Old Believers. Maybe all of them are, the priest, Ilya, Yuri, Granma, the crew."

"Old Believers?"

"They follow the old version of Russian orthodoxy, before the Reforms in the seventeenth century. The Bolsheviks hate them, more than the ordinary church, and they hate that with a passion. People say the Old Believers, they're a bit touched, a cult."

"But their priest looked after the children, and they're hiding us."

"In this time, being in a cult may not be the worst thing."

"Ilya said they'd used this route before. Is it possible that they've smuggled other Old Believers out under the marble?"

"Maybe the ffwl is becoming wise," she said and kissed him, once, twice.

The barge bumped heavily against the side of the lock. From somewhere up above, the sound of shouts and the barking of dogs reached their hiding place. Evgenia put her finger to his lips and the two of them lay side by side, shivering and afraid.

Then, suddenly, the engine and the bilge pump were cut and they heard the metal of the hull ring as heavy boots thundered down the ladder into the hold.

Two dogs barked, then fell quiet.

Jones and Evgenia held their breath as best they could. Outside their hiding place, the animals sniffed and whined, their paws pattering on the marble.

"Nothing but stone down here," came Granma's voice, a little bored.

"The dogs seem excited," a man's voice, surly.

"Maybe a big rat is teasing them."

"We should lift this slab."

"Good luck with that brother. It weighs ten tonnes. You need a dockyard crane to even try – and the All Soviet Marble Works will have your balls if you break off a single speck of their precious rock. The high-ups in Moscow love this stuff. Break the marble for a rat if you dare, but that's on your head, not mine."

A long pause, a decision being made. "Oh, all right mother, stop your nagging. Come on boys, it's time for lunch."

Boots on metal retreated, diminished – and, after that, there was only a silence that went on and on.

Eventually the engine throbbed onwards, south, towards the sea. But something was not right.

"The bilge pump. It's not working." The anxiety in Jones' voice was raw, his whisper too loud. Evgenia gripped his hand tightly, "Sssh."

But he was right. The level of the slop at their feet rose, first soaking the bearskin rug they were lying on, then wetting their backs through their clothes. Taking the tin case out of the film bag, Jones jammed it between his ribs and the marble.

In the darkness, Jones pressed his mouth against her ear.

"Evgenia, what shall we do if they capture us and one of us survives and the other doesn't?"

For a time, she said nothing. Jones listened intently for any sound other than the the throb of the engine, the hiss of the river and the sloshing of the bilge water, still climbing by the inch.

"The Cheka will play games with us. They may let you go."

"They could kill us both, at the drop of a hat."

"If they have me, they won't need to kill you. Before they shoot me, they will force me to write love letters to you, twenty letters for twenty years. So even in 1953 you will think that I am alive when I am long dead. I've told you about this. So you must promise me that, if they take me but let you go, you will hurry to the West and, the moment you are free, tell the world what the peasant said. 'There is no bread.' Promise me you will do that."

"What if you're still alive?"

"I will be dead within a week. Promise me."

"I promise."

"I love you, Evgenia. I have never loved anyone more my whole life." He squeezed her hand. "I shall love you until my dying day."

The bilge level seemed to hold steady for a time – but then the barge hit some rough water and the slop sluiced over their faces. They held their breaths, praying for the water level to go down. But it did not. The slop rose above their ears and they lay with necks angled, arching their mouths to the stone as their precious pocket of air grew smaller and smaller.

One minute...

Ten minutes...

An hour...

Time was meaningless in here. Neither knew how long they had been down here in the dark before they heard Yuri's light steps climbing down the ladder, his curses, the slosh of his boots in the bilges, the sound of the crowbar prising the wooden chocks free – and, at last, saw a faint glow-worm of light.

Evgenia squeezed out first. After she was through, Jones passed her the tin case and, taking one last breath, edged out from underneath the marble. As he stood up, coughing and spluttering, his lungs were heaving.

Soaked with the evil, oily water, Evgenia and Jones clambered up the ladder to see a cold and dismal sun sinking towards the horizon. What had happened to them was beyond words and they had none.

"I could kill Pyotr," Jones said at length.

Stripping down, they washed off the foul water as best they could, then changed into new clothes Yuri had found for them while he tried to dry their boots on a radiator. At least the tin case had kept its seal intact.

Yuri disappeared, only to come back shortly. "Granma wants to see you in her cabin," he said.

The tabby on Granma's lap stopped purring the moment they entered. Her cabin was tiny: a cot where they both sat, a chair for her, and a chart of the river on a small wooden table, with photographs of Lenin and Stalin plastered across the bulkhead. The still occupied the rest of the space.

Nodding to Lenin and Stalin, she pressed her thumbs against the outer edges of the wooden panel where the two portraits hung. The two Bolsheviks swung back to reveal an icon of the Madonna and child. Kissing the icon, she muttered a prayer and crossed herself in the way of the Old Believers.

Then, leaning across to the still, she opened a tap and filled a jug with clear liquid, found three glasses and filled them each to the brim. They drank them all down in one. She poured three more shots.

"How long to Odessa?" asked Jones.

"In two days the sea. From there we hug the coast. Odessa, a week, maybe more, maybe less."

"To Odessa then." Jones made to down his glass but Granma's tone stayed his hand.

"Never had dogs before."

"Granma, you know we almost drowned back there. Drowned because Pyotr didn't bother to fix the bilge pump. He could have killed us."

Her blue eyes had a film of water over them, the mask of her face beginning to crack.

"What is it, Granma?" asked Evgenia.

"Your precious film. Tell me, what's in it?"

"A dead man and a dead horse. A dead village. Orphans, dying, their tummies distended, like balloons."

"Will it make any difference?"

"Yes, Granma, all the difference in the world. No-one outside the Soviet Union believes this famine is happening. This film will prove that our government is lying."

"The Cheka?"

Up above, where Arkady was at the wheel, the barge horn blasted. Granma stood up, surveyed the empty river, gave the boy a lick with the rough edge of her tongue and returned to her cabin, returning to her silent self-absorption.

"You were saying," prompted Evgenia, "the Cheka."

Granma's words came in a rush, tumbling out one after another. "At the very last moment, the Cheka ordered Pyotr to come with them. At that last dock. Son of a bitch, he drinks too much. He'll talk, tell them everything, not just you but the others too. He's my... my..."

Her shoulders heaved. Tears started to run down her cheeks. "He's my only child. He's a fool and a drunk but he's all I have."

Evgenia comforted her, stroking the old lady's hair, whispering into her ear.

At length, Granma continued, "Pyotr is stubborn, like his father before him. He won't crack under the knout. But if they give him a bottle, if they talk to him like they're all pals, then in his cups he'll tell them everything. So you should leave. You should get off the barge before he cracks."

"When?" asked Jones.

"At nightfall. In an hour, maybe less."

"Will he crack?" asked Evgenia. "Are you certain?"

"No. But the risk..."

They left her, the cat once again purring in her lap.

For a moment, the two of them stood on the steps of the cargo hold, looking out upon the world beyond the riverbanks, the sky to the east turning pink. Their quandary was impossible.

Perhaps Yagoda's letter was still their best way out of trouble. Perhaps it could be used to create a story of a secret mission for the head of the GPU. But, for that to work, they would have to be who their other documents said they were: a professional translator and a foreign journalist. Dressed up like barge workers, in stinking working men's clothes, her hair cut short, the magic letter would not be believed.

But Pyotr could deliver them up at any moment. All the GPU had to do was telegram the local militia to hold the barge at the next lock on the Dnieper and they were done for.

"The Cheka," Evgenia said at length, "they grind you down. You have courage, you have determination, you have something precious the world must see. But, in the end, they break you. If we leave this barge, they will sniff us out. If we stay on the barge, they will have us. But for these poor people who have risked their lives to help us, we are nothing but a curse. The same with the Wobblies. It would have been better if we had not even tried."

Overhead, a solitary crow beat its wings against the darkening sky.

"Let's go before we lose the light," said Jones, his hand touching the bag holding the Kinamo and the reel of film.

They told Yuri of their decision who relayed it to Granma. As the barge rumbled to a stop, they shook hands with Yuri and waved farewell to Arkady, who grinned hugely at them, oblivious. Of Granma, there was no sign.

The barge bumped against the ice. Here, the Dnieper had widened, the western bank a dark strip, two miles off. Ice floes close to the hull creaked and see-sawed, settling into a broken crazy-paving as the wash from the engine died down. Jones picked a solid rectangle twenty yards long towards the stern and, when he lowered himself onto it, it barely tilted with his weight. Evgenia passed him their bag and she too jumped down.

Soon, two black dots were making their way across the vast icefield towards the dying sun.

Chapter Twenty-Four

The sky turned blood red, then scarlet. By the time they made the riverbank, it was an inky blue. By the light of the stars, they found a rough track running parallel to the river – but it was potholed and full of sumps of snow and ice which they sank into, sometimes beyond their knees. It was madness to try and go further in the dark. Madness, too, to stay out here on the edge of the steppe with nothing to protect them from the wind from the east, growing stronger with every minute.

After some time, stumbling, exhausted, they came across a black shape looming out of the dark. Crowley's lighter did its job, illuminating a building of the simplest possible design: wooden slats laid diagonally, their ends embedded into a bank of earth, the floor frozen mud, on top of which a filthy sheepskin lay.

"All my darkness sums it up," said Jones. "Do you think that Duranty would ever end up in a fisherman's hut like this?"

Evgenia shuddered. "Never."

"Yes, not his thing. Poor chap, he needs to widen his horizons." Jones was oddly happy. Better the hut than the hole underneath the marble. They scouted around for some firewood but their hoard was pretty pitiful, only a snow-sodden log and a dead bush that burned fiercely for ten minutes before it was done. When the log took hold, its smoke filled the hut, sour and acrid in their throats. It was a mercy when the fire died out. They lay down together, shivering in the iron cold, and waited for dawn listening to the howl of the wind.

"The film reel, Mr Jones? The film reel?" Lyushkov's soft rumble was calm, gentle, almost girlish. For the life of him, Jones couldn't remember where he'd left it. He was always losing things: his hat, his marbles, the film reel. "I am most terribly sorry, Mr Jones," said Lyushkov, "but you give me no choice." They crushed all the bones of his left hand first, then all the bones of his right – and he sat in front of his typewriter in a wet slimy darkness, while Cardiff demanded copy, and he couldn't write a word because he had flippers instead of hands.

"For God's sake, shush, you'll wake up the dead!" cried Evgenia.

Jones surfaced from the nightmare, his chest constricted, drenched in sweat despite the intense cold.

"You were mumbling to yourself, louder and louder. Then you started to scream..."

"I am most terribly sorry, Evgenia." There was something so utterly formal about Jones' apology that she burst out laughing and hugged him. "Ffwl!" she said.

To the east, the darkness was softening, turning from obsidian to darkest blue. Across the frozen river, three miles away, they made out a goods train rattling along the far bank, its wagons defined only by their noise, the guard's van shining a solitary red light at the rear.

Jones studied the train for a time, then said, "If Pyotr talks, they'll find out we're heading for Odessa. All they have to do so is search the westerly bank and, hey presto, they've got us. If we move inland, it's still easy for them. In the snow, underfed and exhausted as we are, we can only move at a snail's pace."

"So?"

"Evgenia, we're on the wrong side of the river. We cross the river, we hitch a ride on a goods train, hide in a wagon, then we have a chance."

"The bridges," breathed Evgenia. "They'll be guarded. Passports checked, everything. It's impossible."

"Who said anything about crossing by bridge?"

"We can walk across the frozen part. But for the channel, we'd have to have a boat..."

"We can punt a floe."

"What is punt?"

"You stick a pole into the water, wiggle it along and you move. It's the only thing that they taught me at Cambridge."

She did that trick she had, of drawing back, her head turned away, as if she was repelled by his presence. "You're not serious?"

He was, very.

After a time they found a long, thin log, a fallen silver birch. Snapping off the branches as best he could, he looked at her like a caveman. "Pole," he grunted.

"Idiot," she said.

"The word does not rhyme with yacht," he said, matter-of-factly.

Foolish as it seemed, she accepted his invitation to go punting on the frozen river. So, long before sunrise, they started back out across the river, Evgenia carrying both their bags, Jones shouldering the pole. By the time they had got to the channel, sunrise was already approaching. Their dilemma was simple. Too small an ice-floe and they could be upended in the river; too big a floe and the pole would not be effective, and, when the sun came up, they would be drifting in the middle of the channel for all the world to see.

Chance made the decision for them. They were tip-toeing at the edge of the channel, studying the floes, when with a jolt the ice they were standing on was suddenly torn clean away. Startled, Evgenia almost fell in, recovered and jumped back onto the solid river ice. Jones, using his pole as a trapeze artist on a high wire, recovered too. The floe, a lozenge about ten feet long, stabilised. Jones walked to the rear and put the pole in, gave it a wiggle and, to Evgenia's astonishment, it began to move back under Jones's direction. It took him a little time to find his rhythm, but soon he was poling with grace and efficiency – and Evgenia had to jog along to keep pace.

"Now, do you believe me?" said Jones.

By way of answer, she jumped back onto the floe, steadied herself and squatted down towards the front, clinging on to the precious bag with the film reel in it.

Sunrise found them midstream, Jones wrestling with the force of the current. Ahead the river curved to the east, offering an end to their struggle. As the sun climbed, swathes of early morning mist came and went, sometimes hiding both sides of the channel from them, sometimes clearing entirely away. Jones was wrestling with the current but somehow winning his battle when the bullets started to fly, zzzing past them, hissing as they hit the ice.

The mist cleared for a spell and, on the western bank, they saw three lorries etched against the skyline, troops on the bank below. Evgenia flattened herself against the ice, while Jones went down onto his knees. The moment they hit the mass of the river ice on the eastern bank, Evgenia jumped to safety, quickly followed by Jones. Bullets whistled overhead, in front and behind them. Then the mist came down again, blanketing them, and they hurried towards the memory of the sun.

The mist was so thick that the coal train had dawdled to a slow walk, so it was the easiest thing in the world for Jones and Evgenia to hop aboard the plate of a wagon, climb the short ladder and then untie the tarpaulin covering the coal so that they could slide underneath it. The coal was caked in soot, sharp-edged, almost fiendishly uncomfortable. Yet, compared to hiding under the marble, it was heaven.

After a time, the mist cleared and the train picked up speed. Jones peeked under the edge of the tarpaulin and looked across the river but could not see the three GPU lorries. Their luck was still holding.

Sinking back, he tried to make himself comfortable on their bed of coal. Exhilarated by their escape, it took a moment for him to realise that Evgenia was crying.

"Why are we doing that? We managed to escape, no?"

"The GPU tried to kill us."

"But they missed."

"That means Pyotr talked. He told them about us. It means the Old Believers... all of them...." She was crying so hard she could not get the words out.

Jones' face hardened as he struggled to come to terms with the evil that was hunting them. In the Hollywood movies the hero would say, "They'll never get away with it", but something held his tongue and instead he simply held onto her as the coal train jolted its way through the mist.

This was not Hollywood, he knew – and, here and now, the Cheka had every chance of getting away with all of it.

Chapter Twenty-Five

The big man had slobber on his beard and dust and straw in his wild hair. He was foully drunk and not a little mad, but there was nothing wrong with his animal instinct. He could smell their fear.

Stopping them on the broad, tree-lined avenue a hundred yards from Odessa train station, the vagabond barked at the top of his voice, "This one's a foreigner. You can tell from his fancy spectacles. What's a foreigner doing all dressed up up in tramp clothes, eh? There's a few kopecks for someone who asks that question, eh?"

Doing a little dance in front of them, he sucked noisily on the teat of his vodka bottle.

"Pretty lady's got herself a foreign tramp, eh? Come on, give us a few kopecks, your secret's safe with me."

It was five o'clock in the morning by the station clock, and not that many people were about – but still the drunk's attention was the worst possible thing for them. They hurried on through the slush – the season was beginning to turn, the snow starting to melt, here in the most southwesterly corner of the Soviet Union – doing their best to ignore him. But he just skipped along after them, barking more loudly.

"Running from a jealous husband, eh, are you my pretty lady? Taking ship to Constantinople, eh? I'll show you the way. Running from somebody, that's for sure."

"Listen, brother, sssh, I'll give you some kopecks," said Evgenia, struggling to suppress the desperation in her voice, "but not here in the street."

They ducked into a dark alley leading to a dilapidated nineteenth century villa, pools of slush on the cobbles. Opening her purse, Evgehnua scrabbled around for two twenty kopeck coins – "that's all I've got" – but in her haste to shut him up a thick fold of one hundred rouble notes fell to the ground. As bad luck would have it, they landed in a cone of light thrown by a streetlamp.

"Ooh, the pretty lady is a rich one too. Smells a bit bourgeois to me. On the run from the Cheka, are we pretty lady? My tongue's going to wag and the nosy ones will start asking questions about your fancy foreign friend."

Jones punched him on the jaw, then in the gut, twice, and slowly the drunk crumpled to the cobbles. Evgenia picked up the fold of rouble notes and they were about to run for it when the drunk said in a voice quite different from the one he'd been using before, "You won't last five minutes on the street. There's Cheka snouts every hundred yards between the station and the ferry terminal. I can show you a way to the docks... but it will cost you."

"How much?"

"Two hundred roubles."

"That's a fortune."

"Not to you, lady."

Her eyes questioned Jones. He nodded.

"OK," she said.

"Money now please," said the tramp.

"No."

"Now."

"One hundred now, one hundred when we're at the docks."

The tramp got to his feet, clutched the hundred rouble note she offered and hid it in his coat, then gestured for them to follow. Hurrying away from the street into the yard of the old, run-down mansion, he jogged down some stone steps into a gloomy basement, Jones and Evgenia following close behind. He turned right, then left, then came to a passageway down which a small boy in a sailor suit stared at them, frozen in terror.

"Not a word about this son, ever, or I will come to you in your dreams and you will never sleep soundly again."

The boy stood stock-still for what seemed an eternity, then

nodded and stepped aside, so that they could walk past him in silence.

Two turns further on, they came to a mouldy wooden trapdoor in the floor.

Reaching into his coat, the vagrant found the stubs of three candles, lit each with a match and shared them with his two customers. Then he lifted the trap and guided them down, down into the old catacombs of Odessa.

The light from their candles flickered in the darkness, illuminating a length of tunnel with a curved roof and dull yellow limestone underfoot. Down here, the air was sweet and clear, the temperature coolish, the labyrinth never ending. Every hundred yards, passages veered off to left and right. Sometimes they sloshed through stagnant pools of clear water, but for most of their journey the ground was dry and the going easy. The most troubling thing about the tunnels was, apart from the scuffling of their own boots, the lack of sound. There was something about the texture of the stone that absorbed noise. Occasionally they had to stoop low to pass from one set of underground chambers to the next; at one point, Jones bumped his head and, rubbing it, slightly dazed, was in danger of getting left behind. The tramp said, "You keep up, Mr Foreigner. If you wander off, you'll go stark staring mad in half an hour. There's too many tunnels down here. You get lost, you die."

At length they came to a stop in a chamber, the floor lined with soiled blankets, the walls decorated with chalk drawings of sailing ships, dolphins, naked women. Though they couldn't hear the sea, the tunnel air smelt differently down here; it carried a slight but unmistakeable salty tang.

"We'll wait a while," said the tramp. "When the day is done, that's the best time to see if we can find a ship that will take you. I'll go with the pretty lady. The foreign gent best stay. Otherwise, someone might sniff out his peculiar origins."

Opening his knapsack, he produced some bread and hard cheese, cut the latter into wafer-thin slices with a curved blade and passed the food around.

Evgenia asked about the origin of the labyrinth. The city had been a boom town under the Tsars, the tramp explained, the fourth biggest in the whole of the Russian Empire after Moscow, St Petersburg, and Warsaw. But wood was scarce and manufacturing brick in kilns ruinously expensive. The solution was to dig down and hew out the local yellow limestone, made of out sea shells millions of years old. They call it coquina.

"The result?" he said. "Odessa sits on top of the biggest labyrinth in the world. That makes it a very special place for smugglers, ne'er-do-wells like me – and the kind of people who have their own reasons to avoid the nosey parkers, eh?"

"What did you do, before?" asked Jones.

He sighed and said: "I was a professor," then fell silent. Jones' candle spluttered out.

"Have you another candle?"

"One hundred roubles."

"Come on."

The tramp leaned forward and blew out Evgenia's candle, then his own. Suddenly they were locked inside a darkness, absolute and entire. Not a word was spoken, not a movement made. The only sound was the three of them breathing.

"Two hundred rou..."

The tramp didn't get to finish the new price, because at that moment, Jones lunged for him – or the place where he thought he'd be. But the man wasn't there and Jones ended up flailing into the stone.

Something shifted and then, from the darkness, came the sound of triumphant mocking.

"Three hundred roubles for a candle," the tramp said. "And a lot more if you ever want to see the sun again."

Jones felt Evgenia's hand on his leg. In the darkness, he leant forward. Their hands met and she passed him something squarish, metal...

Crowley's lighter.

It fired at the very first attempt.

Jones was onto the tramp in a flash, tossing the lighter back towards Evgenia. It went out in mid-air but, despite the blackness, Jones had his target, pummelling him with his fists, finding his gut, his jaw, his temple, left and right, right and left. The tramp kneed Jones in the groin, then punched him on the cheek and tried to skip away – but Jones caught an arm and piled punch after punch in where his neck and head ought to be.

Once again, the tramp lunged at Jones, clobbering him with a punch to the side of his neck. Jones rolled to one side, recovered, grabbed the tramp by his hair and bashed his head against the rock wall, again and again and again...

The tramp was by the far the bigger man, but Jones was fired by a blind fury. Behind them, Evgenia scrabbled around on the rock floor, searching for the lighter. Her fingers came across a knapsack, the tramp's. Frantically she delved into it, before coming across a box of matches. She opened the box, caught one – but it didn't light. The second failed too. Then a blind kick from the tramp knocked her sideways and she dropped the box, the matches scattering across the ground. Scooping a bunch up, she scraped them against the side of the matchbox and, suddenly, there was a flare of brilliant light.

Jones cried out, "Oh God, no!"

Evgenia lit another match and, with that, the stub of her candle.

"I never meant to," said Jones, the words from his bloodied lips trickling to a halt.

Evgenia stared at the mess of blood and bone that had been the tramp's face. He was quite dead.

"I couldn't see," said Jones. "I couldn't see how he was. I... I... I..."

They sat in the candlelight, their heads down, alone and afraid. After a time, Evgenia's hand reached out to Jones's and gripped it firmly. "I'm sorry."

"It is done."

Evgenia shushed him and, holding a candle with one hand, went through the tramp's knapsack. She found two more candles, long and thin, two more boxes of matches, two bottles – one of water, one of vodka – a ball of string, a piece of chalk, a wallet bulging with rouble notes and, folded neatly, a piece of paper. She unfolded the paper and on it was scribbled, in tiny print, a map of an extraordinarily complicated labyrinth. She stared at it hopelessly.

"If that's a map of the tunnels, then that is our way out of here," said Jones.

"It's a map. But there's no way of knowing where we are on it."

"Listen, Evgenia, I hate the dark, I hate being trapped underground, more than anything I hate being in the same chamber as a man I have just killed. So let's go. Let's trust to our luck. Ariadne, she gave Theseus a ball of twine when he went down into the labyrinth to defeat the Minotaur. We do the same trick. Let's go."

Tying one end of the string to the tramp's leg – there was nothing else to fix it to – they walked out of the exit they had come in by, Evgenia leading the way with the first of the candles, Jones stumbling on behind her, loosening the ball of string as they walked. Every time they came to a fork they turned left until they came to an enormous hall, so big that the candle couldn't light it. In the distance came the unmistakeable sound of waves breaking against a beach, then the long withdrawing roar as the wave withdrew. Excited, Jones hurried forward, plunging into the darkness outside the pool of light made by the candle.

"Idiot!" Evgenia cried.

Jones stumbled and almost fell. Following the noise he was making, she too raced out across the cavern – and there she found Jones, holding a broken thread. In his haste to get away, the string had snapped. They tried to find the other end but gave up, taunted by the sound of the breaking sea, taunted by the possibility of seeing the sky at last.

Chapter Twenty-Six

They hurried through the subterranean dark towards the smell of the sea, the blackness edging dark grey. Somewhere near here was a source of light.

Fortune had favoured them at last. Jones and Evgenia stood on the shores of an underworld lagoon, on its pebble beach an ancient rowing boat.

"Shall we?" Jones said

Evgenia didn't need asking twice.

They set off, Jones at the oars, the lagoon narrowing into a tunnel where they had to use their hands to push against the low ceiling to propel the boat forward. Then, before they truly understood where they were and how far they had come, they were out among the breakers, the open vault of the sky overhead. Jones pulled them steadily towards a secluded, sandy cove and the rowing boat came to a rest in the gathering dusk.

Stripping off their filthy clothes and holding hands, they half-ran, half-danced into the frigid sea, and tried to wash away the coal dust that had infiltrated every pore.

Once out of the water, Evgenia said, "Perhaps it would be best to row back. The catacombs are the safest place for us."

"No more holes in the ground, ever again," Jones replied.

There was a place underneath an uprooted tree at the back of the beach. It wasn't much but it afforded some protection from the weather. Evgenia told him that it was best if she went into the city on her own, to try to buy new clothes for him and her, to see if she could find a ship that would take them away. Jones tried to argue with her but knew that she was right and watched her disappear off into the night.

After she had gone, it started to rain and, with that, he felt a growing sense of desolation.

After an agony of time, Evgenia returned a different woman. Gone was the filthy deckhand, in her stead young Soviet woman, hair washed, dressed in the very latest fashion: jacket, red blouse and skirt, and in her hand a suitcase.

"How did you do that?"

"Winnie, I met her quite by accident. She's been singing for some bigwigs in Odessa. Without her it would have been impossible. Here, she gave me some cheese, a bottle of Ukrainian wine, fresh clothes for you too. She's been a godsend."

The suitcase held a man's three piece worsted suit, shirt, red tie, vest, underpants and a pair of shoes. The shirt fitted perfectly, the suit too big – but Jones was no man of fashion. Only the shoes were a failure and Jones had to contend with going out on the town in a deckhand's boots.

"Winnie introduced me to a ship's officer from Copenhagen," said Evgenia. "Their ship has been held for a week but they're hoping it will finally be leaving for Constantinople on the early morning tide."

"And?"

"The officer said he couldn't promise anything. It was, it must be, the captain's decision. The officer and the captain, they're going to be at restaurant where Winnie sings tonight. If we past muster, they'll hide us until we're safely out to sea, then drop us in Turkey with no questions asked."

"Will it work?"

A silvering of the sea: moonrise. She smiled, as much to herself as at him. "We've got this far. Who knows?"

Under the light of the moon, they devoured the cheese and drank the wine, listening to the soft roar of the shingle as it rolled in and out. For the first time since Haywood made his dying wish, Jones believed that they might just have a chance of a life together.

The restaurant was a riot of plush velvet, everything in red. At the back of the main dining area was a little stage, spotlit, and beneath that a gypsy band sawed its way through popular hits.

The Danish ship's officer, Jens, arrived, a burly blond giant. Kissing Evgenia on both cheeks, he smiled formally at Jones in a way that suggested irritation, civilly masked. Shortly afterwards, the captain turned up, a thick-set older blond man. He was polite, punctiliously so, but guarded.

"You're planning to leave port on the early morning tide, Captain?" asked Evgenia.

"We cannot leave without the express permission of the harbourmaster and that permission has been withheld for a week now. Never any answers. Only delay. This will be my last voyage to the Soviet Union."

As he toyed with a glass of beer, a telegram arrived, delivered by a young deckhand. Flipping out some reading glasses, he began to peruse it.

"May I ask, what is your news captain?" asked Evgenia.

He shrugged and said, "I'm delighted to say that our ship is very honoured." He seemed neither delighted nor honoured. "We've finally been given permission to leave on the four o'clock morning tide. The only proviso is that we have been asked to take three special guests dear to the Soviet Foreign Ministry."

Jones beamed. "Who might they be, may I ask?"

"Ah," said the captain, "here they are now."

Professor Aubyn and Dr Limner walked into the restaurant, closely followed by Duranty.

"Jones, old cock, Evgenia!" exclaimed Duranty. "What a coincidence! May we join you? Make it all a bit of a party, eh? Heh, Jonesy, you'll never guess who I got to see back in Moscow."

"Stalin."

"In one. He talked up a storm, about how it was necessary to forge good relations with the United States, blah blah blah. The *New York Times* are over the moon. Let's get some champagne.

The office has put me in for the Pulitzer and are paying for me to go on the razzle in Constantinople."

"Congratulations old man," said Jones, a smile frozen on his lips.

"As I was saying, Mr Duranty..." Aubyn had a sour expression on his face as if he had been sucking on a wasp. "I take a very dim view of how the Soviet authorities have been treating us. We have been wanting to take our leave for two weeks now and only today are we finally in Odessa. Please use your good offices with the Kremlin to ask for an explanation."

"It's always tricky, getting a response. New Soviet Man loves to play it close to the chest, Professor Aubyn."

"You've met Stalin, Mr Duranty."

"That doesn't make me a travel agent, Professor."

"Well, it's not good enough. Our plans have been thrown awry and we should have been on our way back to Washington DC more than a week ago. I really didn't expect this treatment..."

The professor became dimly aware that introductions were in order. He stopped in mid-sentence. "Erm..."

"Professor, Dr Limner, may I introduce – or probably reintroduce – Mr Gareth Jones of the *Western Mail* and his translator, Evgenia? You may remember them from Moscow?"

Aubyn offered a weak half-smile, Limner not even that.

"Captain, Sir, I believe that you will be taking Professor Aubyn, Dr Limner and I to Turkey first thing tomorrow morning. The professor has recommended that the United States recognise the Soviet Union. He's written a report praising how things are done there," Duranty's eyes glittered with mischief.

The Captain and the officer bowed and soon the maitre d' appeared, ordering for more chairs and places to be set at the table.

When the champagne, Duranty proposed the toast. "To a new era in America-Soviet relations! To us!"

Evgenia and Jones repeated the toast, all smiles, and drained their glasses.

Duranty's easy grin clouded. "Champagne is warm. Bloody

peasants." Turning to the maitre d', he barked, "Can you please bring us some ice to chill the bubbly?" Then, turning back to Jones, he said, "Nice suit you've got there, Jonesy. Pity about the boots. What have you been up to all this time? Moscow hasn't been the same without you. We really missed you."

"Researching a piece on Soviet culture, Duranty."

"Good on you. Not much blood and gold in that. But," his eyes were a-glitter as they turned to Evgenia, "but sex for sure."

The party studied the menu and ordered caviar, oysters, foie gras, steak and salmon, all washed down by a good Bordeaux.

"Professor Aubyn's report," Duranty continued for the benefit of the Danish officers, "highlights the progress the Soviet Union has made with food production. Isn't that the case, Professor?"

Aubyn nodded, acknowledging the tribute. The captain sipped his beer and then said, "You reported that the food situation for the people was good?"

"It is excellent," said Aubyn, Limner nodding.

"Why on earth do you think that?" asked the Captain. "Do you not see the people starving?"

"Because it is the case," said Limner, flatly. The Captain turned to Jones and Evgenia.

"Have you not seen the starving people, the beggars pitifully thin, the corpses?"

Evgenia tried to deflect. "It's the Party's..."

But Jones cut in.

"Yes, Captain," he said. "I have."

The captain stared into his beer.

"Captain," said Jones, "may I have a private word?"

"If you're asking about a berth in the ship for you and your translator, my officer has already broached the matter and the answer is yes."

"That would not be appropriate," said Limner.

"I beg your pardon," said the Captain.

"That would not be appropriate," Limner replied. "Mr Jones and his translator have eccentric views and Miss Miranova was unable to suppress her hostility to Professor Aubyn when she was supposedly translating for him."

"She fainted is what you're trying to say," said Jones.

Duranty cut in. "Hey, let's not all fall out boys and girls."

Limner gestured at Jones and Evgenia. "You see, it would be impossible for Professor Aubyn's party to travel in the same ship as these two."

"It's my ship, sir," said the Captain to Limner. "If you want to stay in Odessa, so be it."

Limner stood up, bowed and said, "I shall make the necessary representations to the authorities," then left the room.

The meal continued, more miserably than before, Duranty making small talk about his time with Stalin, the professor moaning about his travel delays, Jones and Evgenia replying as economically as possible. In the background, above the noise from the band, they could occasionally make out Limner talking heatedly down a telephone. Limner returned but said nothing.

After they finished the main course, the gypsy band swung vigorously into action and the red curtain parted to reveal Winnie in her distinctive get-up, Soviet boiler suit and black bowler hat. She started out singing a moody jazz number about unrequited love but her voice faltered. The band struggled on for a few more bars, then gave up.

She dipped her head, then began, "I want to dedicate this song to two friends of mine. They're good people. And I..." Her voice broke. Tears were streaming down her face. "I do not deserve to be called their friend."

The drummer swished a cymbal, inappropriately. She closed her eyes and the beauty and power of her voice filled the room. The last lines went:

"...*Oppressed so hard they could not stand,*
Let My people go!"

She stopped once again, the band staring at her, uncomprehending.

From out of a boiler suit pocket she produced a small revolver that gleamed dully in the spotlights. Her hand shaking, she pointed it at the table of dignitaries. Aubyn fell off his chair and dived underneath the table, Limner half-slid to join Aubyn, the Danes stared, unmoving, Duranty looked on, his face a picture of nonchalant amusement.

"It's a trap, for God's sake!" said Winnie. "I betrayed you. They said, they said I could go home to New Orleans. That's why I did it – but they were just lying, lying like they always do... I just overheard them tell Dr Milner there's no way you two are going on the ship, nor the negress too."

Jones stood up, started to walk towards her. "Winnie!"

She screamed, "Go!", then pointed the revolver at her temple and fired.

In seconds, Evgenia and Jones were out of the door and running. Passing a statue of Lenin, they headed downhill towards the docks. The Cheka were chasing them, shouting, blowing whistles, military boots stamping on the cobbles, voices bellowing for them to stop. Jones turned to block them but he was brought down, fists pumping into his back and the side of his head. Evgenia ran on, the letter from Yagoda in one hand, bag in the other; then she too was tripped up. As she fell to the ground, the tin case tumbled out of the bag and under the brilliant moonlight it bounced down, down, down the Odessa steps until it disappeared into the shadows below.

After a time, Lyushkov emerged, the film reel clasped in his sausage-chaped fingers.

Chapter Twenty-Seven

Lyushkov lit a cigarette and studied the smoke coiling upwards through the open window. Jones sat on a chair on the other side of a desk, his left eye a liquid slit in the blue-black pulp the Cheka had made of his face.

"Good news, Mr Jones. Moscow has decided that you are free to go."

Jones said nothing.

"When your face looks better, naturally."

"Naturally," said Jones, deadpan.

Not so far away, a ship's horn blasted its farewell to Odessa. Much closer, a bird started to trill its welcome to spring, the sweetness of the sound contrasting with the racket from nearby speakers calling for workers to forswear alcohol for the good of New Soviet Man.

"And Evgenia?"

Lyushkov stubbed out his cigarette on the desk and, yawning, stretched himself. Studying Jones all the while, he picked up a pencil from a holder on the table. "Mr Jones, it is my unpleasant task to tell you that Miss Miranova has been diagnosed by eminent doctors of the mind. They have found that she is suffering from acute neurasthenia. As such she is incapable of travel at the current time. You understand?"

"Of course."

"This talk of famine..."

"What famine?" Jones replied.

The pencil snapped in two. A long pause, then, "We have watched your film, Mr Jones."

"What film?"

Lyushkov nodded to a figure behind Jones who moved out of the shadows and tapped Jones on the left side of his face with a short metal rod. His arms handcuffed behind his back, Jones offered no resistance, and nor could he. He did his best to suppress a gasp of pain. In that goal, he did not succeed.

After a time, Lyushkov said, "Miss Miranova suffers from the same terrible delusion, perhaps in an even more heightened form."

"Does she now? Fancy that." Jones tone was the opposite of respectful.

Lyushkov signalled to the figure in the shadows and the pulp was tap-tapped, more forcefully than before.

Jones gasped and coughed up some blood, then uttered, "May I speak frankly?"

Lyushkov nodded.

"Evgenia and I were last seen alive and well by five witnesses, Professor Aubyn, Dr Limner, Walter Duranty and the two Danes. You've got your hooks into the first three, no question. They're all useful idiots. Hear no evil, speak no evil, see no evil. But the Danes? I don't think so. So, sooner or later, you're either going to have kill me or let me go. You've only told me that Moscow has decided to let me go for your own amusement. The question that's eating away at all of you is will I talk about the famine?"

Lyushkov stared at him.

"If I do, you will kill Evgenia," he whispered. "So I won't, will I?"

Lyushkov stood up and walked slowly out of the room.

*

They took him back to the cell. It wasn't so damp and it wasn't so cold. There was even a small square window at the top of one wall through which shafts of sunlight could reach him. I'm an honoured guest, thought Jones.

His theory, that the Kremlin wouldn't like it if he was killed, held true. They fed and watered him and they didn't touch him for a whole week. But the mental torture was far worse than the physical. Somewhere, close by, somewhere under this same Odessa sky, was Evgenia.

Perhaps.

The left side of his face was still a pale duck-egg blue when the cell door opened and Lyushkov's bulk filled the doorframe.

"So."

"How may I assist the Colonel?" Jones' mock deference was not lost on Lyushkov, but the time for beating had past.

"You are free to go."

"By ship?"

"By train. I will accompany you to the Polish border."

"Thank you very much," said Jones, with icy politeness.

The quickest route to the Soviet-Polish border would have taken less than a day but in the event they travelled for three whole days. Slow trains passed through wildernesses of snow and ice, of dead villages with blackened churches and roofless izbas, past corpses lying this way and that, past fields of weeds, empty and untended because there was no-one left to tend them.

Sometimes the escort, five guards, said something banal to Jones and he replied – but, for the whole of those three days, Jones and Lyushkov did not exchange a word.

They arrived at the border at three o'clock in the morning, Stalin time. It had been snowing but now the stars appeared. The border post was guarded by a machine gun nest and, high above it, a spotlit hammer and sickle, blood-red against the night sky. Outside stood a queue of a hundred or so wretches, shuffling in silence in the frozen air. Lyushkov barrelled to the front of the queue. Just before they entered the post, he turned and smiled bleakly at Jones and said: "your face looks good now, yes?"

"Yes."

"No bruises?"

"There were never any bruises."

"And the famine?"

Jones said nothing. The moon rose, its light casting black shadows from the girder bridge onto the frozen white of the Zbruch river below, reversing reality, as if the entire world could only be seen through a photographer's negative.

"The famine, Mr Jones?"

"There is no famine, Colonel."

Lyushkov nodded and handed him his passport and wallet – "nothing missing, Mr Jones" – then pushed open the door. Lenin and Stalin looked down as Jones's passport was stamped.

The formalities did not take long. He had no baggage, none at all. Lyushkov indicated the way to the pedestrian crossing at the side of the railway bridge. Jones started walking and did not look back, not once. He waited until until he was certain he was more than halfway across the border when he started to run.

*

Somewhere in the middle of nowhere in Poland, he'd got the train guard to stop the train so that he could wire ahead, alerting the free spirits of the Berlin press corps – some still existed in 1933 – to his press conference the next day. When he had finished, he took a short-cut and hurried through the railway station buffet and saw a half-eaten sausage on an abandoned plate. He had not the seen the like of it in six months.

He was moving as fast as humanly possible but it took him a day and a night to cross Poland and enter Germany, the morning to get to the German capital. Arriving around noon, he discovered the old Berlin, the one he loved, had gone. In its stead was a city with Swastikas hanging from the station, from all the grand buildings, with loudspeakers at the street corners playing recordings of Herr Hitler's speeches again and again. The manager of the Berlin press club, a Herr Schmidt, dapper, fastidious, greeted him fulsomely, too much so, and led him in to the conference room. Behind the dias where he was due to speak hung a Swastika flag.

A bell hop found him and gave him an envelope with his name on it. Recognising Evgenia's handwriting, he was about to open it when something stopped him.

"Is everything in order, Mr Jones?" asked Herr Scmidt.

Jones placed the envelope in his jacket pocket and gestured at the Swastika.

"Take that away," said Jones, flatly.

Schmidt thought about it for a few seconds, then nodded, and asked the bellhop to remove the flag.

The journalists started to arrive soon after. Once the room had filled up, Jones began: "In the Soviet Union, right now, as we speak, millions are dying of famine..."

At the end, questions.

The hardest one was asked by no-one he recognised: "Got any collateral for this famine story, Mr Jones? Any still photographs? Any film footage?"

"No, I'm sorry."

"Why not?"

Silence.

"You're saying millions are dying, Mr Jones. That's a big claim. It's your word against the entire Soviet Union. And you've got no photographs or film to back your story up?"

"That turned out not to be possible," Jones said and his voice cracked, a little.

"But Mr Jones..."

"...there's nothing more to say," and he closed the press conference.

When he got to his hotel, he asked for a bottle of sleeping pills. In his room, he closed the curtains, undressed, took Evgenia's envelope from his jacket and kissed it but did not open it and then took a fistful of pills and studied them in his hand. There were about twenty or so pills in his palm, gleaming dully in the light from the bedside lamp. His hand started to tremble. Then he threw the pills away and they pattered on the parquet floor. Stooping, he picked up only two and swallowed them and sluiced them down with a glass of water and closed his eyes and had his first proper sleep for time out of memory.

In the night he woke to a rustling sound. Someone was pushing a copy of a newspaper underneath the door of his hotel room. He hurried to the door, opened it and saw, just in time, a man in a black suit disappear down the corridor and take the stairs. Jones checked himself, closed the door and inspected the paper. It was the *New York Times* and it had given pride of place to a column by Walter Duranty. Jones got to the words: "Any report of a famine in Russia is today an exaggeration or malignant propaganda" then ripped the newspaper into shreds.

He sat back on the edge of his bed and opened Evgenia's envelope and started to read:

"My Dearest Englishman, I can imagine you now, playing a game of golf that you love so much..."

He imagined her writing it, Lyushkov staring at her insolently, the man with the cosh waiting in the shadows. When she had finished, he heard Lyushkov's rumble:

"Next letter..."

THE END

Author's Note

Gareth Jones was shot dead in 1935. He was killed in China at the orders of the Soviet secret police – payback for his efforts to tell the truth about the famine. That is the firm belief of his family and mine too.

This book is, of course, a work of fiction. But Stalin's famine, the millions who died in Ukraine and Russia and the lies western journalists like Walter Duranty and useful idiots like George Bernard Shaw told about it were all too real. They faked the news in 1933.

Evgenia is fiction but Stalino, now Donetsk, was founded by Welsh mining engineer John Hughes and her story, or something like it, is not impossible.

Gareth Jones' mother had taught the children of John Hughes. Jones did his best to counter the lies told by Duranty and the other Kremlin conformists but to little avail. Not enough people believed him and Duranty's version of events, that there was no famine, prevailed. Lyushkov was real, too. He had been a GPU officer during the famine and, suspecting that he was about to be purged, he defected to Japan. There, he told the truth about the famine and the atrocities committed by the GPU. At the end of the second world war, he vanished.

Duranty won the Pulitzer and died in 1957 in Orlando, Florida. The *New York Times* still boasts about his Pulitzer to its continuing disgrace.

Big Bill Haywood and Fred Beal both ended up in Stalin's Soviet Union. Though Haywood died there, Beal managed to get out and tell the truth about the famine in a book. Again, as with Jones, his story was so incredible it was not believed.

As a cub reporter for the *Sheffield Telegraph* in 1983, I met Malcolm Muggeridge who had written the truth about Stalin's famine for the *Manchester Guardian* in 1933. Muggeridge wrote that the famine was "One of the most monstrous crimes in history, so terrible that people in the future will scarcely be able to believe it ever happened." Muggeridge wasn't shot but he got the sack. His words hold true even today, especially in Vladimir Putin's Russia where ignorance of Stalin's evil is encouraged by the master of the Kremlin. Putin is, after all, a Chekist through and through.

The Max Borodin in my novel is my tribute to a real Russian journalist. Borodin, 1986-2018, was a brilliant journalist based in Yekaterinburg who broke the story of how Russian Wagner mercenaries were killed by American forces in Syria. A few days later he called a friend to say men with balaclavas were outside his flat. He fell out of his fifth-floor window by accident.

Or so the Russian authorities say.

Lightning Source UK Ltd.
Milton Keynes UK
UKHW040949170720
366708UK00002B/209